Roses are White

The Conti Story

Paul Tripi

This is a work of fiction. Names, characters, places, and incidents either are the product of the author's imagination or are used fictitiously.

Copyright © 2018 by Paul Tripi

All rights reserved. No part of this book may be reproduced or used in any manner without written permission of the copyright owner except for the use of quotations in a book review.

Roses are White

The Conti Story

Paul Tripi

2019

Black Oyster Publishing Company, Inc.

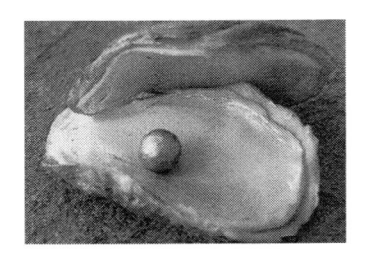

CHAPTER ONE

It was snowing, but that's nothing new in Buffalo, New York, in January. The wind whipped around forming snowdrifts everywhere. Peter Conti, a sixteen-year-old high school student, fought the elements as he made his way to the house of his friend, Sonny Lippa.

"Hey Sonny, what's up," asked Pete as he took off his stocking cap and gloves.

"Nothing much. Al and Ray are on their way over. They wanna go over to Heinz hill and do some sledding."

"Cool, any chance there'll be some girls there?"

"God, is that all you ever think of?"

"No, but I was hoping you were going to say that Jackie Millen and the Fossa twins might be there."

"They might, I talked to Carol and told her we were going and she said that sounded like fun. They could show."

Just then came a knock on the door and Alfonse Espolito and Ray Baldi came strolling in.

"You guys will not guess what we got out there," said Al with a big smile.

"I don't want to even venture a guess," responded Pete.

"A car hood. Do you have any idea how fast a car hood will go down Heinz hill with all of us on it?"

"Oh man, that sounds so cool. Where'd you get it?" asked Sonny.

"From outside the auto shop, man, they'll never miss it. Come on let's go."

The next thing you know the four boys were dragging a car hood down the street in anticipation of an adventure. Heinz hill was loaded with kids on sleds, toboggans, and snow saucers. The hill is a long steep incline running from the parking lot of the old Heinz Boiler factory, long since closed down, to a creek bed that just shouts out danger.

The heavy snowfall had slowed down but you couldn't tell because the wind was gusting and blowing the lighter snowflakes still falling, sideways. Here's something you might not know about Buffalo, New York. When the wind is up it blows harder than almost anywhere else in the good old USA. It gets so strong that sometimes the shops in the downtown area are forced to "put the ropes out."

Downtown Buffalo is located just off of Lake Erie, unluckily positioned so that it gets the full force of a north or northwest wind blowing unimpeded across the lake. That's where "putting the ropes out" comes into play. What is that you might wonder? Ropes are stretched out about waist high next to the sidewalks the entire length of the lake side streets so the people can pull themselves along hand over hand to combat the wind. If it were snowing at the same time, you just wouldn't believe it. You'd have to experience it. It's a trip.

As soon as the boys arrived they positioned their car hood at the very top of the hill and prepared to pile on. They were smart enough to realize they had no way of steering the thing so they moved over as far as they could to one side of the hill. Next they informed everybody who was, or was going to be, in front of them to stand clear by screaming as loud as they could, "get out of the way, we can't control this thing," and pushed off. What happened after that was flat exciting. Do you have any idea what happens when 500 pounds of dead weight is sent flying down a slippery surface with little to no friction to slow it down? Well neither did these boys. But within fifty feet they were starting to find out. They had no concept of their speed; they just knew it was fast, very fast. At that exact moment, they were all sharing the same emotion. Fear. Pee in your pants fear.

By the time they were half way down, Pete was thinking about jumping off. He would have, but they were all hanging on so tight to one another no one could have broken loose from their death grips. A blink of an eye later the whole shoot and shebang went airborne. It only took one small bump and the hood was gliding like a bird. Kaboom was the sound the hood made when it returned to earth, and pow pow pow pow was the sound the boys made as each one hit the slope behind it. It looked like four explosions as each boy barreled into the snow and tumbled. The hood continued down and finally stopped about fifty feet from the creek bed, showing no wear and tear at all. As luck would have it, so did the boys. They all came up laughing and cheering like they just won the Irish sweepstakes or something. They weren't the only ones laughing. Everyone who witnessed the spectacle had joined in including the gaggle of cute high school girls perched on top of the hill.

Jacqueline Millen, the twins Carol and Sarah Fossa, Valerie Stevens, and Rose Marie Marshall, the crème of the crop from Tonawanda High School, were all bundled up and ready for some snow fun. Jackie and Rosey were the adventurous ones and before the other girls were done laughing the dynamic duo were on their way down the hill both riding snow saucers. When they reached the bottom they walked over to the boys.

"Nice play Shakespeare," Jackie said to Pete as the boys were walking back up the hill pulling their hood.

"Jackie Millen," Pete said bowing and then curtsying. "How ya doing?"

"Obviously better than you fools. Is everybody alright?"

"Normal guys would probably be dead but since we're not normal we're all fine," said Sonny.

Rosey responded almost immediately, "You got that right, none of you are normal, and I mean that in a bad way."

"Oh excuse me Miss perfect," said Sonny.

"Kiss my butt, Sonny."

"Move your nose and I will."

"That's so funny, I forgot to laugh."

"Children," said Jackie.

Rosey had to have the last word so she did the only thing she could do without talking; she stuck her tongue out at Sonny. The two girls started up the hill, talking and giggling. The whole way up Pete just stared at Jackie. She was the one. Ever since the fourth grade they had been great friends but although Pete would never admit it, he would have liked them to be much more than just friends.

Sonny and Rosey were at each other throats every time they got together, a sure sign they both dug each other. As they all got closer to the crest of the hill, Sonny yelled, "Hey Rosey, if you think you're so cool. Why don't you prove it and hop on the hood? Or are you all show and no go?"

Rose responded immediately, "Anything you can do I can do better, you dumb dago. Wanna take a ride, Jackie?" she asked her friend.

"Are you out of your mind? Didn't you see what happened a second ago? No way!"

"Come on. I don't want to get on alone and you know the other girls won't. Please!"

"God. If I die, I'm gonna kill you Rosey."

The whole time the girls were debating, the boys were staring at Sonny with looks that could kill. No way did any of those guys want to go down on that hood again, but big mouth Sonny put them in a position where if they didn't they'd lose their manhood before they even got it.

After they yelled the get out the way spiel, the six petrified teens started down what used to be a hill but now turned into a mountain. The only good thing as far as Pete and Sonny were concerned was that the two girls were hanging on to the both of them for dear life. This time each boy was hanging on to the side of the hood and not each other. Where that hood was going was where they planned to go.

They hit a small bump and the hood took flight again. Not far, about four or five feet but far enough for every last one of the passengers to scream out of pure terror. The additional 200 pounds had the thing going even faster than before and there was no denying that these kids were in peril. Half way down, Jackie was crying and Pete was about to join her. Three quarters of the way down it hit all of them almost simultaneously, the creek. There was no way to stop the thing and at that speed no way to exit. As they approached the creek bed everyone hunkered down and prepared for the collision.

A raised lip ran along the top of the creek and thank God for it. The hood, which by the way was totally out of control, hit this little lip. Acting like a ski jump it sent the hood airborne, propelling it far enough to clear the entire crevasse. The makeshift sled started up the small incline that rose from the other side of the creek and came harmlessly to a stop. You could have heard a pin drop when the kids got off the hood. No one said a word. They left the car hood where it came to rest, climbed down and up the frozen creek bed, and headed back to the top of Heinz hill. Even Sonny, who was never at a loss for words, was speechless.

As they approached the top Pete leaned over to Jackie and said, "You are one brave girl. I gotta tell you Jackie, I was scared."

"Scared, are you kidding. I was petrified, Pete. Don't you ever let me do something as stupid as that ever again. And Rosey, Rosey you're crazy!"

When they reached the top, the girls joined and hugged their friends, and quietly left. The boys didn't say much either. They all knew they had pushed the envelope.

"Anybody wanna help me go get that hood?" asked Al. "It's not that I'm worried about getting it back to school. I'm just afraid that someone else might be crazy enough to take that ride. I hate to say this but somebody could die."

"I'll do it," said Ray. "We could get into some big trouble if somebody gets hurt on a count of us. Let's go, Al. See you guys tomorrow."

Al and Ray slid down the hill on their butts and were gone.

"Sonny, isn't Jackie just perfect? I hate to say it but I got it bad for that girl."

"Da," replied Sonny. "I think she's nice but Rosey is the one that cranks my handle."

"Yeah, she's cool. I'll tell ya one thing, they both got a set of balls on 'em."

"No kidding. I could have died when they said they'd go down on the hood. You think I would have said anything if I thought there was any chance they'd say yes? I didn't want to go down again. I thought by saying that Rosey would think I was really brave."

"Well, that backfired, you asshole. You almost killed us all."

"I know. I really thought for a minute there we were gonna buy the farm."

"Sonny, we almost did."

The boys headed home both thinking about the girls. Nothing new, what else do sixteen-year-old boys think about? Pete walked into the kitchen and found his mother standing at the sink doing dishes.

"Hey, Ma, what's the hap?"

"I'm going out on a limb and figure that you mean, what am I doing?"

"Come on Mom, get with it. You're cool. Let loose a little."

"Thanks for your advice, Mister Conti. Now, don't you have some homework or studying to do?"

"Mom, when you have the intelligence level that I possess there is no need for studying."

"Oh, I see, Einstein. But just humor me and pretend like you're studying."

"O.K. Ma, But can I have a little snack first?"

"There's some cookies in the jar but don't eat them all."

Peter's mom, Teresa Conti, formerly Miss Teresa Roma, was the heart and soul of the Conti family. His dad, Thomas, a foreman at the Chevrolet plant, was the lifeblood. Pete's younger brother, Russell, even though he was only eight, was considered the serious one, and his sister Marie, the baby at age three, was, well to put it lightly, spoiled. Peter himself fell under the category of comic relief. They lived in a comfortable home just outside the Buffalo city limits in the small town of Tonawanda, New York. It's a loving family, and although all four of Pete's grandparents were born in Italy, that doesn't change the fact that the Contis are simply your all around All-American family.

CHAPTER TWO

Ah, to be young and in high school. Peter and his friends were traveling through life like a bird soars through the air, effortlessly.

"It doesn't get any better than this," thought Pete as he rounded third base after hitting his sixth homer of the year.

Peter was good at everything. He lettered in three sports. Quarterback of the football team, starting guard on the basketball team, and star third baseman on the baseball team.

He was an A student and was liked by all. Nice resume for an eighteen-year-old kid without a worry in the world. That is except how he can get the one thing he wanted most out of life, a date with Jackie.

"Hey asshole," said Sonny as he walked up behind Pete at his locker.

"I hope you're not talking to me," replied Pete.

"Is there some other gutless guy standing at your locker, drooling over a girl seven lockers away, who doesn't have the balls to ask her out?" asked his buddy.

"I've got plenty of balls. You wanna see 'em?" answered Peter.

"Gross—you're disgusting," replied Sonny with a look on his face like he just bit into a lemon.

"Thanks for the compliment, now what do you want?" asked Pete

"Party over at Rosey's house Friday night. Why don't you show some of those balls of yours, figuratively speaking of course, and walk over there and ask Jackie to go with you?"

"'Cause it would be like asking my sister to go out. We're just too good of friends to ruin it by dating. You know that."

"I know that you're good enough friends to talk to her about it. Ya know she might just be feeling the same way about you. Smarten up."

"God, Sonny. I wish that was true."

"You're stupid! What do you have to lose?"

"How about the best friend of my life, that's what."

"What am I, chopped liver?"

"Well, actually, you kind of smell like it."

"That crazy Rosey challenged me to eat four Big Macs."

"And of course you did."

"That's why I smell a little, you know, gas."

"Oh, you sick bastard—I just threw up in my mouth a little—get away from me—I mean it."

"I gotta go anyway, I'm making myself sick. That woman is going to kill me one day."

"You can say no sometime, you know. Jesus, Sonny—get away from me now!"

It's not like Peter ever had any trouble asking girls out. He was good at that too, but Jackie was another story altogether. Pete had a number of girl friends that he'd dated in the past but right now he was solo.

As he stood there mesmerized by his dream girl the urge was there to ask her but the gamble seemed too high. Peter decided to go to Rosey's party alone.

Rosey's parents were super cool guys. They allowed Rosey to have a select number of friends over as long as everybody stayed under control, the music didn't bother the neighbors, and even though the legal drinking age in New York in 1965 was eighteen years old, absolutely no alcohol. As soon as any of the rules were broken, the party was over.

People were dancing and having a nice time. There was no apparent boozing but you could bet some of the guests were partaking. Seemed like everyone was having a blast. Everyone but Pete, that is. Jackie was there with Ronnie Atom, a nice enough guy who thought he was way cooler than he really was. Pete had enough of watching Jackie dance with the guy and decided it was time to leave. After he danced a dance or two, with one of the girls from the small covey of unaccompanied gals gathered by the punch bowl, he said his goodbyes and was getting ready to take off.

As he walked out, he noticed a little tiff going on between Jackie and Ron. He watched for a second and started drifting over to let's say eavesdrop a mite. He didn't get close enough to hear what the tiff was about because before he was in range, Ron had grabbed Jackie by her arm. She was seriously trying to pull herself away when she was assisted by "guess who." Pete punched Ron so hard in the forehead he hit the ground like a turd falling from a tall horse. Pete stood over him and said, "Now you can get up and try to defend yourself, but all you'll get for your trouble is the beating of your life. Try me," With a look on his face that definitely said he meant business, he said, "If you ever lay a hand on Jackie again, I won't just beat the shit out of you, I'll kill you. Is that clear enough?"

"Is that supposed to be some kind of a threat?" answered Ron with absolutely no thought of getting up.

"No Ron, that's not a threat, that's a promise!"

As the young pugilist turned to see if Jackie was all right, he felt her arms wrap around him.

"Oh my God, Peter!"

"What happened?" he said as he turned back towards Ron with full intentions of finishing something he just started.

Jackie grabbed Peter as he turned, stopped him and said. "Nothing, it's over now."

"What's over? What happened? What the hell did he do?"

"It's not what he did, it's what he wanted to do," she said holding his arm knowing what was about to happen next if she didn't.

There was no power on earth that could have stopped Peter Conti as he pulled his arm from Jackie's grasp and turned to look for the already disappearing foe, except: "Pete, please. Will you just stay with me a minute and hold me?"

"Of course," he whispered as he held her head against his chest. "I'll hold you for the rest of our lives."

She looked up at him and kissed him like a woman would kiss her man who was going off to war. No words were said for a minute or two. They just stood there holding each other.

"Peter," she said softly. "You are the most—"

"Stop," he said interrupting her. "Don't say something you might regret."

"Regret, I've regretted not saying this to you for years. Are you going to make me say the words?"

"No, Jackie. No need. But there is something I need to say to you."

She put her fingers over his mouth and then kissed him again.

All the next day Peter was walking on air because he and she were meeting the very next night at Jake's Bar and Grill, the high school beer joint where kids at Tonawanda High School spent pretty much every weekend night. He was waiting there with Sonny, Al, and Ray. The boys were just kicking back with a few brews while each waited for a woman.

"Me and Kathy are going to catch the new Bond movie at the Majestic. Gold Finger—I love that Connery guy. Anybody wanna go with?" Ray asked.

"Me and Rosey are going over to her sister's to baby sit. Of which I have no problem, if you get my drift?" replied Sonny.

"We'll go Ray, if Pammy says we can," said Al shyly, knowing he's about to catch shit.

"You pussy." Ray laughed.

"Oh yeah?" Al shot back.

"Is that your comeback," interjected Pete.

"I'd have a better one if he wasn't right, but that Pammy Dolan has me twisted around her baby finger."

"Don't let 'im kid ya Al. There isn't a man amongst us, including me, who's not pussy whipped. It's already happened to me and we haven't had our first official date yet," said Peter.

Just then three guys walked into Jake's, apparently looking for somebody. After a short conversation with the bartender, they walked over to where the guys were sitting.

"Which one of you tough guys is Pete Conti?"

"Who wants to know?" asked Peter as he took a sip of his draft.

"Ben Atom, Ron's brother."

"Then, that would be me," said Pete without flinching a muscle.

"Well that's too bad for you cause you're about to get your ass kicked!"

"I only see three of you. You got help coming?"

"I don't think the three of us will have much trouble taking on you four pussies," responded Ben.

"First of all, I don't need my friends. Second you obviously have no idea who you're talking to. And third, this should be fun; I'm looking forward to it. Just wait a second while I finish my beer."

Peter took a long pull on his beer and slowly stood up.

"You got a dime, Ben?" he asked.

"What da ya need a dime for, you going to call your mommy?" asked the inquisitive brother.

"No, I'm gonna call you an ambulance. I'm gonna make sure you're carried out of here on a stretcher. Alive or dead, I don't much give a shit."

Sonny tossed Peter a dime and said, "You need any help, buddy?"

"No, just tell Jackie I'll be spending the night in jail tonight for putting these guys in the hospital and that we'll have to catch up some other time."

"Let's go outside Ben, I don't want to bust up anything in here."

Peter stood up, and in case it hadn't been mentioned, Peter was built like a brick shit house.

"Wait a minute!" said Ben who was obviously having second thoughts.

"Just tell me why you and your buddies teamed up and beat up my brother last night."

"My buddies? They weren't there. I was there alone. I hit your brother one time with a love tap for crying out loud and he dropped like a rock. I was going to hand him his head on a platter for what he said to my woman, but she stopped me," said Peter.

He continued with, "Whatever he told you were lies. Now, if you're willing to take the beating I was going to give him, I got no problem with that. Let's just get this over with now. You're wasting my time."

"Hold it, one second. Just hold it. I think there's been a misunderstanding. Just take it easy. We're just going to go."

Ben and his friends turned and walked away.

"You are cooler than the bottom side of a pillow," said Sonny. "You would have got your ass kicked if you went out there alone."

"Two things. We would have never made it outside. I would have punched Ben in the throat before we took five steps. If the other two would have come at me, I know you guys; no way you're not in it. I really wasn't worried."

"Yeah, but that phone call line was great!" Ray added.

"Small lesson. Why fight if you can talk your way out of it."

"Now I have to go home to change my pants before Jackie gets here. I believe I soiled myself," added Pete with a boyish smile.

They all laughed but deep down inside they had an unbelievable amount of respect for their childhood friend. Always had.

Ray took off to meet Kathy, Sonny headed to Rosey's sister's, and Al was heading home. Pammy was picking him up at his house. That left Pete sitting at Jake's waiting for his life to begin.

CHAPTER THREE

When Jacqueline Millen walked into Jake's she was a vision of grandeur. Absolutely breathtaking. Dressed to the nines and made up like she was posing for Glamour magazine. She was trying to look the best that she could and her mission was accomplished.

Peter looked up from his chair and almost fell out of it. It's funny how someone can look at another person for ten years and really never see them. But this particular moment, seeing Jackie and really looking at her, would stay in Peter's memory for the rest of his life.

"Jesus, Mary, and Joseph," Peter whispered to himself.

"Jackie you look simply beautiful!" he said so loud the whole place could hear him.

"Thank you kindly sir," she replied with a curtsy. "I'd better. I've been working on this look for an hour," she said, smiling with a smile that was so bright she looked like she was doing toothpaste commercial.

"I'm meeting someone here. Do you want to wait with me?" she added.

"What do you mean? What are you talking about? Who?" replied a semi-confused Peter.

"Oh, you. I've been waiting what seems forever for you to ask me out and you have the audacity to ask, 'who.' Peter Conti, for being one of the smartest guys I know, you sure are dumb."

"I was stupefied by your beauty." he replied. "Did that make up for it?"

"In spades," she answered. "You don't look so bad yourself," she added.

"Thanks," he replied. "I took a shower yesterday, just because I knew we were going out. I didn't change my underwear though. No sense in spoiling you."

Jackie just laughed and laughed. She sat down at the table and ordered a Coke. She was just shy of her eighteenth birthday, too young to drink, but it didn't matter, alcohol wasn't her thing.

"What would you like to do tonight?" he asked.

"Can we just talk for awhile?" she replied. "I'm a little hazy on what happened and what is happening between us. I guess I really would like a little clarification."

"Well, interesting comment to start but I'll be happy to give you my take if you will respond in kind," he said with a smug look on his face. "Here goes. About ten years ago a boy made friends with a very nice girl who lived around the corner. They went to the same school together and in fact were in the same fourth grade class. They hung out together, along with a multitude of other friends, girls and boys, and stayed friends all the way through high school. The boy, as he got older, started to look almost exactly like Paul Newman only a little more handsome. The girl looked OK.

"One day, at a party, the guy was walking to his car and saw a small argument going on between this girl and some unfortunate fellow. Our hero walked over there out of curiosity, but just before he got there, he tripped, stumbled and fell. As he fell, he bumped against this unlucky young fellow. The poor guy tumbled down. As luck would have it he was completely finished conversing with the girl, so he left.

"The girl on the other hand, seeing the chance she had been waiting for, for many, many years, threw herself at our hero, offering sexual favors for the unbelievable act of courage he just exhibited. After she showered him with kisses and almost begged him to ask her out, he gave in to her pleading and asked her for a date. And even though he never had an inkling of interest in this girl they got together and that's how we got here."

"Oh, thank you your majesty for clearing things up for me, from your perspective that is. Now let me enlighten you and put some reality into this conversation.

"Some of the stuff you said was true. We have been friends for ten years and you are nice looking but who, I repeat who, was the guy that for at least the last four years has been watching almost my every move at school? I believe that would be you Mr. Conti.

"I should have asked Principal Miller if he would move our lockers closer to one another just to prevent you from straining your ears and eyes. Now, let's get this straight. Thank you very much for helping me out with what turned out to be an uncomfortable situation, but I could have handled that situation myself. And, I kissed you because I have wanted to kiss you for, as you say, many years. I think you are a wonderful person, a perfect gentleman, a handsome man in marvelous shape, a good son, a good brother, a good friend, and a person I would be proud to be associated with. Even though I am obviously way too good for you.

"Now that's how we got here."

"Hmm, now that you mention it, that sounds a little closer to the truth. But, here is the real truth." Peter said as he reached out and grabbed Jackie's hand while staring right into her eyes. "I fell in love with you in the fourth grade. I have always hoped that one day you would be my wife. I think you are the most beautiful woman I have ever seen. And even though I am absolutely sure you are way too good for me, I am hoping beyond hope that you are in some small way feeling the same way about me. If you're not, at least I've had the chance to say this: I've always felt that if I never did, I would regret it for the rest of my life.

"Jackie Millen, I'm head over heels for you!"

Jackie hesitated a second, smiled, and replied "I knew you were slow but I didn't think you were blind. There has never been another boy for me. I never thought for a minute that we wouldn't be together, forever. You are the love of my life. I came here with the same thought. If this night ends with us going our separate ways, at least I would have gotten a chance to tell you that I love you, and that I have loved you what seems forever!"

Peter squeezed even harder on Jackie's hand. Not a word was said for what seemed an hour but was only a minute or two. A single tear fell from Jackie's eye before Peter broke the silence and said, "Just remember who said it first."

Senior year was a blur. Pete and Jackie were inseparable as were Sonny and Rosey.

Jackie was Pete's biggest fan when it came to his sports, but he had other fans too.

"Mr. and Mrs. Conti let me assure you that Peter will get the finest of educations at the University of Miami. We have the highest rated engineering program in the state of Florida and I guarantee you Peter will get more than a little playing time on our football team in his freshmen year," said Walter Bar, the Hurricanes' head football coach and recruiter.

"Coach, first, call me Tom and my wife's name is Teresa. We want you to know that we definitely like everything you're saying here but this decision is solely up to our son. As you're well aware he's had a number of offers and he's still considering almost all of them."

"Well Tom, and Teresa, we at the U want you personally to know we will do everything legally in our power to make sure Peter has all the tools and help we can offer to get him to the ultimate goal of a college degree."

"We're sure of that Coach, but as mentioned, the decision is Peter's."

Peter sat and listened to all the promises and semi-bull that was now a normal occurrence in the Conti home. The big thing for him was the visitations to each of these schools, first class treatment all the way.

"Well Mr. Big Time, have you decided which school you plan on blessing with your attendance?" spouted Ray as the usual boys sat at Jake's.

"I don't know guys. I'm thinking I've got a lot better chance of playing if I go to a smaller school like Villanova or Canisius. They're closer to home and all too."

"Yeah, and closer to Jackie, too. God you're pussy whipped," interjected Sonny.

"Oh my God. If anyone on the face of this planet shouldn't be calling anybody else pussy whipped, it's you!" answered Peter. "If you look in the dictionary at the words pussy whipped, you'd see your picture," he added.

"I'm not pussy whipped. It's called love."

"Yeah, apparently love is not having to say anything except 'yes honey,'" piped in Al.

"Wait a minute. How would you know? You took your cousin to the prom for Christ's sake."

"She wasn't my cousin. She was the daughter of my mother's friend's cousin."

"Never mind. I rest my case," said Sonny. "Anyway back to you, man. Where do you really want to go?"

"I'll tell you guys. I liked The University of Missouri. The campus is spread out and easy to get around in. The facilities are great. Columbia was a neat little town. I liked it, but it's so damn far away. I just don't know."

"You're gonna have to decide pretty soon man. It's almost letter of intent day," said Ray.

"I will. Right now we're in the middle of the baseball playoffs and that's what's on my mind. I'll make a decision in the next week or so."

That night Peter had dinner at Jackie's house. Her mother was busy making a delightful dinner in the kitchen. She was an excellent cook, and Pete enjoyed both the food and the company. Jackie and her fifteen-year-old sister Judy assisted but mostly they watched. Jackie's dad and Peter sat on the patio. Mr. Millen with a beer and Pete drank a Coke. Peter just waited for the question almost every person he'd talk to over the last month or so had been asking.

"So, have you decided on a school yet, Peter?" asked Mike Millen.

"Not really sir, but the University of Missouri is at the head of my list right now."

"Great school. The Big 8 is a tough conference though. You ready for that kind of challenge?"

"I don't know! I met a few of the ball players when I went there and I have to tell you, sir, they're mammoth. I met Rickey Anderson, their middle linebacker, and I'm not kidding, his arms were bigger around than my legs," he said making a circle with his hands as big as a bushel basket. "They do have a great work out facility and according to Coach Lewis, I'm just the right size now." But he did add with a smile, "With a little more muscle in a few areas."

"Sounds very nice Peter. Good luck wherever you chose to go. Mrs. Millen and I have always known you would go far in life and now the opportunity is staring you right in the face. Don't screw this up boy, and I don't mean the football. A college education can take a man a long way in life. I know I've always regretted not going further in school."

"I don't know sir. Seems to me you have all a man can ask for. You have a beautiful home, a good job, and a wonderful family. What else could a man want?"

"Thank you, Peter. That's nice of you to say. Jackie is right about you. You are smart. You brown noser," he said laughing.

With that the women came out toting platters of food. Featuring chicken, Italian style in Peters' honor. They ate like kings and laughed and enjoyed one another's conversation. It was a very nice evening. One that they had had many times before and one that Peter hoped would go on for the rest of his life. The way that Peter and Jackie looked at each other made it obvious to the Millens that that was definitely a possibility.

Not a day went by that the two weren't either together or on the phone. Their lives were entwined and they both loved it that way. If Peter wasn't eating at Jackie's, Jackie was eating at Peter's. If there was such a thing as a perfect couple, this was it.

Saturday's baseball playoff game was between Tonawanda and Kenmore East at their field. It was a big game for both teams. The winner would go on to the regionals, while the loser would stay home and watch. Their season would be over.

Jackie led the procession of cheerleaders to the front of the stands as they started their chants. Of course Jackie was a cheerleader. How could they be the perfect couple without that? It just seemed like nothing could go wrong in the blessed lives of these two young adults. Then it happened.

Bottom of the sixth, Tonawanda was leading by two but Kenmore was up and they had the bases loaded with only one out. THS took the lead on Pete's double in the gap with two outs in the fifth. Ray was pitching a great game but he was getting the ball a little up that inning and the Kenmore guys were taking advantage of it. Ray had a worried look on his face as he rubbed up the ball getting ready for his next pitch. Pete noticing the anxiety on his buddy's face, called time out, and went to the mound.

"Ray, you've been pitching your whole life and you're good. Real good. Remember that when you throw this next pitch. This guy can't hit you. And remember you've got eight other guys out here behind you. If he gets lucky and does hit it, we'll catch it. Now do your thing man. No worries, buddy."

The next pitch came; swing, and the Kenmore batter hit a high foul ball along the third base side. Peter turned and ran back as fast as his legs could carry him. The ball was coming down over his left shoulder and he had his eyes on it all the way. Just as the ball hit his glove, he stumbled over a rut close to the brick wall that ran along the left field sideline and flew head first into the structure. Peter went black.

When he woke up he was in Kenmore Mercy Hospital. He was totally disoriented and scared. The only people in the room were his mother, his father, and Jackie. Jackie and Teresa cried in each other's arms and Tom stood in the corner trying not to cry, but it wasn't working. Peter tried to gather his thoughts but couldn't seem to place what was going on. He tried to speak but he couldn't. Three times he tried to call out but nothing. Finally he spurted out the word "Mom."

Teresa scrambled to her son's side. Reaching out for his hand in a panic she grabbed it and said. "Oh, thank you, Jesus. Thank you, Jesus!"

Peter wanted to ask a bunch of questions but couldn't. Only his eyes could ask. His mother still crying started answering the unasked questions.

"You're in the hospital honey," she choked out. "You've been out two days." She tried to continue but couldn't.

His father standing over his wife's shoulder, tears still running down his face, continued, "You were in a coma son," he said with his tears of fear turning to tears of joy. "We didn't know if we were going to lose you," he said gathering himself so as not to scare his son anymore than he already had.

But Teresa was doing quite well at accomplishing that feat all by herself. Her tears of joy were loud and uncontrollable.

"Honey, please, Peter needs you strong now. Come up here and talk with us."

Jackie dashed into the room, followed closely by the Peter's doctor. All three stood behind him as he examined Peter using some instrument that allowed him to peer deep into Peter's eyes.

"Well, Doctor?" asked Tom Conti almost pleadingly, "Is he alright?"

"Too soon to tell now, Mr. Conti. Your son has had major trauma to his brain. The fact that he even came to is all we could have hoped for thus far. Right now he needs plenty of rest and close observation. He's going to be here awhile."

Again Teresa Conti started to cry but this time she wasn't sure why. Just the unknown was getting to her. The entire time the doctor was speaking, Jackie sat in a chair in the corner of the room and wept.

Three days passed and Peter started to focus much better. His speech was not impaired and his physical condition and appetite were well on their way to where they were before the collision with the wall. His family almost never left his side the entire time. There was always someone there with him, be it his mother, father, or Jackie. Now that he was on his way to getting his strength back, friends were allowed in.

As much as Sonny, Ray, and Al wanted to pimp their buddy, calling him a pussy and slacker and whatever else they could think of just to avoid saying their true feelings, it didn't work. All three lifelong friends were worried sick for days and when they finally saw their buddy, joking and name calling just didn't fit. His eyes were blackened. The left side of his head was still swollen from the incision the doctors had to make to relieve the swelling in his brain. He looked like five miles of rough road.

"Jesus, Peter, are you alright?" They all said almost in unison.

"You oughta see the other guy," he said with a smile that was obviously a little painful.

"What can we do man? Just name it."

"There is nothing you guys can do. I just need time to heal. I have what they call a cerebral concussion and there's no fixing it."

"What does that mean?" asked Sonny, obviously worried as hell.

"It means that when I hit the wall part of my brain detached from my skull. It's gonna be detached, maybe forever."

"Wait, explain that a little more. What do you mean, forever?"

"No problem guys. Everything will be back to normal pretty soon. It just means I'll be getting some pretty bad headaches every now and again."

"Bad ones?" asked Ray quietly.

"Not good, Ray. I've had a few already and they kind of make you sick to your stomach," answered Pete trying not to make it sound worse than it was. "Hey guys, no one told me. Did we win the game?"

"Yeah, we won. They tied it up in the sixth. But our buddy Ray here hit a dinger over the right field wall in the seventh and we won three to two," answered Sonny.

"I don't know how he even saw the ball, he was crying like a girl at the plate," inserted Al.

"I wasn't crying! Dirt flew into my eyes," replied Ray argumentatively. Then he leaned over to Peter and whispered. "No fucking way we were going to lose that game after they carried you off that field. No fucking way!"

"You did pitch a hell of a game Ray. A hell of a game!" Sonny said defending his friend.

"Yeah, you were great, Ray. I'm only giving you shit. You were great. I could barely see you anyway, I was crying myself. Same dirt."

"How long before you're back? Did the doctor say?"

"Well, that's the good news. You guys aren't gonna have to waste your time watching me play any college games. I'm gonna be normal in every way except: no more contact sports. Can't take another hit to the head. I guess I'll go to college but not on a scholarship."

The three friends just stood there. Not a word was said. Their hero, the best damn athlete they've ever seen in their short lives was done.

"You're gonna be alright, that's all that matters. Fuck sports. All they do is make you sweat and smell like Al," said Sonny doing his best to break the tension of the worst news they've ever heard.

"Fuck sports? Fuck sports?" answered Pete.

"Haven't you guys ever heard of golf?"

CHAPTER FOUR

"Peter! You got a letter from SUNY," yelled Pete's mom as she opened the mail.

"Hell, Mom they don't even have a damn football team," he answered.

"Watch your mouth."

"Sorry Mom," he said as he grabbed his letter and walked into the living room to read it.

"What does it say?" she asked inquisitively.

"Well, I'll be. Mom, you are not going to believe this!"

"What? Believe what?"

"It says here, the State University of New York at Buffalo has approved your request for an academic scholarship and are awarding you, Peter Conti, a scholarship which includes tuition and books for as long as you keep a 3.5 GPA. This award is good for the school years starting August 1966 and last until August 1970. For further information contact the Admissions office at 1700 Elmwood Avenue, Buffalo New York. Congratulations!"

"Oh my God! Thomas, Thomas," Teresa shouted out the back door to her husband who was cleaning the garage.

"What? I'm busy." he yelled.

"Come here quick."

Tom darted into the kitchen expecting to see a fire or something. When he didn't see any apparent danger he quickly said, "Jesus Christ, Teresa, what's so damn important that you screamed like the house was on fire?"

"Peter just received a letter from Buffalo State. He got a free ride. A scholastic scholarship. Isn't that just unbelievable?"

"How?"

Just as he got that word out, Jackie came running in from her house just around the corner. Peter had called her just moments before with the good news.

"I can't believe it!" she exclaimed. "I just sent in the request a month ago."

"You sent in the request?" said Peter.

"Yes! You think the only reason people get scholarships is because they can throw something real far? You're brilliant, you idiot. For crying out loud you've never even gotten a B in your life."

"You're right I am exstreming intelagrent ain't I," he jokingly answered.

"Yes, you are and if you plan on keeping your promise to me, I need you to have that college degree we've been counting on."

"Wait a minute. MOM! Jackie's trying to marry me again," he yelled out covering his head with his shoulder to protect against the expected punch in the arm.

"You keep up the good work, Jack. One of these times he'll realize that might just be a good idea," she said as she slapped him on the same shoulder as Jackie.

"Honey, why didn't you tell us about this? It's so wonderful. Thank you so much," Pete's dad said as he hugged Jackie tightly. "I'd marry you myself if I hadn't of made the terrible mistake of marrying Teresa," Tom said raising his shoulder waiting for the same slap. That of course came.

"But thank you sweetheart. We didn't know how we were going to come up with the money to get this idiot to go to college. This is an answer to our prayers."

"Thank you all but it was Mr. Miller who deserves the credit. He was asking me about Peter's health after the accident and I told him what was going on. You know about the offers being rescinded for the scholarships and he's the one who told me what Peter should do. I just skipped a step and did it myself. Mr. Miller gave me Peter's transcripts saying he would need them for applications. He's really sorry how everything worked out. He said he is Peter's biggest fan. No big deal."

"No big deal?" Peter said grabbing her. "Thank you, thank you, thank you!" and he kissed her full on the mouth right in front of his parents, something Peter would normally never do.

"Wow, that was worth it. Now, I expect you to wash my car every week for a year."

"No problem," said Peter's mom. "Of course I'll do it."

"I was talking to Peter, Mrs. Conti."

"I know, I just said that for fun.

"Now you go over there right now Peter and wash this girl's car."

Everybody laughed. But what just happened was a miracle as far as the Conti family was concerned.

Months passed. Peter was enrolled and doing great at Buff State. Jackie attended Millersport Nursing Academy. Ray went to Niagara Junior College. Mr. Conti got Al a job at the Chevrolet plant. Sonny went to the University of Buffalo and Rosey went to work in the family business, a nice growing clothes cleaning company called simply The Tonawanda Cleaners. Everybody was doing well. There was one that wasn't going too well.

The war.

1966 was a time of death and damnation. The war in Viet Nam was raging. Sorry, the "conflict." The United States lost more men in the Viet Nam conflict than you could count but the country still didn't call it a war. Boys were dying every day in droves, and still it was a conflict. In the presidential elections of 1964 Lyndon Johnson ran on a ticket promising the American public that if he were elected he would deescalate the war and start bringing the boys home immediately.

Barry Goldwater, his opponent, on the other hand said if he were elected he would send in everything we have and blow North Viet Nam off the face of the map. Johnson won and America lost. Months after he was elected Johnson sent more boys to Viet Nam than ever before. The casualties were mounting at an unbelievable pace and the country was torn. Half of

America wanted the war to end and the other half just argued that we shouldn't be there in the first place. Brave American soldiers who put their lives on the line every minute they were there, were treated like dirt by an ignorant angry mass of Americans who for some reason took the political uproar of our country out on the troops. Heroes who fought and almost lost their lives defending democracy and freedom were spat at. Our beloved American flag, our symbol of freedom, was burned. It was not a proud time for Americans.

All the while Peter, Ray, and Sonny were constantly worried. Not for themselves but for their friend, Al. Changes were occurring in America, changes affecting the lives of its young men. On their eighteenth birthday every American boy had to alert the American Selective Service board that they were eligible for service in the armed forces. The American Selective Service board had another name. The draft board. America had a draft, a mandatory enlistment into the Army and a pretty good chance to lose your life. If you were eighteen and not enrolled in school you were classified 1A. If you were still in high school you were 1HS. If you were enrolled and attending college you were 2S. Only men classified 1A were eligible to be drafted. That's why Peter, Ray, and Sonny were so worried. Again not for themselves, they were all 2S. But their lifelong friend and companion Al, he was 1A.

"Al, why don't you get your ass in school?" asked Peter standing in Al's doorway.

"What are you doing here?" asked Al.

"I'm sorry, don't you own a TV or a radio, and is it possible that you can't read," shouted Peter. "1As are getting scooped up every single day. Wise up, you asshole."

"Fuck it man. I got no problem putting as many gooks in the ground as I can. Fuck'em if they can't take a joke," responded Al.

"This ain't funny Al. I mean it, man. We've got five dead from our graduating class already, and twenty-five from the school. Smarten up!"

"I ain't afraid, Pete."

"I know that Al, but me and the guys are. Not for us but for you."

"Don't be. I'm a big boy now. Plus Peter, I can't get into any school with my grades. I've already tried."

"Then get your ass to Canada."

"I don't want to. I'm an American not a Canadian. If I'm called, I'll serve. Period."

"Ah fuck," said Peter. "It's your life man, but I had to speak my piece.

"Come on I told the guys we'd meet 'em for a beer over at Jake's."

"Ok, hold it a second. I gotta drain my lizard."

After Al finished using the bathroom, the boys headed over to Jake's. Al really wasn't too happy about it, he was sure he was going to have this same conversation two more times but thought he might as well get it over with.

The day the threesome dreaded came three weeks later. They were sitting at their usual table over at Jake's when Al walked in and threw it on the table. The three boys all looked up at the same time. They didn't have to read it, they knew what it was, but there it was in black and white—GREETINGS.

"How soon?" asked Sonny.

"I'm to report to Fort Dix, New Jersey, in one month."

"Anyway you can get out of this?" asked Ray.

"Nah, Don't really want to. Hell maybe I can become a general in a couple of years."

"More likely you'll be in the brig in less than a week," added Peter.

"Well, this can only mean one thing, let's get started," said Sonny. "Four beers and four shots Jake, and keep 'em coming."

It wasn't long before the boys were commode-hugging drunk. All the regular stuff had been said a number of times. You know---I love you guys---You're my best friends--Good luck Al---I can't believe how handsome I am, (that was Peter's contribution of course)---It's not going to be the same without you, Al.---standard drunk talk. But every one of these boys knew what was going on, they were all scared, and they had good reason.

As they were getting ready to leave, Pete brought up this question. "We walking or should we call one of the girls? Cause if I drive home in this shape I can kiss my car goodbye. Right after my old man kicks my ass, that is."

"Let's walk. Your old man will kick our asses too!" responded Ray.

They split off one at a time and Peter was just about home when he passed Jackie's house. The door was open and the lights were on in the living room so Peter crouched down by the side of the stoop and whispered into the screen door. "Honeeeey. It's me. Come here a sec, a sec, a sec, a minute."

"OK, darling," answered Mike Millen.

"Oh-oh."

Mr. Millen came to the door. Saw Peter crouching by the shrubs next to the stoop, and said. "What the hell you doing, boy? Stand up! Are you drunk? Get in here."

Peter stood in the foyer while Mr. Millen continued his questioning. "What are you doing? This isn't like you. Did something happen?"

Peter lowered his head. He didn't want to cry in front of Jackie's father, but a few tears were welling up. A tear dropped as he explained. "Al got his draft notice today. I don't want him to die."

"I see," responded the understanding man. "How soon?"

"A month."

"I see," he said again. "Peter, not all soldiers die. Most of them live, for crying out loud," he stated and continued by explaining the facts of war to a half man half boy whose only knowledge of war was what he'd heard or what he'd read in the papers.

"I was in France. D-day. I watched a bunch of brave men who were defending our country and our way of life forfeit their lives in the name of freedom. I was and am proud to have been a part of that. I've known your dad for a long time, a brave man, he was in the South Pacific, Guadalcanal, and he came home, didn't he. Freedom comes with a price. Our boys are paying that price right now, I grant you that. But it's necessary. Most of us came home. Most of the boys going to Viet Nam will come home too. Being drafted is not a death warrant. Al will come home. I know it. Al will come home.

"Come on, I'll walk you home. You look like you could use some sleep."

As they walked out the front door, the door to Jackie's room closed slowly. She got back into bed. She was crying. She loved Al, too.

Life went on as usual. Peter went to school and worked. He was a construction laborer in the summer and stocked shelves in a shoe store during the school year. Buff State was in the actual city of Buffalo about eight miles from Peter's house. After his late class he would often stop at the Delaware Grill for a burger before he went to work. He stopped there because it was right on the way to work and the food was delicious.

He was told a number of times by a bunch of people that the Grill was a hangout for some very suspicious gentleman and that the owner, Vito Bonsano, was probably connected. Peter had met the man on numerous occasions before anyone told him that and found him to be a friendly, sincere man, who treated Pete, even though he was a young guy, with respect. Vito took a liking to Peter, probably because he showed some major balls for even going into the place. They talked on a regular basis. Peter would ask Vito a lot of questions about the old country. Peter was proud of his Italian heritage and was like a sponge when Vito would tell his stories. Their talks went on for a while and then one day Vito said, "Peter. I don't think you should come here anymore. Don't ask me why. You don't want to know. Just know if you ever need anything, you come to me. You have made a friend and I am a good friend to have. Capisci?"

"Yes sir, I understand. I'll miss you though," was all Peter said. He kind of knew all along that Vito was probably involved in other businesses. He dressed like he was the president of the United States and everyone around him treated him with unbelievable respect and that fact was obviously noticeable. Vito always excused himself when talking to people when Peter was present; he never let Peter hear any conversations.

Peter finished his last meal at The Grill, a veal parmesan sandwich and started to walk out. He stopped, walked over to Vito, and stuck out his hand then leaned over and as a sign of respect kissed the man on his cheek.

"Goodbye, sir."

"Goodbye, my young friend."

Little did Peter know what turn of events would transpire over the friendship he struck that day, Nobody could have. Peter Conti, all American boy and Vito Bansano, also known as the Don, the head man, Numero Uno, the boss who was respectfully referred to by all made men, soldiers who were members of the Italian Mafia, as Godfather.

CHAPTER FIVE

November 1968, the United States had a new President. Richard M. Nixon was elected as the 37th president and would take over office in January 1969. Peter, as well as every boy around Peter's age, including their parents rejoiced. Johnson is out and Nixon will start bringing our boys back home, soon. Wrong! The war raged on. More boys went to Nam, enough in fact that we were running out of 1A candidates. So in December of 1969 all deferments for all males eligible for the draft were changed to 1A.

When that happened it didn't matter what Selective Service classification a boy had, he became 1A. There would be instead, a lottery. That's right, bingo balls drawn from two bins. One bin had balls marked with everyday of the year, including leap year, and one bin had balls with numbers from 1 to 366, a ball for each day of the year. A ball from bin one would be drawn and a corresponding ball from bin two would be drawn indicating the number dedicated to the corresponding birthday of the eligible candidate. A televised drawing was to be held on December 1, 1969 and boys with numbers below 120 were definitely going to be drafted, boys with 120 to 180 were maybes and boys with numbers above 180 were almost certain not to go. Depending of course on just how many boys the politicians in Washington were willing to sacrifice in a conflict many Americans felt we had no business being involved in, in the first place.

"What do you think, Pete?" asked Sonny

"It sucks, that's what I think."

"I agree but there is absolutely nothing we can do about it, that's for sure," Sonny added.

"But we don't have to like it," Peter said dejectedly.

Ray then stuck his two cents in with, "Maybe the damn thing will end before it comes to that."

"Yeah, and maybe a monkey will jump out of my ass," replied Sonny.

Peter piped in with. "Hell with it, guys. We got a fifty/fifty chance anyway. Let's worry about it if and when it comes. That reminds me. Got a letter from Al," he said while pulling it out of his pocket.

"Hey Guys... Just got off of duty. Time is short. Maybe four or five more patrols and my ass is out of here. Weather continues to fucking suck, gotta be 200 degrees today. Food here fucking sucks. Hi Poa City fucking sucks. The Army fucking sucks. OK you are now filled in on what life is like in Viet Nam. Don't know what the next few weeks will bring. Just looking forward to getting my dago ass out of here and back home. Looking forward to seeing my family and you guys. I hope you fucking guys never have to come to this God forsaken hellhole. That's all I gotta say about that. Hey, need a favor though. Can one of you guys get one of your women to fix me up when I get home? If I don't get laid by somebody without slanted eyes in the first week I'm back I'm gonna kill myself. Let that be on your heads. Gotta go. They're bombing the fucking camp again. Really. Gotta go. Did I mention this place fucking sucks. See you all soon. Love you guys, Al."

"Man every time we get a letter from that guy he makes the place sound like a vacation spot. I don't think he likes it there," said Sonny.

"Yeah it sounds great," added Ray sarcastically. "I'm just glad the fucker's alive!"

Pete said as he looked at his watch. "I gotta go. Jackie's car's in the shop and I told her I'd pick her up from school. I gotta go, I'm late already."

Peter took off and raced to get Jackie. He arrived just as she exited the school.

She jumped into his car, gave him a kiss, and with a giant smile on her face said, "All A's. 4.0. Perfection. Thank you, thank you all. Oh please, no applause, please."

"What? You get your grades?"

"Do you have your hearing aid turned off? A—4.0---all A's---perfect."

"Oh, then you did get your grades." And up came the protective shoulder. "I'm kidding honey—spectacular—phenomenal—magnificent---very good---very good indeed," he again jested.

"That's all. Take me home."

"I'm kidding. Great job, babe. I mean it."

"Too late. Just take me home."

"Come on. I'm sorry. Really, let me see them."

"OK," she said, excited again as she pulled out the grade sheet from her purse.

Peter scrutinized the report and after careful review said, "Congratulations honey. I know you were sweating out your final on medications but you nailed it. Great."

"I know, Mrs. Holden said I got them all right. Perfect. I'm a genius."

"Yes dear, you certainly are," Peter said with a smile. He wasn't about to make the same mistake twice in less than five minutes.

They started home and out of left field Jackie said, "If you have to go, I want to get married first."

"What? What are you talking about?"

"I'm talking about Viet Nam. If you have to go I want to get married first."

"I'm not going so this is a moot conversation."

"You heard me. I mean it."

"Jackie, this is not the kind of conversation or decision people make, like you're talking about getting a haircut. I've got college to finish. I want to have a decent job. We need to save up some money for a house. There's a ton of stuff to consider before we do anything."

"I said my piece and I mean it," she said with her arms folded.

"I am not having this conversation now. THE END."

"Will you consider it?"

"I said THE END."

"And I said will you consider it,"

"IF and that is a very big if. I get drafted, we can talk about it, but not until. Agreed?"

"OK. I love you, ya know."

"Da."

"Well is that your reply?"

"No. I meant to say I love you too. Women, you can't live with them and you can't live with them." Up came the shoulder.

Peter dropped Jackie off at her house and drifted home. After dinner, Pete's dad was reading the paper in the living room and sipping on a cup of coffee. Pete sat down on the couch next to his dad's chair and serious as could be asked, "Dad, will you tell me about WWII?"

Tom put down his coffee and paper, looked right at his son and said. "What do you want to know, Pete?"

"Everything. How'd you get in the Marines and why? What was it like? And Dad, were you scared?"

"Was I scared? Every single second of every single minute." He answered, but he had plenty more to say. "We were all scared. But we were there for a much different reason than the young fellas who are fighting now. We were attacked. You know all about this stuff, you've read about it in the history books but let me tell you son, there is no feeling on earth that can send a guy off eager to fight than when bombs start dropping on his country." He continued as he explained the circumstances of his enlistment.

"We were playing a little football over at Front Park. A bunch of us all heard the news together that the Japanese bombed Pearl Harbor and we were officially at war. Hardly anything was said; we got our stuff and headed over to the Marine recruiting office, basically because that was the closest to the park on Niagara Street. We got our asses in line, and the next thing I knew I was a Marine. There was no real thinking about it."

"Tell me more, Dad."

"Peter, guys don't talk about what happened during times like that. You almost don't remember details. It's like you just exist. You do what you're told, when you're told, and you do it to the best of your ability. Why? Not so much because you might die if you don't but because someone else, one of your buddies, might die. I was on a lot of teams as a young guy. But none like this one!

"I know you're thinking about a bunch of crap right now, what with Viet Nam blazing, and the draft lottery and stuff. You mother and I talk about it every day. We don't know what will happen. Nobody does. But if you end up going over there, and hear me good Peter, give it everything you got.

"You know how and why guys become heroes? I'll tell you why. Because they're scared, so damn scared that they do unbelievable stuff at unbelievable times, protecting themselves, their men, their ground, their very existence. They are ruthless. If someone needs to be killed, they kill them! There isn't hesitation, not for a second. It's war. The other guy isn't a guy, he's the enemy. You ever hear the expression 'he who hesitates is lost?' Heed that one. I pray every night that you don't have to go. I pray that this freakin' thing will end tomorrow. But if it happens, if you have to go, son, be the best you can be."

There was no more to be said. Peter got up from the couch and walked out of the room. Tom watched him the entire way.

The boys got the news early the next week. Al was wounded. How bad, they didn't know. All they knew was that a bomb found a foxhole Al was in and that he was in bad shape. They kept in constant communication with Al's mom. She assured them that the moment she knew anything they would know. Ray was the first to hear.

"It ain't good guys!" Ray told his friends sitting at their regular table at Jake's.

"How bad?" asked Sonny

"He's blind in one eye and they really don't know the condition of one of his legs."

"At least he not dead," said Pete.

"He might as well be," Ray mumbled.

"What are you talking about? You know how many guys would love to have just come home? Read the papers, boy. I hope like hell his leg is OK. I hope like hell he can walk again. If it's possible, Al will. If he comes home and all he lost was an eye, then thank you, Jesus. That's all I can say, thank you, Jesus."

"You're right, Pete. We all know what that letter could have said. You're right."

They toasted their buddy and right in the middle of Jake's, they all prayed.

"Well, I was going to wait for a better time to say this but I guess there is no time like the present," Sonny said changing the subject and the mood.

"Tell us what?"

"What you're planning to wear for Halloween," said Peter and then added, "I think I'll dress up like a pirate, how about you Ray, are we going trick or treating together?"

"You asshole, no this is not about Halloween, I was thinking you might want to come to my wedding!"

Ray spoke first, "What is wrong with you? Why buy the cow when the milk is free?"

Pete spoke next. "What the hell is that suppose to mean? I've heard that forever and it don't make sense." He stuck out his hand and said. "Congratulations buddy, that's one lottery you surely won!"

"I think so, guys. I'm twenty-two, I'm in love, and with all this shit going on, Rosey really wants this, so . . . ."

"When?" asked Pete.

"That's the thing. I asked her that same question and she said yesterday. That means really soon. This woman does not fool around and quite honestly I'm afraid of her."

Ray just shook his head and said, "Here we go again. Jake, three beers and three shots."

"Yeah, I know, and keep 'em coming," answered the bartender. "And my name ain't Jake. When are you stupid bastards gonna stop calling me Jake?"

"We know that, Bobby. Jake just sounds better," Ray replied laughing.

"Shit." Pete thought. "This is not going to go over too good with Jackie."

The wedding day did come fast. And everything turned out perfect. Rosey looked like a million dollars and Peter told her that while they were standing at the reception line at the Knights of Columbus Hall. He also told Sonny he looked pretty good too maybe not quite like a million dollars a little more like a hundred dollars. All three laughed and hugged.

It wasn't what you would call a giant wedding. It was simple, only their immediate families and close friends were invited. That's what Rosey wanted, and that's what she got. When it came to the best man's toast, Ray, one of the groomsman, said, "Quiet please. Peter Conti, the best man, would like to make a toast."

"One quick toast first. To Al, wish you were here. Come home soon," Peter said raising his glass, and all drank.

"Well, where do I start. I met Sonny two weeks ago in jail. I was arrested for jay walking, of course I was completely innocent. It's true I was, in the middle of the street, but I had just run out there to save a couple of young orphans who were trapped by the moving cars. I was hit in the hip saving them. No big deal. That's why I'm limping a little right now. Sonny was in there for male prostitution. He got caught in the back seat of a car with a seventy-four-year-old black woman. But that's neither here nor there. He said he was getting married in a couple of weeks and since he didn't have any friends due to his bedwetting problem, would I consider being his best man. So here I am."

Everybody was laughing and booze actually came out of Sonny's nose with the bed wetting line.

"No, No, there's no truth to that at all except for the bed wetting thing. No the truth is I met Sonny in kindergarten almost six years ago. Oh hell, that was sixteen years ago. Man time flies when you're having a good time. Sonny is a friend that is with you through thick and thin, no matter what, no matter when. He always has been and as sure as I know my own name, he always will be. I'm sure he knows that's a two way street. I am honored that he chose me to be his best man! (Even though it really pissed Ray off). I've known Rosey almost as long and all I can say to her is: What is wrong with you girl? Let me rephrase that. Rosey you found the perfect man for you and Sonny has the perfect woman for him. I couldn't be happier for both of you. So with that said let's raise our glasses as I say, long life and happiness. Salute!"

Peter went back to his seat to a rousing round of applause. He stopped just before he got to his chair and ran back. Stuck his arms in the air and said. "Wait a minute please, wait just one minute." The room became quiet again.

"Guys," he said to Sonny and Rosey, "Ever since Sonny asked me to be the best man I have been wracking my brain trying to think of the perfect gift. I wanted it to be special. I wanted it to be something you guys would have for your entire marriage that would remind you of me every time you saw it. Finally it hit me. I hope you enjoy this heartfelt gift."

With that Jackie, the maid of honor, walked out with a very large package and handed it to Pete. Peter handed it to Sonny and Rosey and said "Enjoy."

The laughter was riotous as Sonny opened and showed his guests a life size picture of Peter. All four of them hugged.

November came and went fast, and before you knew it, it was December first. Lottery day.

The boys were all together at Jake's, along with fifty others. The place was filled with mixed emotions. All eyes were fixed on the television screen awaiting the first balls to be pulled.

"Well here's to you guys," said Ray as he jerked back a shot. "Good luck."

"You too, buddy," Sonny said sipping a beer.

"I thought you'd be watching this with Rose," said Pete.

"No, she didn't want to watch. She said she'd wait till I got home and I could tell her in person what number I drew."

"That's funny, that's what Jackie said."

"You know guys, think about this, if we get a high enough number we won't get drafted at all and if it's not real low, it might take a long time before we gotta go. Maybe the whole shoot and shebang will be over," Ray added confidently.

"Yeah. Good thoughts, Ray."

The lottery started. After ten or so balls were pulled the date April 8th was called. A guy in the bar yelled. "That's me." The next ball was drawn with a number. The entire bar was silent waiting for the call. "194." The place erupted.

"Drinks are on me, Bobby. Set em up," screamed Eddy Arnald.

This went on for a while before the date called was May 26th. Ray stood up and yelled. "My turn."

Peter and Sonny stood shoulder to shoulder with their friend waiting for the next ball to be drawn.

"244" was the call. All three guys raised their arms in victory, grabbed their shots and down they went.

"Congrats you asshole. That's the number I wanted," laughed Sonny and hugged his pal.

Pete just high-fived Ray and laughed.

Another date was drawn. January eleventh was the date. Big Jim Amith yelled. "Me."

Next call. "Number one."

"I've never won a single God damn thing in my life and this is what I win. This is funny!" He put his drink down and just walked out of the bar.

When November 22nd was pulled, Pete's birthday, Pete stood up and shouted. "I'm up." Again the boys stood shoulder to should. The call came. "Seven."

The bar went silent again, as it had every time one of the guys got a lower number.

"Fuck!" shouted Ray.

"Oh, well. Shit happens," Peter uttered, really not trying to be funny at all.

"Jesus, Pete, I don't know what to say," Sonny said obviously saddened by the number.

"Nothing to say. I'm going in. Shit part is. I'm going pretty soon." Pete drank his beer down, but this time not in celebration. "We still got you to go Sonny, at least that's one low number eliminated."

Fifteen minutes went by and still no June first; Sonny's birthday wasn't called. They just sat and waited. They all had a beer in front of them but really none of them were drinking.

All Pete could think about was Jackie. Yes his parents were going to take it bad too, but all he thought about was Jackie.

Finally Sonny's day, June one came. One more time the boys stood in unison. "330." Again the boys threw their arms up in victory. Sonny was elated but tried to not show it too much in front of Peter.

"Yeah," yelled Peter "Yeah."

"I don't know how I feel right now," said Sonny.

"What are you talking about? You got a wife to worry about. And you Ray, you're a lover not a fighter. We won guys. One out of three. We won Yeah, of course I had to get it broken off in my ass but like I said before, shit happens. And just so you guys know, it ain't the gooks I'm all that worried about. I gotta go face Jackie."

CHAPTER SIX

GREETINGS came ten days later. Peter had to report to Fort Dix, New Jersey, January 15th. He read the letter closely. It said his induction would commence at the downtown Buffalo Civic Center, 1001 Jefferson Avenue, on February14th. There was a list of things you could take with you and a list of things not allowed. It suggested the inductee should take a bus, a cab, or get a ride because after induction the entire group would be hopping a bus to the Fort. He read it three times before he called his dad over.

It was Saturday morning and Tom was just coming home from getting a haircut. He was taking his shoes off when he heard his son call.

"Hey, Dad."

"Yeah Pete, what's up?"

"Got the letter."

Tom walked slowly, with his head down, into the living room. He was in no hurry to read it. He read it a couple of times and said, "Well son, you've got a month to get all your stuff together and get into a little better shape."

"Better shape. I'm in pretty good shape dad, I'm always in shape," he proudly said.

"I hear you, son, but you're going to want to be in a lot better shape than you are now, trust me. Basic training is hell."

"Geez, dad, I bet a bunch of guys show up there who couldn't even run around the block."

"Yeah, and those poor bastards will wish they were dead in less than a week. They'll have you running five miles every day in the first week. You'll be doing pushups because the little bit of hair they let you keep isn't laying just right. I'm telling you son, you are really going to want to be in shape. It will make things a lot easier for you, trust me on this one."

"I understand, Pop. What do you think I need to do?"

"A lot of pushups and a lot of running. A lot."

"OK Dad, will do," Peter said, turning away while putting the letter back into the envelope. Before he turned all the way around he felt a hand on his shoulder.

"I'll tell your mom. You'd better call Jackie. She'll want to know right away." He spun his son around and hugged him. "In case I haven't said it in awhile, I love you Peter." He turned and walked back into the kitchen.

Jackie was getting out of her car when she saw Peter coming around the corner.

"Why are you walking?" she shouted to him.

"Just felt like it."

"I'm dying for a cup of coffee, want one?" she replied.

"You got any whiskey?" he said knowing she'd pick up on that.

"Already," she answered back, and her head dropped.

She put two cup on the table and grabbed the pot that was percolating on the stove. She poured his cup and then her own. She was very meticulous in doing so but was obviously thinking about something else, when she said, "I don't care. We can just go down to City Hall and do it there."

"NO Jackie. I don't want to get married like that. You deserve a big wedding and you're going to get it."

"We can have a party when you get back."

"Please Jackie! What is the difference?"

"There's a difference to me."

"What?" he said. "That I will love you more. I can't love you more. That would be impossible."

"It's not that. I just want to be your wife."

"You will be. I promise."

"Not good enough."

"I can't have this conversation again right now. I gotta go," and he got up to leave.

"Aren't you going to drink your coffee?"

"No, honey. I've really gotta go."

"Are you upset with me now?"

'Of course not. I just have a million things to do and less than a month to do them in, that's all. I'll be back in two hours and we'll go out for dinner, six thirty, just the two of us. I promise, we'll continue this conversation then."

"Promise?"

"Promise," he said as he kissed her and left out the back door, knowing she was just about to break into a tear fest.

Peter walked back into his house to his mother, sitting at the kitchen table, crying.

"Oh, Peter," she said and she stood up and hugged her son.

"No, time for that, Mom. We knew this letter would be here any day and it's here. I've got a bunch of stuff to take care of and I'm going to need some help. Starting with, you, I need you to help me at the jewelry store. I've got two hours to buy an engagement ring. Will you help, Mom, please?"

They headed out the door for Rickman's, their family jewelry store, before you could say Jack Robinson Peter told Mr. Rickman what he had to spend and Jackie's ring size.

He brought out a tray of rings that did nothing but confuse Pete. "I like them all, Mom."

"Here, this one. It's the right price and she'll love it."

"I don't know Mom. I sort of like this one."

"No Peter, this one. Take my word for it. I'm absolutely positively sure."

"Mom?" Peter asked shaking his head a bit.

"Well she came here with me a little while ago when I picked up your father's watch."

"Mom!"

"It's the ring, Peter. It's already sized. Now pay Mister Rickman and let's go. You only have an hour before you have to pick her up for dinner."

"Mom. How do you know that? Does she know I'm getting a ring, right now?"

"No Peter, she just called a second before you came in to tell me to tell you she'd be fifteen minutes late for your dinner date."

"Mom."

"I swear it, honey. Nothing was said about anything other than the time. Honest."

"OK. Thanks, Mom. I think I'll let you keep your position as the best mother in the entire world. How's that?" he said as he kissed her and away they went.

As they walked out the door of the store Teresa Conti could not stop from having these mixed feelings. Her son was drafted today, one of the worst days of her life. Yet she was feeling so happy just then. "Finally," she thought.

Peter knew fifteen minutes meant at least forty-five minutes so he showed up at Jackie's at 7:15. As he pulled up so did she.

"Sorry honey, I couldn't get out of the store. But it will be worth it, you'll see."

"Ya know is it possible to get a little closer to the agreed upon time. It doesn't matter tonight but do we have to be late to everything every time?"

"Quit your complaining! I'll be just a minute. I want to put this on."

"OK but I'm counting to sixty."

While she was changing, her parents came into the kitchen where Peter was patiently waiting.

"Peter we heard. Good luck. We will be praying for you," said Mrs. Millen.

"You'll be fine kid, just don't volunteer for anything," added Mr. Millen.

They started walking out and Peter grabbed Mike's arm and whispered.

"Mike." Jackie's father recognized Peter wanted a private word and let his wife continue on her way.

"What's the matter, buddy."

Peter pulled the ring box out of his pocket and opened it up for his future father-in-law to see.

"Is this OK with, you?"

A big smile came over the man's face. He stuck his hand out and said, "Welcome to the family, Son."

"I won't say a word to the missus. I'll let Jackie do that. But speaking for both of us, we're thrilled. Couldn't ask for a better son-in-law. Congratulations."

"Well, she hasn't accepted yet."

"Ha ha ha ha. Are you kidding? Just have good footing when you ask her so she doesn't knock you down. Now put that away. She's coming."

She looked so sexy her father almost blushed. She had on a low cut black dress that looked like it was painted on her.

"Well, was it worth the wait?" she asked.

"Is that what you're wearing? I said you should wear something nice.

"No wait, for once I don't want to kid. Wow, wow, wow. You look beautiful. No you don't just look beautiful, you are beautiful. Well, Jake's is out of the question."

"Jake's! Jake's!"

"I'm kidding. I've got a nice place picked out. I'm not saying where, it's a surprise. It's nice."

"OK, that's better."

As they were walking out the door Mike yelled out. "Hey Mister Conti. Have my daughter back home by ten. It's a school night you know." He got a slap in the back of head for his joke.

Darone's, one of Buffalo's finer restaurants, overlooks Lake Erie at the mouth of the Niagara River. When Peter phoned ahead for reservations he asked if he could reserve a table with the best view possible. They don't normally reserve special tables but Peter explained the circumstances and they were happy to oblige. Dinner was great. The food was exquisite, the wine was perfect, and the ambiance was spectacular. Jackie started to ask Peter if he had given any more thought to the conversation they were having earlier. He stopped her in the middle of the conversation and said.

"Jackie, not now, and not tonight. I promise you we'll have the talk. But not here not tonight, okay?"

"But Peter?"

"Jackie, tomorrow, OK, tomorrow. We have a bunch to talk about tonight but no talk of marriage. Please, not tonight."

"OK," she said obviously disappointed.

They held hands most of the night. Peter simply couldn't take his eyes off of her. She really was a beautiful woman. They had an after dinner drink and Peter called for the check. The waiter walked over with the check and Peter said. "Just give it to her."

The waiter placed the leather folder holding the check in front of her and walked away.

"God, Peter. I swear. You are something else. I hope I have enough to cover this."

"Well, see how much it is first," replied Peter.

She opened the folder and just stared. Peter who is normally a shy guy, got down on his knee in front of all the other diners, and as she picked up the ring from the folder he said, "I have been waiting to say this since I was eight years old. Jacqueline Millen—will you marry me?"

Without hesitation she answered. "Yes! Yes! Peter I will marry you! I want to marry you more than any woman has ever wanted to marry any man since the beginning of time. I love you Peter. I love you with all my heart."

He reached into the folder holding the ring and gently slid it on the ring finger of her left hand. When he kissed her he could hear the sound of applause in the background. The other patrons in the restaurant had obviously gotten wind of the proceedings and applauded at the sign of the acceptance and the kiss. He stood up and politely said to the onlookers, "Thank you. I'm the luckiest man on earth!"

He sat down and everyone went back to what they were doing. The two lovebirds just stared at each other for a few moments. Before Jackie could say anything Peter said, "I hope this will do until I get back. I want a big wedding. A shindig. I want to show you off to every member of my family and every friend we've ever had."

"OK, darling. Whatever you want," she said with tears of happiness running down her face.

With that Peter waved for the real check. The waiter came over handed Peter the bill and said. "The wine and drinks are compliments of the Darone family—Congratulations!"

They left the restaurant, but didn't head home. The night was just getting started. Peter got Jackie home by ten all right. Ten the next morning.

With the holidays and all, the days went by like minutes. January 14th was on Peter like stink. He had gathered everything he was allowed to bring and was mentally and physically prepared to face whatever was coming. He just didn't know what that was going to be.

The Contis had a big going away dinner for Peter the night before he left. Sonny and Rosey were there, Ray too, of course, but he was solo. You know, woman troubles. The Millens were there, along with a multitude of Peter's aunts, uncles, and cousins. It was like a small banquet. Teresa had filled their family room with various and sundry folding tables and chairs and made room for all. It was very nice. The main course was, by Peter's request, his mother's famous spaghetti and meatballs, a large portion of fried calamari for an appetizer and a salad that Jackie's mom, Patti, brought. For dessert, tiramisu, made by Jackie. It was a wonderful evening.

After the festivities ended, and everyone had wished Peter all the luck in the world, Sonny said to Peter, "What do you want me to do for you when you're gone?"

"What's to do? Hold down the fort."

"I mean it, man. Just name it."

"Well, can you make sure Jackie's all right?"

"I would of done that without you asking."

"I know that, buddy. I also know you're a worrier. But don't. I am going to do just fine. You know me!"

"You know, Peter." Sonny said hesitating a moment.

"I know, Sonny." Peter interrupted. "You don't need to say it. I do too." They hugged.

Peter thanked his parents and headed out. There was nothing said when Peter and Jackie left. Neither set of parents expected their children home that night.

The next morning Peter and Jackie ran back to Peter's house, picked up his stuff, grabbed his parents, went out for an early breakfast, and headed over to the Civic Center. The mood was upbeat but there was definite tension in the air. The unknown is always scary no matter what the circumstances. These circumstances had the possibility of a deadly outcome and there wasn't a one of them that didn't realize that.

Peter decided it was his duty to put everyone at ease. As they were standing in the parking lot beside the building ready to say their goodbyes, Peter hugged his dad, hugged and kissed his mother, and kissed Jackie a loving goodbye, he then said, "I have an announcement. I am going to be fine. I give you my solemn promise. I will come home. I will do nothing stupid. I know you will all worry, but don't. I know what I'm doing and I'm going to be absolutely fine. Nothing happens to people who are loved as much as I am. I know it in my heart."

"Do you remember what I said, son?"

"Yes sir. Every word."

"Peter you will write us and tell us everything that's going on? Won't you?"

"I'll do my best with that Mom. But you know, I'm probably gonna be pretty busy. I'll write when I can."

"Do you have everything you need?" asked Jackie, who had been noticeably quiet.

"I've got all they'll let me have. I'm fine!"

As he turned to go he added. "You know, not everybody goes to Nam."

No answer came from anyone in the group. They all knew the chances of that happening.

"Bye, I love you guys!"

"Bye, son." his parents said simultaneously.

Jackie held her emotions as long as she could. As Peter started to walk away she flung herself at him and with tears flowing she whispered. "Please come home to me, Peter. I can't live without you!"

"I will. That is a promise. I will be back. I love you, Jackie, I love you."

He picked up his duffle and away he went. All around him the exact same scene was being repeated over and over again.

Hello, Uncle Sam!

CHAPTER SEVEN

As the throng of young men entered the building, Peter spotted Jim Amith, a guy he knew from high school.

"Hey Jim. Ain't this the shits?"

"Fuckin' sucks!"

"Tell me how you really feel," said Peter, laughing.

"Any idea what we're supposed to do? Where we go?" asked Jim.

"They'll tell us, Jim. If they don't, just follow the crowd."

Just then a mean-looking guy, apparently the man in charge, in uniform of course, yelled out. "All right children, get into some sense of order here. All the guys with last names from A to E stand right here, you're number ones." He pointed to a square painted on the ground five paces from where Peter was standing with the number one painted in it.

"F thru J in that box, from now on you're called number twos.

"K thru O right over in that one, you're three.

"P thru S, you guys are four, right over there.

"T thru Z, you're number five, in the box right behind me.

"If you're not in the right box get in it now.

"All right. Number ones, I am Sergeant Riker. Shut your mouths and follow me," he said as a squared jawed, well-built man wearing a perfectly maintained starched uniform, a drill sergeant's circular hat, and sunglasses, even though he was inside the building, stood in front of box number one and screamed out. "This way, ladies."

"Where do you think we're going?" Jim whispered to Peter.

"I don't know, but I wouldn't talk if I were you," answered Peter.

They were walking so fast it was more like a trot. They went down a couple of flights of stairs and were led into some kind of a locker room. "Strip down to your skivvies, keep your socks on, stow your gear in a locker, except for your induction notice, lock it and take the key. Then line up, with your notice in hand, against that wall. If you were not smart enough to remember your notice, when you get to the first window give them your name and social security number, they'll give you the papers you need. Now line up."

Peter answered before Jim even asked. "I don't know, Jim."

"This is where we find out if you ladies are healthy enough to be in this man's army. For those of you with your notice go to the appropriately marked window, hand them your notice and wait for them to stamp it, then move forward to the hole in the wall ahead of you. Hand your paperwork through that hole and then stick your arm through it."

When it was his turn, Peter handed his letter through the hole on his left. Someone on the other side took it, grabbed his index finger, and stuck it with a pin or something. Peter didn't exactly know what they were doing 'cause he couldn't see a thing except a blank wall. After a minute, he was handed back his document and his hand was shoved back out the hole. He stepped forward and stood behind the guy in front of him. When Jim was done and stepped up behind Peter, Peter said, "Blood test."

The line was still moving and at the end of the hall was a good sized men's room. They were handed a big beaker and the sergeant yelled instructions. "OK ladies, stand in front of a urinal and put about two inches of piss in that jar. Don't fill it up; you won't like what you have to do with the excess. You got it?"

The ordeal ended with a doctor's examination. When it was Peter's turn, the doc checked his reflexes, did the whole open your mouth and say ahh thing, and checked his body out part by part. When it was time to peer into Peter's eyes with the little magnifying glass light thing, the doctor asked, "Ever had a concussion?"

"Yes sir, I was hospitalized with a concussion when I was in high school."

"I see," he said as he took a little closer look.

"Have you been having much trouble with it?"

"Well, I do get some pretty bad headaches."

"Are you having one right now."

"No sir, not right this minute,"

"OK, then get your ass over there with the rest of the guys. You're fine."

Peter got up walked over and got back in line. The physical was over. The only test of his life that he would have loved to fail, he passed. Jim followed. They were led back to the locker room where they dressed, retrieved their stowed gear, and headed out to the buses. Before they entered the bus, heading to Fort Dix, they were asked to stay in line, turn to their rights, raise their right hands and repeat after the speaker. "If you do not agree with what you just swore to, take three steps forward, the rest of you pile in the buses."

"Welcome to the US Army."

The buses arrived at the Fort early that evening. After a meal, if that's what they call it, they were led to a barracks and assigned bunks. Jim made sure he had the bunk right next to Pete's.

"For those of you who don't have the ability to remember, I will repeat my name." the sergeant yelled out. "My name is Sergeant Riker. I am your babysitter for the next thirteen weeks. You can call me Sergeant or Sergeant Riker, but do not call me Sir. That is reserved for officers. Your response should be and will be in unison and loudly, YES SERGEANT."

"Yes Sergeant," was their response.

"I can't hearrrr you."

"YES SERGEANT."

"That's better. Reveille is at oh five hundred. At that time you will be issued all the things you will need to exist here at Fort Dix. After that you will be taught the proper way of stowing your gear, and the proper way of making your bunk. You will be taught these things one time and one time only. For thirteen weeks you're mine. If I were you I would listen to everything you are taught. You will eat and shit the army way. You will learn how to stay alive and keep the guy next to you alive. This is no game gentleman. This is life and death. And you can bet your asses, you won't die 'cause you weren't in shape. Be ready for hell. You got that, ladies! Now hit the rack. Hell starts at oh five hundred."

Sergeant Robert Riker was a twenty-year man. He had already served two tours in Nam. And was awarded the bronze star for heroism under fire along with a purple heart for wounds he suffered while earning that star. He was and is a full-fledged hero. He acted and sounded like a hard man but just the opposite. He volunteered to be a drill sergeant. He watched too many men die over there not to try and help. He was hard on his men because he wanted them to live, every last one of them. Now he had a new batch of raw recruits and he would do everything in his power to make them the best soldiers they could be, no matter what.

When the minute hand hit the twelve, signaling five a.m., Riker stood in the middle of the row of bunks and loudly blew the whistle that usually hung around his neck.

"You have fifteen minutes to be cleaned, dressed, and standing in front of your made bunks. Is that clear? Starting right now." And he gave a short burst on the whistle again.

Thirty men scrambled in different directions making sure those orders were carried out. Nobody wanted to face the wrath of Riker.

They were issued their gear, returned to the barracks and put on their fatigues, the uniform they would wear for the next three months. Next they were taught the proper way to stow that gear along with their personal belongings. When they were finished with that, Sergeant Riker showed them the army way to make up their bunks. The second he finished his demonstration he screamed.

"OK ladies, now you try it."

Riker seldom spoke. He yelled his orders. But that's not the nature of the man. That was his job. To keep these boys alive, and discipline was just one of the things they needed to learn. He didn't give a lick if they liked him, but he would teach them respect and the consequences of not following the rules. He would teach them the meaning of following orders.

After he tore apart most of the bunks, he made them try again and again until they were remade to his specifications.

"Now that's how you make a bunk. I expect your bunks to look like this every morning. If you sit on them, remake them. If the major comes in here for a surprise inspection your bunks better look like this and your lockers too. Now head over to the mess tent. I wouldn't eat too much though. We're going for a little jog when you get back. Be lined up in front of the barracks at oh nine hundred. Dismissed."

All that running Peter did the previous month, on his father's advice, paid off in spades. Guys were dropping like flies and it was impossible to even count the guys who lost their breakfast. By the time they hit the two-mile marker Riker had seen enough.

"Fifteen minutes, ladies. My mother did better on her first day, for crying out loud."

Four or five of the guys were still standing strong when they stopped and Sergeant Riker made a mental note of who they were. Peter was the first name on Riker's list.

After they limped back to camp they were given a needed rest, had lunch, and headed over to the administration building for classes.

Peter did as he was told, how he was told, and when he was told to do it. He was always alert and studied what he was supposed to know. He was always at the head of the pack and was always quick to lend a hand when needed. He was a model recruit, and it surprised no one when Sergeant Riker called Peter into his office. They all knew what was going on in there.

"Conti, I like you, so it pains me to do to you what I'm forced to do."

"Yes Sergeant, and what would that be, Sergeant?"

"I'm forced to make you the platoon leader of this here bunch of loafers."

"Yes, Sergeant."

"Yes Sergeant? You don't even know what that entails!"

"Yes, Sergeant. I don't know what that entails, Sergeant."

"You are now accountable, if someone fucks up, you'll get the blame, if someone's late for anything, you again. These men need a leader and I think you can be that man. Are you up for that challenge?"

"YES SERGEANT."

"Then don't let me down. Dismissed."

When Peter exited the Sergeant's office the rest of the platoon saluted him, even though you only salute officers. That was their way of accepting Peter as their leader. They all knew it but two minutes later Sergeant Riker came out an announced it. They were starting to become a unit.

The training became more intense. Five mile runs with full pack. Night marches. Survival training. Pushups, more pushups, and of course a lot more running. They almost never walked anywhere. It was always double time. Ten mile marches. More classes. That's how it was for weeks. Army way this and Army way that, run here run there, eat this, and shit there. Everything you need to know to kill somebody fifty different ways. They were becoming a well-oiled machine. Now the competitions were starting. First Platoon was at the head of almost every category and mainly for one reason.

First came the rifle range. Best shot in the entire camp. PFC. Peter Conti. 1st Platoon.

Next came the mile run. Fastest runner on the base. PFC Peter Conti 1st Platoon.

Obstacle course, best time. That's right. PFC Peter Conti 1st Platoon.

Obstacle course, best accumulated time. 1st Platoon Peter Conti Platoon leader.

And it went that way for thirteen weeks. If Peter didn't win the contest he was near the top. When graduation day came around all the guys were trying to figure out where they would be heading when Sergeant Riker came into the barracks and yelled, "Conti Front and center."

"Yes, Sergeant," he yelled.

"Follow me Conti, the major wants to see you."

Peter had no idea what was going on. He hadn't done a single thing wrong and had followed every rule to the letter.

"Wait here, Conti."

Sergeant Riker walked into the major's office with Peter just outside.

"Are you sure about this boy, Bob?" asked the major.

"Yes sir, dead sure, I'll stake my reputation on him. He's diligent, intelligent, a born leader, he can shoot the eye out of a snake at a thousand yards cook him up and make it taste like lobster. He's fast, strong, toughest guy in the camp, and fearless. Sir, I'd be honored to fight side by side with this man. He's the best I've ever had."

"That's high praise coming from a soldier like you, Bob. Send the man in."

Peter walked into the major's office, saluted, and stood at attention.

"At ease, soldier." The major hesitated for a second or two and said. "Private Conti, your record and accomplishments here during training camp have been exemplary. Soldier, we have a unit for men like you, men who show unusual skills, courage, and special abilities. It will mean additional training but when you have completed that training you will be part of the most elite, most feared force, this man's army can offer, Special Forces, son. Welcome to the Green Berets."

Riker stood in the corner wearing a smile. He was proud of what Peter was able to accomplish and he hoped that he had some small part of making him the soldier he turned out to be. As they walked out of the major's office Riker told Peter how he felt.

"Congratulation, Soldier. You deserve this. If there is anything I can do for you, you let me know. I said this behind your back and now I say it to you face. I'd be proud to fight beside you, Pete. Good luck," he said as the two men shook hands.

Peter was honored. Once you go through basic training all the information and conversations you've had with the civilian population become moot. All the, be careful, don't volunteer for anything, and the don't be a hero advice goes by the wayside. You're a soldier. You do your duty to the best of your ability. Your reason for living, your purpose, is to defend your country and all the people who live in it. That exact moment, with the major's words still ringing in his head, Peter knew what his duty was. He was going to train and learn everything he possibly could. He was going to heed his father's words and "be the best that he could be." Peter Conti was going to become one lean mean killing machine.

Special Forces training was intense and then some. They were taught how to fire every kind of weapon the army had to offer and fire it on target. Not just the standard M-14, which had a limited range, but assault rifles that could kill a man from 2000 yards. That's over a mile away. They were taught numerous ways to kill a man with their hands, their feet, their fingers, their thumbs, knives, bayonets, rocks, ropes, hell they were taught twenty ways to kill a man with a spoon. They learned to disarm, disable, and dismember the enemy. They became fearsome soldiers, with the skills to go on missions in small forces and get the job done. Even if the force was one.

Their physical training wasn't any picnic either. There were numerous parachute jumps, that went without saying; being in the Airborne Division was a prerequisite to being a Green Beret. No, that was like falling out of bed for these guys. But being dropped out of a helicopter in the middle of the Everglades with nothing but a knife and a compass and expected to meet up with their comrades in a certain number of days, now that takes some skills. Brass balls too. After that was accomplished, they were dropped in the desert with the same equipment and the same orders. Their next assignment required a two-man team. Two men were issued their knives and compasses again, but this time they were also given a twenty-foot rope. You see, this assignment was to scale a mountain, free hand, using just the rope, get to the top, tie the rope around each other's waist so that there was three or four feet separating them, and wait. Wait for what you may ask. They stand there until a helicopter that is dragging a rope with a hook on the end, flies by and hooks the rope tied to the men. The men would then slam together and be lifted and brought safely to the ground. Are these guys tough or what?

Competition between these soldiers was fierce. They were the best of the best and they wanted to prove it. The rifle range was a good place for that. All twenty Special Forces trainees were poised to show their prowess. They were shooting assault sniper rifles at 200 yards to start and there wasn't one shot that stayed from the bull's eye. At 500 yards ten soldiers scored four out of five bulls and ten were still a perfect five of five. Peter was one of them. At 1000 yards three soldiers had a miss but were still four out of five, magnificent shooting, but not good enough. Only Peter Conti and Lee Roy Sikes, a country boy from Birmingham Alabama, were left. They were shooting at 1500 yards, almost a mile from the target. Two rounds would determine the winner of this competition. This wasn't training at all now, this was a sporting event. Lee Roy had the first shot and didn't waste it.

"Bull's eye." the spotter shouted out as he pulled his head back from the fixed binoculars.

"Nice shooting, Lee Roy," said Peter.

"Thanks man, have at it."

Peter took careful aim. He adjusted the tripod. The rifles they were shooting were equipped with powerful scopes but the wind was a big factor, plus the drop that the projectile would lose over the distance traveled. Peter took all that into consideration and squeezed the trigger.

"Bull's eye," the spotter yelled again.

Lee Roy set up for his final shot, and squeezed the trigger.

"Miss," shouted the spotter.

Peter took his final shot and didn't miss. Two bull's eyes from almost a mile away, that's not good shooting. That's incredible. Peter gained the respect of his peers, and acclaim of his superiors, that day.

Training continued. They were taught to survive on nothing and gain weight while they were doing it. They could see in the dark better than an owl. They could hold their breath underwater for an extraordinary length of time. They could walk into a room, turn off the light switch, and kill a man before the lights went out. These were dangerous men. The best our country could offer. When training was over, the mission had been accomplished; these soldiers joined an elite group, a group respected and feared. Wherever they went the other troops would stare. These were special soldiers. These men wore the symbol of strength and honor, the badge of courage; these men wore and were the Green Berets.

It was a proud day in Peter Conti's life when he stood with his comrades in front of the troops at Fort Bragg and was awarded his silver wings and his green beret. He had all ready been promoted to corporal when he entered Special Forces training and now along with the wings and beret was given his sergeant stripes. He had come as far as you can in a relatively short time. Sergeant Peter Conti, Special Forces, Green Beret.

The Green Berets were not just respected by their peers. They were known and famous to the American public as well. This was a small group of men who carried respect wherever they went in or out of the army's realm. Such was the case when Green Beret Peter Conti stepped off the plane and walked down the gate at the Buffalo International Airport. Soldiers were always looked at when home on leave. When you have on the Green Beret, you're stared at.

"Hey soldier. Do you remember us?" Came the call from Peter's proud father standing with his wife, son Russ, daughter Marie, and of course, Jackie.

"Yes, sir, I have a photographic memory," he said putting down his duffle and hugging each and every one of them, lingering a little bit longer when he had his arms around Jackie. There were no tears, just smiles from all. Russ picked up his brother's bag and they all headed towards the exit.

"My brother's a Green Beret," yelled Russ proudly.

"He's my son!" yelled Tom, and everybody laughed.

"We were not kidding back there, son. Special Forces, Green Beret, God we're proud of you, Peter."

"It's nothing, Dad. But I will tell you, this green hat gets a lot of respect."

"I'd say it's the man wearing it that's getting the respect, Peter," interjected his mother.

"Thank you, Mom. I think that's the first time you ever referred to me as a man."

"Your boy days are way behind you now, Peter." She smiled. "But to me—"

"Don't say it, Mom."

"Tell us everything, Pete. Tell us what you had to do to be a Green Beret?" questioned his obviously proud kid brother.

"A bunch of stuff. Just a bunch of army stuff."

"Did you have to kill anybody?" Russ continued.

"Not today. But the day's not over yet. You might find out if you keep asking so many questions."

"Those are all good questions though," added Tom "What was the hardest thing?"

"The desert. They drop you in the middle of the desert and all you have is a canteen of water, your compass, and a knife. You had the coordinates and four days to find your unit. You get pretty thirsty."

"I don't want to hear anymore," said Teresa "Tell us fun stuff."

"Mom, there isn't any."

Jackie hadn't said a word. Just held onto Peter's hand as tightly as she could.

"We're going straight home, I hope?"

"Gotta stop at Nana Conti's, son. She was so upset about missing your going away dinner, she's been complaining the whole time you've been gone. We told her a hundred times you knew she was out of town 'cause her sister was sick. But she's been so upset."

"OK, Dad. No problem. I'd love to see Grandma."

They stopped, Pete's nana stuffed food into everyone despite their claims of not being hungry, she kissed her grandson way too many times, and they left.

"OK, can we go home now?"

"Well," said Jackie. "Honey would you mind stopping at my house for just a minute? My dad said he knew you'd be too busy to stop by later and they just want to say hi and welcome you home."

"Dad, drop us off at Jackie's. Yeah, I'm tough all right," said Peter, and Jackie laughed.

Shortly after the brief welcome home from Jackie's parents, Peter got settled in and he and Jackie headed over to Jake's to meet their friends. When they walked into Jake's there was a loud roar, led by Sonny and Ray. Hugs everywhere. "Missed you, man," said Sonny.

Every bit as anxious to greet Peter, but slow in getting up, was Al.

"God damn, it's good to see you, Al," said Peter brushing past a number of out-stretched hands. They hugged. "You look good, man."

"Thank you, you lying son of a bitch. But you're the one that looks good. Green Beret, I'll be damned. Peter Conti Special Forces Green Beret. You are one Bad Dude."

"Shut your hole. It's just a job."

"Don't tell me that, mister, I know better." They hugged again.

As Peter was greeting the rest of his old buddies, their wives and girl friends, his three lifelong buddies knowing it would embarrass the hell out of their friend started singing "The Ballad of the Green Berets" from the movie. Peter just stood there and laughed.

"How was that, Pilgrim?" asked Sonny doing his best John Wayne impersonation. John Wayne was the star of the movie "The Green Berets."

"OK, that's enough of that Green Beret bullshit. Stop or I'll be forced to kill all three of you motherfuckers."

Everybody laughed. They partied into the night.

Peter spent most of his time with Jackie and his family. The four friends were together a bunch too. There wasn't a lot of conversation about Viet Nam and Al seldom talked about his time there at all.

One night, the four boys were alone. Jackie, Rosey, and Kathy (Ray and Kathy were on again off again and they were on again then) were off shopping. The boys were sitting around just talking. The Viet Nam subject was brought up. Peter told his friends he had his orders. He was going to Da Nang, July 25th. He hadn't told his parents although they asked a number of times. He kept telling them his orders read to report to Fort Bragg, but he knew that was just a jumping off spot. He planned on telling them after he got to Bragg. Why worry them now. That included Jackie of course. The boys told Peter their lips were sealed and wished him good luck. Just then Al spoke. He hadn't told the boys what happened to him and he wasn't planning on it. It just came out.

"They were bombing the base again. It was a regular occurrence," Al said softly. The boys stopped what they were doing and gave Al their undivided attention.

"When the sirens went off I was in the mess. I left my shit on the table and ran out. We had foxholes everywhere. Over by the laundry was an extra large one and I jumped in.

"The next thing I knew I was lying outside of the foxhole. I couldn't move a muscle. I knew I was in bad shape but I couldn't move to see what was wrong or missing. I knew I couldn't see out of my left eye. I was extremely weak. I just lay there hoping someone would come soon. I lay there for what seemed hours. I was on my side so I could see feet walking around. I saw bodies in front of me but I couldn't tell how many. Why weren't they coming to help me, was all I could think. A medic came by. He was checking the bodies in front of me. He just left them there. He finally came over to me. I guess he was checking me out but after a second or two he just left me. I wanted to yell out, wait, I need help but he was gone. I waited again. This time I was blacking out a few seconds at a time. You know, like when you're dozing off in a chair. Finally another medic came by. I could see him standing over the bodies in front of me. What is he doing I thought. Then I saw. He was removing their dog tags. They were all dead. I was saddened beyond belief. If I could only have moved maybe I could have saved a few of them. Then, finally the medic came over to me. He bent over me and when he removed my dog tags, I knew I was dead. I couldn't believe it. All I could think of was that your mind doesn't stop when you die. It's impossible for me to explain the terror I felt. I just dreaded the moment they would close the lid on my coffin. Oh God I thought. Why?

"I lay there thinking is this forever. For eternity will I be looking up at the top of my coffin? I started to doze off again and I was elated. Now I get it. I will soon fall asleep and that will be the sleep of eternity. Thank God, I thought. Just before I dropped off for good, a medic knelt down by my head and screamed, 'This one is not dead. Get a stretcher over here.' I woke up in the hospital a few days later. My left eye was gone. I had a couple of chunks out of my chest and my leg didn't work. I couldn't feel it at all.

"As I lay there feeling so very sorry for myself, I started looking around. There were guys in there with no legs. There were guys in there paralyzed for life. I saw things that made my injuries look like a toothache. I thanked God that day and I've been thanking him every day since.

"I've never said that to anyone before and I don't think I'll ever say it again. Only to you guys, only to you."

Not a solitary word was said. The three of them just looked at Al. What could they possibly say? Sonny popped a beer. "Anybody want a beer?"

"I think we can all use a shot, Sonny," said Peter.

Sonny grabbed the bottle. He opened it and through the cap away, the signal that the bottle wasn't going anyplace till it was empty.

Sonny picked up his shot glass and he said, "To Al."

Al pick up his glass and said, "Thank you Sonny, but I'm already home. I've got a better toast—to Peter."

CHAPTER EIGHT

"Da Nang, what a shit hole," thought Peter as he stepped off the transport that brought him there from Fort Bragg.

He grabbed his gear and headed over to the base camp outside the city limits. He was to report to a Captain Henderson for his assignment. After making an assessment of the surroundings, he was directed to the one and only permanent building on the camp. He pulled his orders from his top pocket and walked in. "Sergeant Peter Conti, reporting for duty, sir."

"At ease, Sergeant." He grabbed the orders out of Peter's hand and read them. "Get yourself situated. Private Planter will show you to your quarters. Report back to me at oh eight hundred."

"Yes, sir."

A moldy tent greeted Peter as he stepped through the flap. "Jesus," he thought. He flung his stuff on the cot and opened the back flap to get a little airflow through the tent.

The camp was bustling. A group of men threw a football around, and some just lay around listening to music. Peter walked over to the latrine and when he came out he heard someone singing . . .

"From Niagara's speeding water sweeping to the sea. Stands my dear old Alma Mater glory be to thee.

From our hearts a chorus sounded, sounded far and nigh, here's to you my Alma Mater Tonawanda High."

"You have got to be kidding me," said Peter as he walked over to where Jim Amith, his high school pal, was singing.

"Is this a small world or what?" he said to Jim as he stuck out his hand.

"Holy shit. Peter Conti a Green Beret. Are you kidding me?"

"Shit man, somebody had to do it," answered Peter.

"Congratulations, Pete. You got a bigger set than I thought."

"I don't know how to respond to something like that."

"The normal response here to almost anything is to say, hey you got a beer."

"OK, hey you got a beer?"

"Glad you asked. Grab a stool and make yourself comfortable. I'll rustle up a couple. Have you been home lately?" Jim asked as he reached into a bucket and grabbed two cold ones.

"Just left there a little over a week ago."

"Anything new?"

"Are you kidding, there hasn't been anything new in Tonawanda in a month of Sundays. No man, same old place."

"Never thought I'd miss that place but I surely do."

"Hey man, fill me in about this hole," Peter asked as he took a long drink.

"Oh, it's really nice."

"If you stray too far from the camp at night alone, you have a very good chance of being killed, for a starter. We're hated here, the locals all wish we would die or go home. The food stinks, the hookers are diseased, the beer is almost always warm, you've got to know someone to get ice. I know someone by the way. Every time you go out on an op you figure it's your last, the hours are long, the pay stinks, you have a perpetual case of athlete's foot, the weather is ridiculous, and it's almost impossible to sleep. Other than that it's fine."

"Jesus Christ," Peter muttered.

"I don't think he visits here," was Jim's response.

"How long have you been here?"

"Eighty-one days but who's counting. The truth is when you're here days don't matter till you're a short timer—twenty-one days. Then days matter. You got orders yet? I'm sure that you're not staying here with us peons."

"I'll find out in the morning, and I don't plan on peeing on anyone."

"Well, buddy. It's good to see ya. Welcome to Viet Nam."

Peter reported to the captain exactly at 0800 as ordered.

"Do you have my new orders, Sir?"

"Yes, Sergeant right here." He pulled an envelope from his drawer and read them before he handed them to Peter. "You are to report to Po Jing, by August first, connect with four other Green Berets led by a Captain Olsen, and await further orders from a Major Eller. That's all that it says."

"How do I to get there, Sir?"

"I have supply trucks heading there tomorrow; you can catch a ride with them. Report to Sergeant Meyers at the motor pool in the morning oh seven hundred, he'll direct you to the caravan."

"Thank you, Sir."

"Good luck Sergeant. Dismissed."

Peter spent the next few hours in his tent writing and sending off letters to his mother and to Jackie. Didn't say much, just reassure them that things didn't seem too difficult as of yet and that he missed them. He had decided that he really didn't want to give them too much information and worry them anymore than they all ready were.

After he grabbed some food at the mess tent he made a pass around the camp, feeding his curiosity and locating the motor pool. When Jim Amith was finished with his duties the two friends got together for a couple of brews. Not too much was discussed as far as where Peter was headed, he said some small town north. He did tell Jim he would be leaving in the morning.

"They don't tell you much here, just where to go, what to do when you get there, and what time to get back. Never why."

"Don't need a why. That's not my job," answered Pete.

"Yeah, Pete, but sometimes you'd really like to know why."

"Is this your base camp? Do you know?" asked Jim.

"I don't know shit except I'm outta here in the morning."

The two friends spent the rest of their time reminiscing about Tonawanda and high school days, Pete said his farewell and left. He had no idea if he would ever see Jim again. In wartime, no one ever knows.

Peter caught up with Sergeant Nicholas Meyers early the next morning. Meyers was a cantankerous weathered soldier who'd been around the block a few times. This wasn't this man's first dance. Meyers told Peter he was informed that he'd have a passenger and that they would ride together. They would be in the lead truck.

Four trucks loaded with supplies going to Po Jing took off right on time. Their orders were to drop their load there, fill up with their needed supplies and head back to camp that same day. Each truck had a driver and a soldier who rode shotgun. It was only about a two-hour trip, but as always when traveling in the jungles of Viet Nam, hazard was involved.

"Green Berets, huh. You guys are some bad ass sons of bitches," Meyers said, like that was a given.

"That's what they say."

"We've been told you guys can jump into an enemy foxhole with just a knife, kill everything that moves in there, and come out without breaking a sweat."

"I heard that too."

"You don't talk much, Conti."

"You know Sarge, I'm just busy keeping my eyes peeled. There's gooks here in Nam you know."

"Yeah, I heard that myself."

After awhile they came to a narrow spot in the road, not that it was much of a road. The over-sized trail was not only narrower; the jungle was thicker there too, so Meyers slowed down a bit.

"Now's a good time to peel back those eyes. We've lost a truck or two in this area before."

Not a minute after he said that, a bullet enter the windshield and caught Meyers in the shoulder. Pete grabbed the steering wheel with his left hand and turned the truck angling it between two trees. He shut it down and pulled Sergeant Meyers out and laid him next to the truck. The back trucks followed. As all the men huddled together at Sergeant Meyers' side, Peter spoke. "Anybody see where that shot came from?"

"I think I saw a puff of smoke from the top of that crest, Sergeant," answered Private Johnson.

Three more shells hit the lead truck as they spoke.

"I see it. Just left of that clump of trees on the right. Anybody else see that?"

"Yes, Sergeant," came the response from a number of the men.

"Johnson, see to the sergeant's wounds. I'm sure there's a first aid kit in every one of these vehicles, and sit tight till I get back. I am in command now that Sergeant Meyers is out of commission. I'm going to do some recon of the situation."

He continued with, "Take up positions guarding the trucks and supplies. Private Rogers, is it? Grab the set of walkie-talkies I saw under the front seat here. Keep listening for my orders. If you don't hear from me or I'm not back in two hours, turn around and get back to the camp. Is that clear?"

"Yes, Sergeant," was said simultaneously.

Peter, armed with an M-14, a knife, and a couple of grenades, took off. Seconds later he was out of sight. Moving like a cat. Headed to where those shots came from.

Five hundred yards from that clump of trees he saw movement in the bushes. He settled in, becoming almost invisible with his surroundings. Two Cong were sneaking their way apparently to the trucks. They had the misfortune of passing directly past Peter's location. Peter let the first one pass. As the second one passed, Peter grabbed him, covered his mouth with his hand and plunged a knife directly into his back. Peter ripped the knife upwards piercing his heart. Immediate death. The slight commotion made the lead man turn to investigate. He got a thrown knife, the knife Peter just pulled out of the other guy's back, stuck in his forehead for his trouble. Peter had dispatched these two without even a sound. He then pulled his knife out of the second man's head, wiped it, and hunkered down, well hidden, to listen for more of their friends.

After five minutes of silence Peter headed again for that clump of trees. It wasn't but another 100 yards and Peter ran into another unfortunate foe. He broke the man's neck before he even saw Peter. Fifty yards further up he crossed a small ravine that just screamed out trap. He skirted the small indentation and circled back. Sitting in wait were three more soldiers, eyes peeled on the ravine crossing. They heard a shot and there was only two. They started to scramble but before they could dive into any hiding spot, there was one.

Peter slithered towards the remaining gook, his heart pounding. Moments later he heard a slight rustling of a bush to his left and his M-14 spit out a volley of three rounds. Peter moved a few yards from where he fired so his enemy couldn't pinpoint his exact location and waited. He had no idea if he had dispatched the third man. After what seemed an hour but was probably only minutes Peter silently meandered to a spot where he could view the area behind the bush he fired into. There lay number three, dead as a doornail.

As he was surveying his surrounding he heard two more shots coming from the spot he was advancing to. Apparently they were still firing on the convoy. They sounded like they were coming from high up. Peter figured, sniper. Probably perched in a tree. Often times snipers have spotters, guys who do the targeting for them. Peter searched the trees for both possibilities, when suddenly another shot was fired, badly timed for that sniper. Peter located the shooter, and within seconds he had the spotter too. Pop, ten seconds later, pop again, two quick shots from Peter's M-14. Two Viet Cong dropped like acorns falling from a tree. He searched the area for more enemy soldiers. None found. He called in.

"All clear, eight enemy soldiers down."

"Yes, Sergeant, Good work, Sergeant. What are your orders now, Sergeant?"

"First, how is Sergeant Meyers?"

"Complaining, Sergeant. Wants to know where you went, Sergeant."

"Sounds like he's as tough as he looks. Sit tight, I'm on my way back. I want to check our backside before we take off."

"Yes, Sergeant."

Peter circled back. It wasn't over yet. Four more enemy soldiers were approaching the truck following the road behind them. The key word here was where. Peter intercepted the rear attack before it started. He strangled one, knifed one, and shot the other two. He left the bodies where they lay and headed back to the trucks.

Peter took a moment to gather his thoughts. He just killed twelve men like he was squirrel hunting on a Sunday morning. He's been on Viet Nam soil less than seventy-two hours and he'd already taken lives. His head was spinning a bit but he surveyed his situation and it only took a few moments for reality to set in. What he did was save lives, nine of them. This is war. More words of advice from his father struck home. "If you have to kill someone you kill em. It's war." That being said, Peter still walked to the road with a heavy heart.

Peter got back to the trucks, informed the men of the happening, like it was nothing special, and helped get the sergeant back in the truck. Of course this time Peter was doing the driving.

The other men got back into their trucks. Knowing that what they had just witnessed, no matter what Sergeant Peter Conti Green Beret called it, was something special, more than special, it was flat out heroic.

"What the hell happened out there?"

"I went to see who was doing all the shooting. It kind of pissed me off that one of their bullets went awry and hit a friend of mine. When I was walking out there, two gooks came running out of the jungle, tripped, and fell on my knife. Danced with another but he was dead tired. Three more decided they didn't want to breathe anymore so I obliged them. I shot at the other two, who were up in trees, I probably missed 'em but luckily they fell out of the trees and killed themselves. Then on my way back I stumbled into four of their buddies who must have been lost, why else would they be headed to our trucks. They won't be finding their way back at all. I'll tell ya Sarge, it ain't safe out here."

Meyers had a painful laugh and stuck out his hand. "Thank you, soldier. You're something else. I've always knowed it but now I'm sure. Green Berets are some bad mother fuckers"

Moments later, Peter gave the sergeant a full and actual report, which was required since Meyers was the man in charge. Meyers took mental notes knowing he would have to report all this to the captain when they returned. What Meyers didn't say was he wanted to make sure of the facts so that Peter Conti got the credit he deserved. People get medals for what he'd just done.

They pulled up to the supply depot at Po Jing about noon. Men were running around in every direction, it looked like an ant farm. Peter helped the sergeant out of the truck and into a nearby jeep. Peter didn't care whose it was and he didn't ask.

"Johnson, come with me," he ordered.

"Rogers, you ever been on this duty before?"

"Yes, Sergeant."

"Then you know what to do; take over here. Johnson and I are taking the sergeant to the infirmary and will return shortly. If you have the new supplies loaded before we return, just stay put. You got that soldier?"

"Yes, Sergeant."

They didn't need to ask directions. Johnson had been to the camp at Po Jing numerous times, and knew where the infirmary was.

"Who dressed this wound?" asked the doctor.

"Private Johnson here, Sir," answered Peter.

"Good job soldier. You stopped the bleeding and there is no sign of infection. Very good job. I'll patch this man up in no time but he'll be staying with us here for a little while. I'll write this up, just give the paperwork to his commanding officer."

"Yes, Sir," answered Peter.

They moved Meyers to a bed; Peter tagged along and stayed till he was settled in.

"Any word you want to send along?" asked Peter.

"Yeah, tell them loafers to get their asses right back to camp. Tell them I expect the motor pool to be spic and span when I get back. Have them tell the captain I'll be back as soon as I can."

"Will do, Sergeant."

"Oh, and Sergeant. Thanks for everything."

"No problem Sarge. I'll be here for awhile I think. I'll be back to make sure your not bothering these pretty nurses too much."

"Thanks again, and Sergeant, call me Nick."

"It's Pete, Nick."

After Peter got everything straight with the men at the supply depot he went hunting for the Green Beret named Captain Olsen. He wasn't difficult to find. Most men knew where the Green Beret unit was. They're highly respected soldiers at any camp. He dropped his gear on the ground in front of the first tent, tapped on it like he was knocking, stuck his head in, and said.

"Sergeant Peter Conti looking for Captain Olsen."

"Two tents down," came the response from the sergeant sitting on his bunk.

"Thank you, Sergeant."

Peter moved the two tents down, and did the same routine.

"Sergeant Peter Conti reporting for duty, Sir."

"Jesus, Conti. Hell of an introduction."

"I'm sorry Sir, did I say something wrong?"

"No, not that. It's all over camp already about the new Green Beret who wiped out a small platoon single handed before lunch."

"Well, it wasn't a platoon captain. Charlie just had a small patrol out as a welcoming committee to greet us, Sir."

"Well done, Sergeant." he said gladly, knowing he would be working and probably fighting alongside this man in the very near future.

"Do you know our orders, Sir?"

"I don't. I was told to wait for a Major Eller to show. He'll have our orders."

"How many Green Berets are in this unit?"

"With you, there are five of us.

"Now, go grab a bunk in the first tent, with Sergeant Burk. Get yourself situated. We'll all go for chow together and you can meet the rest of the men."

"Yes sir. I may have just met Sergeant Burk a minute ago when I was looking for you, Sir."

"Good. Go get comfortable. See you shortly, Conti. Welcome aboard. Dismissed."

As Peter grabbed his duffle and started walking back to the first tent, possibly his new home, he didn't know what to think. Earlier he actually killed men. Took some of their lives with his bare hands. Felt the life drain from one man while he was killing another. This was like a nightmare. The worst part was it was just beginning. He came to this conclusion, "Whatever I'm suppose to do I'll do. No sense in worrying about it. I've got a thirteen-month tour here and it's just getting started." One thing did become perfectly clear to him: whoever said "War is hell" knew what they were talking about.

"Not necessarily Pete. They make their living as loners. Getting too close to one another will only, in their minds, make it easier to be targeted. No, my guess is we'll encounter these men throughout our journey, at about the same pace. Good question though. Keep them up."

CHAPTER NINE

Peter stuck his head in the first tent again.

"Sergeant Burk? Captain Olsen said I should bunk here with you. My name is Conti, Pete Conti."

"Welcome, Conti, Pete Conti. Name's Nigel but my friends call me Nitro. Throw your stuff down and make yourself at home."

"Thanks Sergeant. Does that name Nitro, have anything to do with explosives?" Peter asked sarcastically.

"It has everything to do with explosives. There ain't a thing that's ever been built that I can't blow up."

"You don't have anything in here that can go boom, do you?"

"Nah, they frown on that here." he laughed. "How long you been over?"

"I'm green."

"Well, if you're the hotshot that just made the grand entrance into camp, it don't sound like you're too green."

"Jesus, man. How fast does word travel in this camp?"

Nitro responded with, "You can't take a shit without everybody knowing. Hell, what else is there to do? Besides, everybody likes to hear when Charlie takes it in the ass. Nice going, Conti! Every time a fellow

Green Beret comes up smelling like a rose, it just builds on our mystique. GIs think we're gods. I love it. Welcome."

"Thanks Sarge."

"Call me, Nitro. What did happen out there this morning, man?"

They talked for a short while. Burk had to go check on something he was cooking up. He has to work on the outskirts of the camp, for obvious reasons. Peter got organized and got as comfortable as he was going to get. He was anxious to meet the other guys but more anxious to know what their orders were, and where he was going to fit in. He started jotting down a note to Jackie but decided what happened in Nam was going to stay in Nam. She and his entire family are worried enough.

At 1700 hours, Captain Orin Olsen stood at the flap at the two sergeants' tent.

"Chow," he shouted.

Peter stepped out and of course recognized that standing next to the captain stood two more Green Berets.

"Burk with you?" asked the captain.

"No, Sir," said Peter saluting the captain and the other officer standing next to him. "Said he'd catch up with us at the mess tent."

"Peter Conti, this is Lieutenant Joseph Lavaca and Sergeant Tom Tully, the rest of our interesting group."

"Lieutenant, Sergeant, good to meet you."

"Po Jing Pete. Wow. He's real. Sorry couldn't resist that Conti, but man you stood this camp on its ear.

Hell, by the time the boys are done passing this story around, you will have killed an entire platoon single handedly," said the Sergeant Tully with a big smile on his face. "Good job, Sergeant, it's good to have a man like you on our team."

Sergeant Thomas J. Tully, enlisted in the army in '64, became a Green Beret in '65, second tour in Nam. All Green Berets are more than efficient when it comes to weaponry but some are what you would call, let's say specialist on one weapon in particular. Tom was Viet Nam's answer to William Tell. What an archer. Put a bow in this man's hands and he could hit a dime tossed in the air from 100 paces. He could do the apple thing but he hasn't been able to find a volunteer that would put the apple on their head. It wouldn't take a genius to figure out the handle Tully was labeled with. Everybody just calls him "Tell."

"Italian?" asked the Lieutenant.

"Yes, Sir. Full blooded."

"Paisan. Welcome aboard. Gotta ask. If you just got to Nam, you probably just had shore leave. I would seriously appreciate it, if you wouldn't mind telling me, what your mother made for dinner the night before you shipped out?"

"No problem, Lieutenant. We had veal cutlets, sliced thin and breaded, with fresh lemon, I don't know what your family calls fried eggplant but we call it mulenjohnny, a side of penne, salad, and fresh bread."

"Stop it, you're killing me, you bastard. Why did I ask?"

Lieutenant Joseph Anthony Lavaca. ROTC University of Pennsylvania, class of '68. Went directly into

Special Forces training and shipped into Viet Nam as a Green Beret six months before. They said he could walk across a stick of butter and not leave a footprint. He moved like a cat and could be as invisible as a ghost, a good man to have on your team.

They shared a meal consisting of some form of meat, no one knew exactly what kind of meat but meat all the same, canned potatoes, and green beans. Lavaca complained the entire meal. They all wondered what their orders would be, but no one speculated. The captain said he really had no idea but that when he found out, they would find out. When that was, he didn't know, but he expected Major Eller to show up with their orders, any day. Waiting was always hard but waiting in camp when the fighting is all around you was a whole lot better than anywhere in the jungle.

"Sarge, I mean Nitro, what's the story with the captain? He didn't say much at chow," Peter asked as the men entered their tent.

"Good man and a fine officer," came the reply.

"Yeah, I could guess that, but what's his story?"

"He's at the end of his tour. That I know. The word is that if you were going to rob a bank, he'd be the guy you'd want to draw up the plan. He's a brainiac. Is that a word?"

"I don't know but I get your gist."

"Well, I think I understand this little group. According to what you've told me about the lieutenant and Tell, we have a team made up of Robin Hood, a Ghost, A Brain, and the Mad bomber, kind of sounds like a pretty formidable team. I'm still trying to figure out where I fit in."

"Oh, the captain checked your shit out as soon as he knew you were joining this team. He said you're our marksman."

"We can all shoot man. I don't get it," replied Peter.

"Yeah, we can all shoot, but the word that came down from HQ is you could shoot the dick off a hummingbird from a mile away. If I had to make a guess here Pete, I'd say, sniper."

A few days later Major Eller rolled into camp. He didn't waste a lot of time getting with Captain Olsen's unit. He informed the captain he wanted him and his men in the debriefing tent at 0800 the next morning. He told him to make sure they were fed; it could be a long meeting.

"That's all I know. Let's meet tomorrow morning at the mess tent at 0700. It wouldn't be a bad idea to hit the latrine before the meeting," said the captain to his men right after he got the word. He made it sound like it was going to be a long one.

"Shit. Long does not mean good," thought Peter as he and his roomy were walking towards the mess tent that next morning.

"What do you think, Nitro?"

"No idea. But I'll tell you Pete, long meetings aren't good. Whatever the major's got in store for us, you can bet we'll be taking a toothbrush."

They ate breakfast and were still sitting at the table, sipping coffee and waiting. They were all wondering what was in store for them but were only minutes away from finding out. The mood was somber but these were confident experienced men, except for one that is.

"Are five-man units usual?" Peter asked no one in particular.

"We aren't just any five-man unit, Sergeant. We're a five-man Green Beret unit. Big difference," answered the captain.

"Hell, Pete, I've been on a couple of gigs with just two guys," said Tell.

"Don't get your panties in a bunch there, Pete," said Nitro. "We'll protect you."

"Thanks Sarge, I'm totally relieved."

They all laughed.

"I can't believe they have the audacity to call this food. They should come up with a new word to describe this shit," complained Lavaca as usual.

They all laughed again.

Exactly 0800, the major entered the tent. Olsen's unit was seated and waiting. After introductions, Major Eller got started.

"Men, I would like to start this morning by letting you all know that your country has great confidence in this unit. You have been hand selected based on the innate skills that you not only posses but that you often display. There is no doubt that these abilities will be tested to their limits but we are confident that you men have what it takes to accomplish this challenging task. This mission is of great importance to our campaign. Your success will help speed up the ultimate goal of victory. Any and all information disclosed here today is on a need to know basis. Surprise is the key to its success."

One of his aides stepped in and handed the major some documents. While they were speaking Lavaca leaned over to the guys and said, "What the fuck, they want us to kill Hitler or something."

"Joe!" said the captain, but he couldn't stop a small laugh.

"You're a couple of wars behind, bud," interjected Nitro.

Peter smiled too but this was starting to sound like a little more than he was expecting, considering this was his first official mission.

"Sorry gentlemen."

"Fong Lo Peak is the observation outpost and fortified base camp guarding the pass to Fong Lo City. Gentlemen, we need that city. Problem is we've lost too many men trying to take it. They can see every move we make before we even get close. We need to take their eyes away. We can't get to the objective because the only access to the base is over a bridge that they have heavily guarded. Every attempt that we've made to cross that bridge has been averted, and we've paid a heavy price.

"We think a stealth unit might be able to infiltrate their way through the jungle force, penetrate those defenses and take out the unit guarding the entrance to the bridge. Once the doorway is clear the waiting back up force will hit the other side with everything we've got. Penetrate the camp and cripple the operation. Once they're out of there, we'll blow the bridge. That's the objective, people. I've been given the task to lay out a plan of action but since this is a stealth operation I would prefer to have input. Let's start out with questions."

"He forgot to say 'without firing a shot,'" whispered Lavaca.

The captain shot a look at the lieutenant and asked, "What kind of numbers are we talking about, Sir?"

"It's not the number of men they have guarding the bridge, it's where they are. They have two five-man pill boxes guarding the entrance. Two men in the hole and three on the outside guarding each location. The kicker is there are also two four-man towers that oversee both sites. We do not have a count on the men they have scattered in the jungle leading up to the bridge. There is no centralized camp for these men; it's a guerilla force that acts independently. No one said that this was going to be easy, but it's got to be done."

"What about the backup force. Isn't there a problem that they are seen by the observation outpost?" asked Lavaca.

"Doesn't matter. We always have men positioned there. As far as they're concerned there will be nothing out of the ordinary."

"Time frame, Sir?" was the captain's next question.

"The sooner you men can get into the field the better. Our mission this morning is to put a plan of action into motion. I have maps of the area that we'll go over and a movement schedule if possible."

"Major, do you want the bridge to be in a condition that it could possibly be repaired when we take over the location?" asked Nitro.

"No, Sergeant, blow it to smithereens."

"Yes Sir, I hear you loud and clear."

The major and captain scrutinized the map and a number of different approaches were discussed. The amount of equipment and supplies needed would have to be at a minimum for stealth tactic purposes. A night attack was also discussed but discarded because they didn't want to fight the guerilla force with so close a venue. After considerable discussion Captain Olsen suggested they break for lunch, at which time he would contemplate the situation and formulate a plan based on his men's individual skills. They broke for lunch.

"You like apples, Pete?" asked Nitro.

"Yeah."

"Well how do like them apples," he jested.

"I don't know what to think. I think the captain will come up with something," answered Peter, but not too confidently.

"I don't like the unknown with Charlie in the jungle. We can't see 'em and it's hard to kill what you can't see," said Tell.

"Does anyone else think this food taste like actual shit?" spouted Lavaca with a disgusted look.

"Christ Lieutenant, can we eat once without your commentary?" Tell Tully said while making a face.

"Sorry, Tell, but fact is fact."

Nitro interjected, "I know I can't use timers. We gotta be sure all our men are back over that bridge before it blows. Hell I'll just use a plunger."

"A lot a shit has to happen before any explosions gonna take place," said Peter.

"Don't sweat the small stuff kid. This will be a walk in the park," answered Tell.

"The hard part is eating them fucking K rations." Lavaca said pushing his plate away.

They finished their meal without the captain in attendance. He stayed back just grabbing a sandwich so he could get down on paper what he thought would or could work. The major came there with the basic plan but left the intricacies to Olsen, after all that's what he did best. The captain was jotting down positions for each of his men but to an untrained eye it just looked like he was doodling on the map. The major interjected a few things but only so he felt like he was participating. The orders were almost nothing but the objective. The final plan was left up to Olsen.

The other four men re-entered the tent and were all ears when Captain Olsen took over the meeting. He pinned the map on the corkboard behind him and started.

"This is nothing but a rough draft. We'll hone this thing as we go along. At any time feel free to interject your thoughts. This is not a standard offensive. We are a team here and your thoughts and ideas are welcome. Nothing can be cut in stone. There are too many variables for us to think we can follow a plan till the end but we need something down as a guide. Here's my plan:

"Every weapon we use will have a silencer. Stealth means undetected. If you have to use a grenade or whatever, our cover will be blown but go ahead and use it. If you need it to save your life go for it. We'll change our plan. Hopefully we can get through the jungle without making too much noise.

"Look here at the map." He pointed to the rising mountain. "This is the foot of Fong Lo Mountain, we are going to use that as due north and draw a straight line here along the base. I'll draw a semi-circle from the east point of the line to the west point making it look like a half circle. The center of the straight line at the bridge is the hub and I'll draw three lines from the hub out like spokes, making our drawing look like half a wagon wheel. This far left side," he pointed to the triangle he made on the left side of the wagon wheel, "is where we will attack. They will of course be guarding the entire area our wagon wheel covers, so if we're quiet we'll cut their force down by two-thirds. And we'll have the mountain to protect our left side. Any questions so far?"

"Captain, do you think they'll have the bulk of their men closer to the bridge?" asked Peter.

"Not necessarily Pete. They make their living as loners. Getting too close to one another will only, in their minds, make it easier to be targeted. No, my guess is we'll encounter these men throughout our journey, at about the same pace. Good question though. Keep them up."

"Hey Cap, what about bodies? The gooks seeing a buddy or two with their throats cut don't you think that's a pretty good tip off that something's going on?" Levaca questioned.

"We'll have to address that, Joe. We'll do the best we can to hide them, time permitting. We're definitely going to move faster than I'd like. The longer it takes us the more chance there is of that happening."

There were no more questions so the captain continued. "OK, this is how I see it will work the best. And

Major, I apologize for breaking protocol but we have one captain, one lieutenant, and three sergeants on this mission and we will be talking in whispers the entire time from now until this mission is over. I am going to call my men by their names. Initially we will start out with Nitro on the left, Joe you'll be approximately fifty yards to his right, I'll be fifty yards to Joe's right and Tell you'll be fifty yards to mine. We will move at the fastest speed we can that will allow us to stay as undetectable as possible. Every two hundred yards we will stop and hunker down camouflaged the best we can and listen. Yes, Peter, before you ask, I'm coming to you. OK Peter—first and foremost make damn sure you recognize each one of us by something on our helmets or something—that's critical—now, with a silenced assault rifle you will climb a tree. If something is moving anywhere near any of our locations. Shoot it. Next—when we settle in, climb down, move the distance that we traveled, and climb back up. And so on. We'll do that four times."

"Sir, what about vision? Two hundred yards is not a problem for a shot but the thickness of the jungle could get in my way."

"Get high, Peter. Get as high up as you can."

"Yes, Sir."

"The fifth time we'll be two wide and two wide. We'll need to because the distance we need to cover will be shrinking—look at the pie shape on the map guys. Joe takes the lead left, Tell lead right. Any help will be coming from the right and Tell you can dispatch them more silently then we can using your bow. Nitro second row left, and I'll be second row right. Peter you are going to be climbing your ass off. When the bridge is in sight start tightening up. Everybody got that so far? Any questions? Anybody got anything to add?

"I like it Captain," said the major.

"Thank you, Major. My men and I will work out the details on equipment and the positioning as far as distances, according to the terrain and the thickness of the jungle."

"Do you have a plan once you reach the pillbox positions?"

"Sir, I have some ideas but I'm pretty sure that will be worked out—let's call it, on the job."

"Good work, Captain! Now let's talk about when."

CHAPTER TEN

The men gathered at the airfield, which was situated at the north end of the camp. Peter was the last to arrive. He had to make a stop at the infirmary; Sergeant Meyers was being released and was going back to the camp at Da Nang that morning. Peter stopped by to say good-bye.

"I feel just fine, Pete."

"They were a little worried when the fever hit, Nick, but I told the nurses not to worry. I said you were way too ugly to die."

"Oh thank you, Rock Hudson." And they both laughed.

"Any idea where you're headed?" asked Meyers.

"No. Going to Huzhou and getting orders from there, that's all I know."

"Well buddy, keep your powder dry. And thanks again for hanging around here as much as you have. Listen up Peter; I want you to know you made a friend here for life. You understand what I'm saying?"

"Of course, Nick, it didn't need saying but since you started I'll finish and say friendship is a two way street and you're welcome on my block anytime."

"Po Jing Pete, my buddy, man."

"What the fuck is this 'Po Jing Pete' thing Nick? I mean it man. I've heard that a few times now."

"It's your handle now, Pete. Get used to it."

"Come on, Nick. All I was doing was trying to get from one place to another. It was not that big of a deal. The only big deal to me was that I didn't shit in my pants."

"Yeah, sure. Well, it was a big deal, a real big deal, especially to me. Just accept my thanks."

"Fuck you. I gotta go before I'm late."

They shook hands. It was the kind of handshake that were they Indians it would have signified they were blood brothers.

Sometimes friendships come and go, but wartime friendships are forever, they're cut in stone. There's a special bond made when men risks their lives for one another, a friendship that only men who've been there really understand.

"I was hoping you guys already left," said Peter as he walked up to the rest of his team.

"No way, we could never leave you behind," replied Nitro. "Every unit needs the guy who provides comic relief."

"Stop, you're killing me," shot back Pete.

"You think the food will be better at Huzhou?"

"No, Joe. But we can all hope," answered the captain. "Mount up; let's get this show on the road."

They hit Huzhou and were in their assigned tents by the middle of the afternoon. Their plan was to go over strategies one more time. Then coordinate with Major Eller who would be in charge of the backup force. First they were going to eat. They were all starved.

"I say acceptable," said Pete, as he tasted his meal.

"It's good," interjected Tell.

"I like it," was Nitro's take.

Joe piped in with, "Have you ever taken a bite out of something from the refrigerator that's obviously had gone bad?"

"Stop right there, Lieutenant. We are actually enjoying our food this evening and do not want your commentary," said the captain who meant every word.

"I was just going to say—"

"Stop. Don't make me make this an order."

"I was just going to say that it's not all that bad."

They laughed, ate their meal, and headed to the captain's tent for a chalk talk. They were ready. Captain Olsen would finalize the timing with the major in the morning, and the team would prepare their gear, weapons, and supplies for their departure. It was Saturday night and they planned to be crawling in the jungle Monday at dawn.

They took a jeep to what the captain deemed as the starting point, and hopped off. Tell had his bow and a good supply of arrows. They all put silencers on their rifles and hand guns. Along with field rations, they had grenades, two knives each, and a strangle wire. It seemed like a lot but it's not much more than they usually carry. Peter had an assault rifle made specifically for long-range shots, equipped with a silencer. Nitro had a backpack full of his specialty items. They were as ready as they were going to be. Before they took their positions the captain stuck his hand out palm down. He usually did everything by the book but with these guys he did things differently. Even though it was a military operation he still felt this was more of a team effort and wanted it to that way. Peter walked over put his hand on top, next the lieutenant's hand topped Peter's, then Nitro's and finally Tell's.

"Let's get it done!" Captain said as he pulled his hand away and headed to his position. Nitro, Joe, and Tell followed and Peter started climbing the tree that he thought had the furthest visibility.

They started. First hundred yards, no enemy encounters. They moved another hundred and still nothing. The four lead men settled into cover and Peter climbed down, snuck up and climbed again. Fifteen minutes later they were on the move once more. Joe saw movement ahead of him and drew his knife in readiness for what must be a silent attacker. But Peter saw the movement too. Poof was the sound his rifle made and the unit had made their first kill. Joe slunk to where he heard the body fall. Charlie was alone and he was deader than a doornail. Joe stuck him in a bush and covered up a few of his parts that were sticking out. He moved out again. Tell heard a noise to his right. He drew an arrow from his quiver and waited, perfectly motionless. The silent shaft was unleashed and, kill number two. Poof, poof and Nitro owed Peter his life. Not ten yards from him two men hung from a tree branch, sort of a tree stand kind of a thing, but they weren't going to be needing it anymore.

When the men had traveled their second 200-yard section they met a small stumbling block, a giant field. Captain Olsen was able to signal his men to gather.

"Plan change. First we wait for Pete."

Peter slunk to where they were huddled.

"Good shooting, Pete," said Joe.

"Yeah, thanks Pete, I owe ya," Nitro whispered.

"Pipe down and listen up. We're gonna low crawl this field and get to that creek bed," ordered the captain.

"You got a plan, Cap?" asked Joe.

"Not yet but I will by the time we get there."

"Crawl as a group, Cap?" asked Pete.

"Spread out twenty yards apart. See that pile of rocks to the right of that dead tree? Gather there. Move out."

They slithered through the high grass all the time wondering if they would bump into someone they didn't want to. Luck was on all their sides. They met at the clump of rocks and all ears were on the captain.

"OK guys, here's what we'll do. We keep this spacing and stay the twenty yards apart and we lose our sniper. Peter, take the left flank."

"Should I leave the assault rifle?"

"No fucking way. We'll need that for sure down the road."

"Yes, Sir"

"OK, pop your heads up slowly. You see those boulders that look like an archway about 200 yards ahead of us? That's the next meeting spot. Slow down a bit boys, I think Charlie is all around us now. I can smell 'em. Let's go."

They got their spacing and started their drive. They didn't get far when Tell nearly crawled up a gook's ass; the soldier was heating up something on a one-man burner. He never got to taste it. The only thing he got was a knife slit across his throat. Tell put out the burner and hid it with the body.

The captain was busy too. He dispatched two Cong who were having a smoke break with two silent shots from his .45. Those two found out that smoking was hazardous to their health. The action was heating up and these men were living up to their reputations. Nitro was crouched behind a tree and started to move when a gook thought he detected Nitro's movement. The man slithered in to investigate. Not a lucky break for that soldier. It cost him his life. The team kept moving forward and met at the boulder.

"It's getting crowded out here, Captain," whispered Tell.

"It's gonna get worse," interjected Peter and added. "Seventy-five yards to our left is a small patrol. I counted five. I couldn't take them all myself without making noise. What do you want me to do, Cap?"

"Where are they exactly? Can we jump them without being seen?"

"I don't think so, Cap, our best bet is to circle and pop them sort of simultaneously, that would be the quietest."

"Then that's what we'll do."

"Keep in our order. That's how to determine your target. When we're in position, be at the ready. The signal will be when my target falls, kill yours. Meet right back here. Move out."

They were back in less than an hour. Mission accomplished.

"Good work, Pete," said the captain.

"That just might give us a little undefended space. Joe, do your Houdini act and scout up front about a hundred yards and then report back here. I think they could be grouping up now. We're less than a half mile from the bridge."

"Yes, Sir." And off went Joe.

"Take a rest here boys. You've earned it. Anybody hurt at all?"

There was no response, which was good news.

It took the lieutenant a good hour to scout out their route. You can't be invisible and fast at the same time.

"I got good news and bad news, Sir. We're clear for a hundred yards. That's the good news, the bad news and you can't see it from here but there's an overhang under that set of rocks," Joe pointed forward and slightly to their right, "a small camp, Sir. I counted eight men, four tents. I think they're all in the camp. I didn't see anybody outside it and I covered the entire area. They're cooking."

"OK, we need to move fast while they're all together. Same plan."

Joe interrupted, "Can't do it, they're up against a rock wall sir. But we can cover them with a half circle."

"Even better. Let's hit 'em fast and hard, guys and get back on track. I can guarantee you someone's gonna notice they're losing men pretty damn soon. Use your rifles or hand guns, I don't care, just do it as silently as possible and ASAP. Don't let any of them get a shot off 'cause if they do we're discovered. We'll be trapped in the middle of a bunch of these mother fuckers, Move out and make every shot count."

They moved quickly, following Joe and his planned-out route. Got in position in a hurry and rushed the group of men while they were eating lunch. They didn't know what hit them. One minute they were talking, laughing, and enjoying a meal, the next. . . .

"Drag them over and dump them down that crevasse and let's get out of here. Joe, take the lead and find a spot we can regroup."

"Yes, Sir."

It didn't take the lieutenant much time and he found something even better than a place to regroup. He found what he thought was an avenue right to the bridge. He returned as soon as he spotted it.

"Cap, we're almost sitting on a creek bed that runs all the way to the bridge. I can't say how well it's patrolled or guarded but I can see a spot where we can enter."

"Did you climb into it?"

"Yes, Sir. It's dry and ranges in depth from three to eight feet."

"How's the cover on the banks?"

"Varies, from high brush to clumps of trees."

"OK, that's our way in. Give me a second to think this out."

While the captain was scratching out a plan in the dirt, Peter and his cohorts took that time to eat a little something. They were fast and efficient and were ready to go in less than ten minutes. Peter handed the captain a packet of food, he literally swallowed it down, took a long drink of water, pointed to his scratching on the ground, and said, Nitro, Tell, and I will slide down and travel the creek bed. Joe, I want you to scout the right side of the bank and Pete the left. We'll hang back from you two but only about twenty yards, that way we're all covering each other. If either of you run across anybody or anything suspicious get back to us immediately, unless it's a single and you can dispatch of them without noise. I don't want to get trapped in this creek bed. We'd be sitting ducks."

"Understood, Cap," whispered Pete.

"Yes, Sir, loud and clear," was Joe's response.

"Peter let's try the best we can to stay in eye contact. If we don't, we could end up on our own."

"Yes, Sir."

"Lead the way, Joe. With any luck we could reach the bridge in a couple of hours," said the captain as he was burying his lunch packet. "Let's go guys."

Within minutes the threesome glided silently over the bank into the creek bed and Joe and Peter started their scouting. Peter and Joe were moving at a steady pace but not fast. One would move while the other watched, and then the other. It was too difficult to do both at once. As Peter slipped between a clump of trees and the bank, Joe saw him wave his arm. Joe waved back to the captain and the three men exited the creek bed.

Peter had a soldier moving towards his position. Pete couldn't make out if he was alone so he just sat tight where he was. The enemy soldier ducked down to get under a low tree branch. That turned out to be a very unlucky move for him; you see, that branch was on the tree Peter was standing behind. As soon as the enemy soldier stood erect, Peter grabbed his head and with one quick twist broke the man's neck. Peter laid the dead body in some tall grass, signaled an OK to Joe, and Joe signaled the OK to the captain. They were on the move again.

From there all was quiet. They moved steadily until they came to a section of the creek bed that was too shallow to provide cover for the guys moving in it. Joe waved Peter to stop and fall back. Peter was thinking the same thing. They both moved back to meet with the rest of the team.

"The bridge is in sight, Captain," said Peter "Can't be but two hundred yards."

"Any sign of men?"

"Nothing moving, Sir."

"Joe?"

"Too thick on the right. I maybe have twenty-five feet of visibility."

"OK Time to alert the major of our position."

The major was elated with the success and efficiency of the team, thus far. He informed the captain that the force was in position. They confirmed the time frames.

The captain barked out orders but still made them sound more like a game plan. "We need to move.

Here's what we're going to do. A two-man team, Pete and Joe, will attack the right side targets and us three will take the left. Stay as silent as possible but that might not be possible for too long. We need to move through the jungle directly towards the pillboxes, taking out the guards and anybody else on the ground. When the towers are in sight, Peter you and Tell go up in the trees and from that position take them out. They've got to have their heads up to see anything and every time they try, you know what to do."

"Now for the machine gun nests."

"Let me interrupt, Captain," Nitro said as he grabbed his goody bag. "Lieutenant, if you can get close enough to toss this at them it will take care of everything. Stay low and as protected as possible, this shit doesn't take prisoners."

"What is it? How volatile is it? Can it blow while I'm carrying it?"

"It's a C-4 explosive extract. It can't blow till you stick this detonator in it. But when it goes...."

"OK, I got it. Show me what to do."

Nitro gave a one-minute demonstration and handed each member a charge. He told Peter. "If you got anybody left in your tower when the nest blows just make sure they keep their heads down cause they will have a clean shot at us, Tell, you do the same. I'll take it from there."

"Guys it's been a hell of a day so far, but if we don't get this done, it's all been for nothing. After we've done our thing, jump in the nests, if there's anything left of them. Stay in them. Do not follow our troops in but once they're out, Nitro—do your thing. After it blows, we'll follow the troops back to camp. Good luck team. It's been a privilege."

They split up, Joe and Pete started off to the right and Olsen's group started moving forward.

Peter and Joe moved through the jungle like ghosts. Joe saw movement to his right and slunk towards it. Poof a shoot from his silenced .45 and he was moving forward again. Peter was having a dance at the same time. He quietly took care of his task, wiped his blade on a big leaf and he was moving again too. One hundred more feet and Joe fired again. Peter heard something directly in front of him, he was too open for his liking and five seconds later he was ten feet off the ground in a tree. The approaching soldier was moving slowly and quietly. Didn't help. Poof, Peter's .45 slug entered the man's head right between his eyes. The captain's team was experiencing the same kind of encounters with the same results. Peter and Joe were approaching a clearing. They had a clear view of the tower, and twenty-five yards in front of the tower was the machine gun nest. The two men slithered behind a single tree.

"I'm going up." Peter mouthed the words and pointed.

Joe mouthed, "I'll stay here. When I can I'll take the nest."

Peter found a perfect spot. He had clear vision and ample mobility for the rifle to maneuver and there was plenty of cover. He could see four soldiers as reported. One had binoculars around his neck. Two were sitting on the side talking and the last one who had his back to Peter was lighting a cigarette. Peter took aim and fired. One of the guys sitting on the rail fell. The other three scrambled. It took the man with his back to Peter a second to turn and see what happened. Too long. He went backwards when Peter's second shot hit him in his forehead. Almost at the same time a guard fell from the opposite tower. All hell broke loose. Both machine guns fired continuously, only they were just aiming into the jungle. None of the team was visible. The guns stopped but the men chattered to one another. A minute later one guard poked his head up so he could peer through the binoculars. Bad for him; a shell entered the right lens of the binocular and continued into his head through his right eye socket.

The fourth guy hunkered down in the tower, afraid to move. He made his last move when he looked up to see where the explosion came from. It was the machine gun nest targeted by the captain's team. Nitro had just done his thing. He didn't have much of his head sticking up but he couldn't resist seeing what blew. It was enough of a target for Peter. The man saw that it was one of the machine gun nests, but it was the last thing he ever saw. Moments later there was a second explosion, this time it was the tower that Joe targeted and turned it into little sticks flying in the air.

The machine gun in front of Peter fired into the jungle again. Non-stop. Within ten minutes they had to stop to duck the barrage of shots coming from the multitude of American soldiers who just arrived. They ducked for only a few seconds but that's all Joe needed to hurl his weapon of destruction. Good-bye to them, it was over. The troops rushed the bridge. They were taking plenty of fire but the heavy artillery that was pummeling the mountainside cleared the way for them. Once they crossed the bridge it wasn't long and the battle was over.

Everything else went as planned. Total victory. The blowing of the bridge was nothing but a formality. The five Green Berets caught up with the main force and proudly marched back to camp.

What was it that Peter's dad told him when he was describing a hero? He said: "They do unbelievable stuff at unbelievable times."

Captain Orin Olsen, Lieutenant Joseph Lavaca, Sergeant Thomas Tully, Sergeant Nigel Burk, and Sergeant Peter Conti—heroes.

CHAPTER ELEVEN

Back at camp, Peter and Nitro dumped off their gear and were headed to the captain's tent to meet the rest of the team as ordered.

"Sit down team, and make yourselves comfortable." The captain had a folding table and chairs set up and on the table were two bottles of Crown Royal and five glasses.

He poured the shots, and as they all lifted their glasses the captain said, "To the four bravest men I've ever had the privilege to fight alongside."

Before they drank Tell said, "That's funny we were all gonna say that same thing."

They laughed and drank their shots down. Just then the major poked his head into the tent.

"Come in, Sir," said the captain as all the men started to stand.

"Sit down men, sit down. You've done enough moving around for one day."

As he walked into the tent the boys couldn't help but notice the half gallon bottle of Crown the major was holding.

"Thought I'd drop off something for you and your men, Captain."

"Thank you, Sir. Won't you join us?"

"Damn, I was hoping you'd say that." Everybody laughed.

They talked over the mission but no particulars were discussed concerning the taking of lives. It was more like after we cleared the camp under the overhang, or Pete's shooting cleared my path, that kind of a thing. Matter of fact, it was Nitro who said the thing about Pete's shooting and when he did, he filled everyone's glass again and said. "To Po Jing Pete, the best shot I've ever met."

After they all drank, the major couldn't resist. "Sergeant Conti, I've got to hear this Po Jing thing."

"Major, you ever get yourself in a situation out of pure stupidity?"

Everybody laughed again and they had another shot. You could bet the major would ask one of the other guys when Pete wasn't present. These were fighting men, fighting a war and taking lives, not because they wanted to but because they had to for God and country. When you take another man's life. When a letter has to be sent to a family that their son or husband will not be returning. That's not something these guys brag about. It has to be done so they do it. It's as simple as that. Yes, men talk about what they've seen or heard other guys do. But that's to brag about that man's courage or his acts of bravery. Yeah, the boys kidded Pete with his nickname but every one of them knew what he did to earn it.

Then the lieutenant had a toast. He looked at his glass of whiskey and said, "To the best damn meal, referring to the booze, I've had since I've got to Nam," and everybody laughed again.

Getting serious for a moment the major asked, "Captain, any idea of the number of men you encountered on your way to the targets?"

"Not exactly, Sir. Well over fifty, Major."

"Damn! Fifty! Guerilla fighters. Right in their own back yard. Damn!"

"I do want a full report of exactly what took place. What you did out there was something special. You brave men are perfect example of the fighting spirit this country needs at a time like this. What you did wasn't just a mission to blow up a bridge; it was a mission to save American soldiers' lives, a lot of lives, my men's lives. I could not be more proud of each and every one of you and I feel like it's a privilege to be celebrating this victory with you. Thank you, and I don't mean for the drinks. To the Green Berets."

They all drank.

"Well, that being said, I'll leave you gentlemen to your well-deserved getting plastered." He stood up to leave. When he did all the men stood up and saluted.

The major gave a perfect salute right back and said. "It's been an honor." And he left.

The captain opened the second bottle and said. "I hate to say this but should we go get something to eat?"

"I am going to assume you said that to add joviality to this party," said Lieutenant Lavaca.

Just then from the outside of the tent flap a voice called out. "Captain Olsen?"

The captain opened the tent flap and a soldier rolled in a cart filled with a Thanksgiving-like dinner, turkey with all the trimmings.

"Compliments of the major, Sir."

"Sweet Jesus, I think I'm going to cry," said Joe.

"Thank you soldier, and thank the major for us. Dismissed."

They ate like kings and drank like sailors on leave. It was a night of celebration, and for good reason. Yes, mission accomplished, but they were past that celebration. They were celebrating something else. There wasn't a single one of them who thought when they set out on this mission, that all of them would be coming back. They knew the odds of that happening. That's what they were celebrating. That was a victory all by itself.

The group stayed at Huzhou for three months. Went on routine patrols. Nothing out of the ordinary if you consider fighting a war 13,000 miles from home ordinary. There is seldom downtime in Nam but for this group that's exactly the situation. Peter took this time to write a letter home. This time not to Jackie or to his mother this letter was addressed to Thomas Conti, personal and confidential.

Dear Dad,

Everything you said has come true. Thank you. The being in shape when I hit boot camp to the concentrating to be my best at all times. I don't know what the outcome will be for me but I do know your advice was the best advice you have ever given me. I've had a few situations here already, just like every guy here but I want you to know I'm thinking about you every step of the way. I know what kind of great father you are to all of us kids. I know the power of your love has carried me to the man I am and the man I hope to be. What I didn't know till now is how brave a man you are. When you are thrust into a situation like this one or the one you lived thru, you have to be brave. I've only been here a short time and that fact has never been clearer. For you, just the length of time you spent like this must have been a nightmare. I can't say I ever thought about what you did in WWII. I just took it for granted, but now living some of it I've never been more proud of you. You are one hell of a man, and Dad, I love you.

That's enough of that. Now for what's going on here. I am in a small unit with four of the best guys I've ever been privileged to know. All Special Forces Green Berets. The other soldiers think we walk on water and I'm pretty sure these four guys do. We are having a bunch of down time right now but you know that never lasts long. Yes, I'll be careful. I miss you all so much it's impossible to put it into words. I hope mom isn't worrying too much. Tell everybody that I love them. See you Dad.

Pete

The down time as expected didn't last long; a private stuck his head into Peter's tent and reported that the captain wanted the team to gather together for some new orders.

"We're headed to Da Nang. There's a detail of Green Beret forming there for some additional training. We're all to report to a Major Millington the day after tomorrow. Just bring what you'll need for two weeks; we're coming back here when we're done."

"Chopper, Captain?" asked Tell.

"Picking us up at 0800 tomorrow."

"What kind of training, Cap?" asked Nitro

"Get ready to laugh Nigel, Explosives."

"Why me then, Cap?"

"Hell Nitro, maybe they can use a little help. I don't make them, I just carry them out."

"Will we be assigned tents or can I just bunk with Nitro?" asked Peter "I'm just getting used to his disgustingness."

"Unless they already have us assigned I don't think that will make a difference."

"Hey Pete, you've been to Da Nang before haven't you?" Peter stopped Joe before he asked.

"It's good," Pete said.

Everybody laughed and left. They needed to get their gear together. As Peter walked towards his tent he thought. "Da Nang, good, I'll get a chance to catch up with Meyers and Amith, I wonder how my high school buddy and that old coot are doing."

They took off on time and hit Da Nang right on schedule. They reported to Major Millington and were told to grab a tent in the south section. He said, "Just ask where the Green Beret bunk, you'll find it easy enough. Tomorrow morning report to the rifle range area at 800 hours."

They settled in. Met a few guys who didn't know any more than they knew and went back to their tents for some snooze time.

"I'm going for a stroll." Pete told Nitro. "Got some friends here I want to look up." With that said Peter took off, first stop the motor pool.

He walked in and was just about to ask where he could find the Sarge when he noticed him working on something over at the tire rack. He walked over and said to his back.

"Anybody see a Sergeant Meyers over here? I'm supposed to kick his ass when I run into him."

Without turning the Sergeant Meyers said. "I hope you brought your lunch and a lantern." He laughed. "Pete Conti, I figured you went home and the dogs ate you." Turning he said, "It's sure good to see you."

"Same here Nick." And they shook hands.

"What brings you to these parts?"

"Training. Going to teach us to blow things up."

"How long you here for?"

"Two weeks."

"Good we'll get a chance to catch up. Good to see you're still in one piece."

"Yeah, Charlie's doing his damn best to change that but I'm hanging in there. How's the shoulder?"

"Hell, nothing but a slight inconvenience. It's good buddy. Really is good to see you! You free for dinner?"

"Yeah. Just got to show up at 0800 for training."

"Then meet me back here sixteen hundred hours. I'll steal a jeep and we'll head into town."

"I'll be here. Gotta check on a buddy first. I'll ask him to join us if he can. Is that OK with you?"

"Of course, any friend of yours."

"Great. See you later."

Peter strolled over to where Jim Amith's tent was before. He had no idea if he'd still be stationed there but he took the chance. When he got there, he tapped on the tent and another soldier stuck his head out.

"Yes, Sergeant. Can I help you, Sergeant?"

"I don't know, Private. Do you know a private named Jim Amith? He's a friend of mine."

"Yes sergeant. I knew Jim."

"Knew?"

"Yes Sergeant, Jim's group went out on bivouac about three weeks ago. They never came back. I'm sorry to be the one to tell you."

"Jesus Christ. Thanks, Private."

Peter went back to his tent with a heavy heart. Death was constant there but it's something you just can't get callous to. Especially when it's a friend. Peter didn't know Jim all that well, he was just a guy he went to high school with, but once they entered the army together he got closer to the guy. Peter was saddened. Things like this were just a constant reminder of where he was and what was going on. Life and death is no game.

"Al was right, this place fucking sucks," Peter said to himself as he walked back to his tent.

When he got there Nitro was sawing some zzzzs so Peter took the time to send a couple letters off to Jackie and his mom. He didn't mention any thing about Jim Amith. He kept telling them that he's out of harm's way and that he's pretty safe where he's been. That he's met some good friends. You know a bunch of small talk. If they knew what kinds of things he's done in Nam in less than half a year, they'd be worried to death. Jackie hardly ever left Peter's thoughts. He tried not to think about her whenever he was on a detail. It would cloud his thinking and maybe change the way he would do something. You know trying to be too careful is dangerous to your health when you're crawling around the jungle trying not to be killed. But during his free time, she was always with him.

Peter and Nick spent as much time as they could together during those two weeks and their friendship was completely cemented. Peter learned how to blow things up "Real Good", Joe found a little place in town that would cook some stuff up that he actually enjoyed, Tell and the captain did their jobs professionally as always. The trip was a success as far as every man was concerned, except for Nitro; he was bored the entire time. In his own words "This was like teaching Mozart to play Chopsticks."

They headed back to the camp at Huzhou and life went on. Then one morning Nitro walked into the tent, saw Peter lying on his bunk and said, "Captain Olsen wants to see you in his tent in ten."

"What for?"

"Yeah, like he told me?"

"I bet my ass I'm in trouble for something."

"That's my guess."

"Well, no time like the present," said Peter and he took off.

"What's up Cap?"

"I don't know. Major said he needed you for a special project. I told him I'd send you over at 1500."

"Am I shipping out?"

"I don't know a thing, Sergeant."

"OK Captain. Thank you, Sir."

Peter couldn't help but wonder what this was going to be and why him. He didn't have long to wait. He walked into the major's office anxious to find out.

"Sergeant Conti reporting as ordered, Sir."

"At ease, Conti. Have a seat. Sergeant we have information that two important players for the VC are having a meeting in their camp at Hi Cong. Colonel Wei So and Colonel Chu Fong are having a planning meeting. We'd like that meeting not to happen. The meeting is Monday morning, at the HQ building on the west side of their camp. It's in the morning but we don't have a time. Here is the layout of the camp. Your mission is to use that assault rifle of yours and make sure that meeting doesn't go off as planned. They will have numerous guards around these men but our guess is they will meet outside the building and go in together. So that one doesn't appear to be the leader. That's your opening. We can drop you safely within two miles of that camp but from there you'll be on your own. Find a spot where you can get a shot and take both men out, if possible. Here are their photos. Make sure if you can't get both, that Colonel Chu Fong doesn't walk away."

"Is there an exit plan?"

"Right here." The major pointed to a spot on the map. This second big hill or small mountain, whatever you want to call it, that starts at this creek a half mile due east of the camp. We'll call it point A. Get to the top of that hill and outfit yourself with a triangular waist rope harness. A rescue helicopter will be there at exactly 1400 hours. He will be dragging a pick up hook, after you're lifted from point A he'll fly you here to point B in the Poe River. He'll take you down to approximately ten feet and they'll cut you loose. Swim to point C, this flat spot here, they will land and pick you up and bring you home."

"What time is the enter drop?"

"Sunday night about three hours before sundown. That will give you time to hide your chute, get the hell out of there, travel the distance to your estimated location and take cover for the night. Get into a firing position early Monday morning. Execute your assignment and exit at point A."

"Yes, Sir."

"Report to the airfield Sunday at 1500 hours. You'll meet with a Captain Rogers, who will be your pilot. Do you have any questions?"

"No, Sir. I understand, Sir."

"Then good luck, Sergeant."

0300 Sunday afternoon Pete was at the airfield and at 0315 they were in the air. The jump went off without a hitch; he hit the ground at the predetermined spot, hid his chute, and slithered through the jungle. He hadn't seen a soul until he was approximately half way to his destination. Two VC were on patrol just ahead of him. He decided to stay clear. If he was to dispatch them and they didn't return to wherever, he might bring suspicion to the mission. He made it to within a half mile of the camp, found a tree that had a high clump of branches that he could use like a hammock and spent the night hidden up there.

When the sun rose the next morning he was already searching for a spot in a tree near his present location where he would have clear visibility of the HQ building. The range was about 700 yards which was a longer shot than he wanted but was far enough to give him the time he needed to get out of there before too many troops would be on him. It was a bright and sunny day, which worked in his favor in two ways. The sun rose at his back, giving him no glare, and when he was shooting, anyone looking from the ground to where the shots were coming from would be looking directly into the sun creating maximum glare. The sun was perfect for Peter's needs.

He found the tree with the exact view he needed, climbed it, and got ready to execute his orders. He had his targets memorized but didn't think it would be necessary. The colonels' cars would be quite noticeable and Col. Chu Fong was a much bigger man than Col. Wei So. Small detail because his intent was to take them out together. Chu Fong was just going to be first.

He stayed motionless for three hours before the colonels' cars showed up. One from the north got there about two minutes before the one from the south. Two men exited each car before the colonels did and surveyed the area and then the two colonels exited. They walked to each other and as they shook hands a bullet struck Col. Chu Fong in his head. All the men immediately scrambled and hit the ground, hiding behind the cars before Peter could get his second shot off. Peter thought for a second and then in a rapid fire manner put two slugs each into both of the cars' gas tanks. It took another shot a few moments later fired into the concrete street to supply the spark and BOOM, BOOM, both cars went up. There was death and destruction everywhere. Peter couldn't be totally confident that Col. Wei died in the blast but the odds were against anybody living hiding next to those cars. He got down from his vantage point and headed to spot A.

People ran around the camp like ants. They didn't know exactly where the shots were fired from but they knew the direction and a good number of men were sent running into the jungle that way. Peter was moving faster than he wanted to, but out of necessity. Luck went his way. He did bump into one soldier, who wasn't so lucky. They saw each other at about the same time and in old West style Peter drew his side arm and didn't even slow down to see if the other guy was dead. He knew he hit him and that's all he needed to know. He continued through the jungle and hit the creek at the base of the mountain about 1100. It was an easy climb, mostly just a steep hill kind of thing and he was at the top in less than two hours.

The most dangerous part of the mission was an hour away. When he was lifted he would be a sitting target for anybody on the ground. Their plan took into consideration that the searching soldiers would not climb looking for the sniper. Why would a sniper put himself in a place that had no retreat? So Pete did have that going for him. But still dangling from a rope under a helicopter with so many men shooting were not good odds.

The chopper showed up on the dot. Peter was ready and up he went. He couldn't hear shots the chopper was too loud. But he could swear he could feel a few brush by him. All else went as planned. No problem with the drop and the pick-up and Peter was in the major's office before sundown.

"Good work, Sergeant."

"Went exactly as planned, Sir."

Peter gave the major the details. Couldn't give him an exact count of the men that perished during the blast but gave him a count of how many were hiding when the cars went up. That was almost the same. He was positive that Col. Wei was a casualty as well.

"I'd like a full report on my desk by this time tomorrow, Sergeant."

"Yes, Sir."

"You're a dangerous man, Sergeant. I'm certainly glad you're on our side. Excellent job Dismissed."

CHAPTER TWELVE

Peter slid into his tent. Death was nothing to him now. It was like going to work and selling shoes.

"How'd it go?" asked Nitro

"Mission accomplished," Peter said as he plopped into his bunk.

"How many?"

"Don't know, maybe ten."

"Oh you are a bad mother fucker, Pete."

"Thank you, Sister Teresa. I'm tired, Nigel. When the fuck is this shit going to stop?" Peter said frustrated.

"Me, I'm a lifer. But I figure you're out of here in about five months."

"I don't mean us. I mean the whole fucking thing."

"Can't think like that. Gotta just do what we're told. The high ups make those kinds of decisions. You're just tired man, get some rest. You'll be alright in the morning."

"Yeah, you're right. I am beat. Killing people is tiring work," Pete said sarcastically, and he turned over to get some rest.

"Pete, when you wake up, let's get the guys together and go into the shit hole they call a town and tie one on. I think we can all use it. What do you say?"

Some muffled sound came from Pete's bunk but Nitro took that as a yes.

Four of the guys headed out right before mess. Joe wanted to eat in town before they went to a watering hole. They had a decent meal although they were not 100% sure of what the meat was. They were thinking water buffalo. But it was good. After a beer or two there, they were on their way.

A broken down shack would be the best way to describe the saloon they entered. It was smoke filled and crowded. Almost the entire clientele were GIs. Intermingled throughout were Vietnamese woman selling their bodies and business was good.

The more sober you were the less likely you would partake. After all the movies they're forced to watch warning them of the many diseases these woman carry you have to be either desperate, drunk, or just stupid to fall trap to their wares but like I said business was good.

Green Berets are like celebrities to other soldiers. When they walk into any place where there are other soldiers, a small hush forms for a second or two and then everything is back to normal. There was no difference here.

"A bottle of whatever you call that shit you pawn off as whiskey," yelled Nitro.

"What you want?" came the reply.

"Whiskey." He said again holding his hands apart signifying a bottle. "And four glasses," he said holding up a glass already on the table and four fingers.

"You'd think these stupid mother fuckers would understand the words they hear five hundred times a day. Wouldn't you?"

The guys hit the bottle hard. But no matter how much you drink you cannot erase memories that will stay with you a lifetime.

The next month was spent doing nominal tasks. It was almost like a vacation for the team. It was like the proverbial shoe, they were just waiting for the second one to drop.

It dropped the next morning, when Captain Olsen who at that time was a short-timer was called into Major Eller's office.

"I've got a mission here Captain, that I need your team to carry out. I know you're out of here in two weeks but before I put another man in your position I thought I'd run it past you. I'll leave it up to you. You want in on this or you want out?"

"Stop there, Major. We're a team. I'm in. I'll leave when it's my time to leave."

"I thought that, Orin. Assemble your men and we'll meet back here in an hour."

"Yes, Sir."

An hour later the men were seated around the major's conference table.

"This is the train bridge over the Tong River. This is the reason we keep fighting the same battle ten miles to the north. Troop transports. We need that to stop. It's well guarded of course. You'll need to infiltrate its defenses and then blow the thing. Sergeant Burk."

"Yes, Sir."

"What we want is three separate charges, first one here on the north end. We've had spotters coordinating the time schedule of the trains. We want the first charge to blow while the train is on the bridge. The second charge at the south end, eliminating a retreat, and the third charge to fell the bridge. Is that possible?"

"Of course, Sir."

"Good. Captain, your job, along with your team, is to get the sergeant under that bridge, and after it's blown, get your asses out of there."

"Understood, Sir. When do we leave?"

"In two days they have a large transport of men and supplies crossing that bridge. It will be on the bridge at exactly 1400 hours. We've tracked the schedule long enough to know they're on time ninety-five percent of the time. We hold the ground almost all the way to the bridge. You'll have about a mile to cover to get into position. We'll have a back up group at your starting position that will charge the bridge if you don't succeed. They'll be waiting for you if you do. We're hoping for the latter, of course."

"We are too, Sir."

"Any questions? No? Good luck gentlemen. That will be all."

"Cap. No way, Sir? Now? Doesn't the major know you're a short time?" asked Tell.

"It was my decision Tom. Besides you guys would probably get lost out there without me."

"You're probably right, Captain," said Peter. "But two weeks. Come on Cap, we can do this one without you."

"I'm in. As long as were together, we are still a team."

"The lieutenant could find the bridge if they'd just put a bunch of meatballs in a bowl on it," added Nitro to bring some joviality to the conversation.

"Oh, man could I go for a meatball sandwich right now," said Joe. "I wonder what kind of disgusting material they'll try and pawn off as food for lunch? I'm hungry."

Peter sat contemplating writing a couple of letters home. No matter how long you're in Viet Nam the feeling of gloom hangs over your head. How long can this team stay lucky? Is this the mission that they don't return? You don't want to think that way but how can you not. Death surrounds you daily and their missions shout it out. He put pen to paper and wrote.

Dear Jackie,

To say I miss you would be the biggest understatement in the history of the world. There is not a moment during down time that goes by that you are out of my mind. Don't worry when I'm working my mind is always on my work. I get strength knowing I'll be in your arms soon. I promised I'd be coming home and I will. That is a given. I just want you to remember that. I know you worry about me, how could I not, you say that about ten times each letter, but don't. I've got four guardian angels looking after me here. Yes, there is danger here. I won't try and convince you there isn't. But we've got it under control. I can handle that. What I can't handle is thinking about how much you're worried.

I'm coming home. Just remember that. I'm coming home.

My team, you know, the guys I've told you about, and I are going on a little trip here in a couple of days. I guess I'll get a chance to see a little more of the countryside. I'm looking forward to it. Tell the guys I said hello. Tell my folks I love them. Tell my brother and sister I'm thinking about them and most of all, tell yourself Peter will be coming home soon and our life will be wonderful. I love you Jackie. Like birds love the sky and people love milk with their Oreos. God, that was beautiful. I'm like a poet. Got to go we're having a sing along by the campfire and I've got the marshmallows. I'll write you again soon. All my love!

Pete

The two days went fast. The team was prepared and in position as ordered. This was a simple transport. Since they occupied the ground between the camp and the drop off point they drove there in jeeps. The captain went over timing with Captain Taylor who was in charge of the awaiting troops. After the short meeting of the captains, the team hit the jungle. Silent invasion. Slinking and skulking were second nature to them. Invisibility was as easy as A B C. Killing's another thing, thank God you never get use to that. They weren't in too far when Joe stumbled onto a threesome drinking probably tea or coffee or something hot. Peter was on Joe's right and caught Joe's signal to come to him. Peter, knowing what that meant and guided by hand signals, maneuvered into position. On Joe's next signal there were four poofs and three dead VC. Peter drifted back into his alley and they continued. An arrow went flying through the air and North Viet Nam was another man short. Nitro engaged his share and so did the captain.

Each small secretive encounter was as dangerous as the next. Somehow the team was still intact, but for how long, how long could their luck hold out? Joe heard a rustling in the bushes off to his right, where Peter was supposed to be. It was way too noisy for it to be Peter. Joe knew something was wrong. He safely, not to give up his own position, rushed to investigate. He stumbled across a soldier with a wire wrapped around his neck and underneath him was Pete. Yes he strangled the gook to death but in the process he fell backward, jammed himself between two tree stumps. He was stuck. Joe almost laughed out loud.

Here are two men fighting to stay alive, one with a dead man lying on top of him. And the situation was actually funny to Joe. Maybe it was time for these guys to get out of the jungle. Joe lifted the dead man off Pete and pulled him out of his sticky position. They proceeded. They were about 100 yards from the train bridge when they regrouped. As always there was unmentioned and unseen joy when all of them showed up unharmed.

"Nitro? You can see what we've got. What are you thinking?" asked the captain.

"I've got three charges set up with time delays. I was thinking we break up into two teams, and an eye. I was thinking you and me Cap will be team one and we'll set a charge here on the near south side as planned. Team two needs to do some climbing and place a charge in the middle of the bridge and also set charge one on the north side. I was thinking Pete could cover us all with that popgun of his. No worries about detonation. I have them set up to set themselves off using the shock waves. The whole fucking bridge will be shaking. It's beautiful. I'll have to detonate charge one with a remote when the train's on the bridge. I do have the other two charges set to blow on a remote if the tremor charges don't work. We shouldn't need 'em though. Well?"

"OK, let me think a second," said Captain Olsen.

"Cap, no offense to Tell, but that's a lot of climbing. Tell can shoot as well as anybody including me. I think I should go with the lieutenant. What do you say, Tell," asked Peter.

"I'll do what you say, Cap. But I can cover you guys, Pete's the athlete," responded Tell.

"Nitro is there any special reason you need to set that first charge?"

"Not a special reason. They all just have to be fastened to a major support. You can see all five of those from here."

"OK, here's what will do. One team. Joe, you and Pete set them all. All three of us can cover a lot better than one and you guys are going to have to pass all three spots anyway."

"Nitro, is there a distance limit on those remotes?"

"No, Sir, they'll work easy from here."

"OK, we'll keep them with us, that way no matter what happens if you guys get at least one charge set the bridge will be out of commission. I want that train but the bridge is the must-do.

"Let's move down to that plateau right there under that overhang. That will give us cover from the top and get you guys closer. We'll start from there. Move out."

They arrived unscathed and unmolested at the spot under the overhang. Nitro pulled out the remotes from his bag of tricks, checked the charges and gave the bag to the lieutenant.

"There are bungee cords in the bag. They'll do just fine to hold 'em on." The charges are numbered one, two, three. Place the number one charge right there on the north side. The furthest one to us, charge three goes in the middle."

"Got in Nitro," said the lieutenant.

"You've got three hours, Lieutenant to get them things set. If the going is easy and you think you can get back the same way, get back here, but be sure you have plenty of time. If not, go to the other side and make your way across the water and back to the jeeps."

"Yes, Sir. Let's hit it, Pete."

Their luck just kept getting better and better. Pete and Joe got to the base of the bridge unseen. Not a shot was fired from their scrutinizing teammates. They climbed the wooden girders and set charge two in the strategic spot that Nitro pointed out before they left. Planted charge three in the center again pointed out by Nitro and did the same at the north end with charge one. All went well; they were almost off the trestle when they heard the train.

"Move Pete, go man, the fucking train is early," yelled Joe.

The two men moved across the decking like monkeys. With twenty feet of trestle left, the train entered the bridge.

"Fuck," yelled Nitro, as he readied the remote for charge one. "It's an hour early."

"Come on boys," thought the captain as he watched his men jump to the bank.

When Peter hit the ground his ankle turned under him. He went down. Joe hit safely. He grabbed Peter by the arm threw him over his shoulder to carry him out of the way of the soon to be coming debris. The train was quickly approaching the north end of the bridge and Joe knew the charge had to be detonated. He was almost under some cover when BOOM. The explosion was deafening. Debris scattered everywhere. A large portion of the track and bridge were gone. The bridge held but was weak and the train wobbled. Joe got Peter on his shoulder again and up the bank to near safety when the second explosion hit. It was only a matter of a few seconds and the train bridge and everything else was going to collapse into the river. When the third explosion went off it was a formality—the bridge was already coming down and the train was already in mid-air. Everything gone. Total destruction.

Minutes later Joe with Peter on his shoulder reached the other members of the team. Nitro and Tell were already on their way to help when the captain yelled out, "Is he alright, Joe?"

The three men laid Peter on the ground. He was out cold.

"What happened?"

"I don't know. We jumped and Pete twisted his ankle or something. I picked him up and tried to get to cover. He must have got hit with something from the explosion. I didn't feel it though. I was shaky 'cause the fucking explosions almost knocked me off my feet."

"I don't see any blood. Maybe he got hit in the head. I don't know but he's out cold," said the captain. "We gotta get out of here. We'll take turns and carry him out."

Nitro grabbed Peter's arm before anyone else got a chance to. "I got him, let's go."

They made it back to the jeeps without any encounters. The VC must have scrambled to safety when they heard the explosions. Peter was still out when they got there. They got him in a jeep and back to camp as fast as they could. He was in the infirmary before the second jeep got to a full stop. Nitro carried Peter like he was carrying his own brother. 'Cause to him, he was.

There was no celebrating that night. The entire team held vigil at the infirmary. The next morning Peter regained consciousness but was in an out for a couple of days. The major had a team of doctors look at Pete. His men were highly regarded by the major and he was going to do all he could to show it. Finally they let the team in to see him.

The first one to talk to Pete from the group couldn't wait to say, "You mother fucker," said Nitro.

"What are you talking about?"

"You're done. You're going home."

"What are you talking about?"

"Home, you know Mom, Dad," (He made a cute little face with his fingers under his chin) "Jackie. Home. Your head's fucked up. You're done."

The captain interrupted. "How you feeling, Pete?"

"I'm shaky, Cap."

"You had a massive concussion, Peter. Severe trauma. Nitro's right. They want to send you stateside."

"Damn. What happened? I don't see Joe or Tell—are they alright?"

"We're right here, ya baby. We blew that train and bridge to kingdom come."

"Damn."

"Yeah, with only two injuries. Your head, and I got a fuckin' hernia carrying your ass back to the truck," added Nitro.

"Damn. I remember jumping and twisting my ankle and that's it."

"I picked your ass up and carried you out of there. You tell your mother that so she'll bake me something nice and send it," said Joe.

"Damn."

"You know guys, the doc said just a few minutes, let's get out of here. I think Pete needs his rest," Cap said as he started rounding his team up. "We will be back, Pete."

They did come back, every day. There was a bond there, a lifelong bond. It wasn't said, it didn't have to be, but these guys were linked for life. A week went by and Peter's head was finally clearing up. Arrangements were being made to ship Peter stateside to a base hospital and it looked like it was going to be Fort Bragg in North Carolina. All the guys were together in Pete's room, when the captain broke the news.

"When's the last time you'd been in North Carolina? 'Cause you're going there Monday."

"Well Sir, at this exact moment it's my favorite place on earth."

"Glad to hear that Pete, 'cause I'm going with you."

"Damn," said Tell.

"No shit," said Joe.

"God damn," added Nitro.

"That's great," responded Peter. "How'd you swing that?"

"My tour is done. It's my time I had to be stationed somewhere and after a little conversation with the major, and a string or two pulled, I'm going with you."

"That's wonderful, Captain. Just great." Peter was thrilled with the news.

So was the rest of the team. They were sad 'cause the team was breaking up but overjoyed it was like this and not another way.

"Gentlemen, the bottom line is this. When you're showing off your medals just remember who your leader was," Cap said with a smile.

And as un-soldier like and completely against every army regulation, the captain received four middle finger salutes, almost simultaneously. He was serious though. The major had informed the captain on several occasions that the bravery, merits, and accomplishments of this team would be rewarded.

Even the major showed up at the hospital when they released Peter for his trip to Fort Bragg.

"I wanted to wish you well, soldier. I'm glad you're all here together. I knew when this team was first assembled it was going to be a very good one. How good I didn't know. Now I do. I'm proud to have known you all. I've been in this man's army for twenty-nine years and I promise you I've never said that to any other team before. Safe travels Captain, Sergeant, and you three let's see what kind of trouble you can get in on your own." He saluted and walked out of the room.

"Good man the major," said the captain, and he got four "Yes, Sirs" right back.

They said their good-byes at the hospital. If respect had an odor it would have been lingering in the air.

Off to America went Peter and the captain. Good-bye Viet Nam.

CHAPTER THIRTEEN

Fort Bragg, North Carolina, might as well have been called Paradise, to Sergeant Peter Conti. Peter, now in the base hospital, was sitting in the chair next to his bed, staring out the window when his doctor Captain Brato walked in.

"How are you feeling today, Sergeant?"

"Captain, I'd be fine if someone would just answer the phone. It won't stop ringing."

Dr. Brato laughed and said, "That should start subsiding a little more each day. I suspect the ringing should disappear altogether in a week or so."

"That's good news. What else can I expect?"

"You will have intervals of some nausea, along with some dizziness, headaches, and you might have blurred vision, but that should move in and out."

"How long?"

"Can't say. Your brain has suffered substantial trauma, causing the swelling and subsequently the pressure. Until it goes back to normal you will experience these symptoms. We'll keep you here for a while for observation and monitor the situation."

"Any idea for how long?"

"Let's keep an eye on you for a few more days before I give you that answer, OK."

"Yes, Sir."

"What am I allowed to do and what am I not supposed to do, while I'm here? I feel OK physically."

"Your body will let you know what you can and can't do, but not much. The headaches and dizziness are going to be sticking around a bit."

"Am I allowed to move around the hospital?"

"Again, Peter, you are free to do what you think you can. I just think you're not going to feel like doing too much. My advice is to rest. Just rest for a few days and then we'll see."

"How about guests? I got a buddy stationed here."

"No problem. Just keep the visits short. Remember rest is the key here."

"Yes, Sir. Thank you, Doctor."

"I'll be back to see you on my next round. Just rest now. If you need anything just buzz for your nurse."

"Thanks again, Doc."

Peter's head was spinning in more ways than one. His life, in the blink of an eye, had become a giant question mark. He still had time to go on his enlistment. How would he serve that? His guess was as soon as he was cleared for duty he'd have a desk job, but where? Too much to think about and quite honestly he didn't have the mental capability to deal with it. He decided to test his legs a bit and walked down the hall. Right outside his door was a fellow patient doing the same.

"Hello, Sir," the man said.

"It's not sir, Sergeant Pete Conti's the name."

"Sergeant Dan Woods. Nice to meet you. Conti, you're already known here on the floor. You're Po Pete."

"Yes, I guess I am."

"Heard what you did over there. Glad to see you made it back."

"Thanks, me too."

"Hey Dan, what exactly have you heard?"

"Wiped out a whole unit of gooks at Po Jing. Single handed."

"The story is greatly exaggerated," Peter responded. "There wasn't anywhere near that many."

"Pal, it was enough for us to hear about it over here at Bragg, that's all I know."

"Well, that was a hundred years ago," said Pete.

"What are you in for, Po?"

"Yeah, call me Pete. Head thing. I'll be all right. How about you?"

"Head thing, I work at the motor pool here at Bragg. A battery fell off a shelf and beaned me. How stupid is that?"

"Sounds like bad luck to me. Hope everything turns out for you."

"How about you?"

"Same kind of thing. It's nice to meet you Dan but I gotta get back to bed. Take care."

Peter turned around and went back into his room. He sat back into his chair. He was tired of lying in that bed, dozed off for what seemed to be a second when he heard a stirring. He woke to see his buddy the captain dropping a box on his bed tray and was turning to walk out the door.

"Hey Cap. I'm awake."

"How's it going Pete?"

"I feel like a bomb went off in my head. Oh yeah, it did," Pete laughed.

"Good to see you're feeling better."

"Thanks, Cap. You assigned yet?"

"Talk about being miscast, they got me in intelligence."

"God, are they hard up."

"That's what I thought, but at least the chance of a gook cutting my throat is way down."

"How you feeling about that?"

"Don't get me wrong Pete, I'm glad to be out of there, but I do think about the guys. I wasn't as worried about them when we were together, as I am now."

"Yeah, I know what you mean. Can't worry though, those hard asses can take care of themselves."

"I know but that fucking place just ain't safe," Cap said and they both laughed.

"Anything new," asked the captain.

"Same shit. Rest, time will tell, don't know anything right now, same kind of bullshit."

"Well, they can't tell yet. It's gonna take time. But are you feeling any better?"

"Yeah. I feel good. The fucking headaches stink, I got a little ringing still going on but it's better. I can't read for long without getting sick to my stomach, and when I get up too fast I almost fall but honest everything is a little better every day."

"That sounds great buddy. I can't stay now. You get some rest and I'll be back later. If you promise me you'll take a little nap, I'll bring a surprise."

"I got enough candy. In fact if that's candy you put over there take it with you."

"Fuck you, that's good candy. Never mind I was just trying to trick you into taking a nap. Obviously I have no business being in intelligence. See you later."

"See ya, Cap. Thanks for coming and thanks for the candy. It is good."

Captain Olsen headed out the door and just as he was disappearing he said, "Take a nap."

Peter did take a nap. It seemed like a long day. He woke. Got cleaned up, by himself. He was getting tired of the nurses do everything for him. Got in his chair and stared out the window.

"Honey! Oh my God Peter, are you all right?"

Peter turned and his spirits jumped from low to super high.

"Mom!" Peter tried to get up but tried too fast and ended up back on his ass in the chair.

"Don't try to get up son. Just sit there your mother's on her way," said Peter's dad.

Teresa Conti gingerly hugged her son but there was nothing gingerly in Peter's hug back. As his mother stood up from the hug, in coming, Jackie wrapped her arms around him and kissed him like he was a soldier coming home from the war ('cause he was). She was the only one crying, completely out of happiness. She kissed him again and said, "Peter, Peter this is like a dream come true. I don't care that you're in the hospital. You're home. You're home. You're alive. Thank you, God."

"I'm speechless," said Peter with a smile on his face you could hang your coat on. "How did you know how to find me?"

"Now you do owe me," said the captain peeking around the door.

"Damn, Cap. I don't know how you did this but thank you."

"It was Tom, I mean your dad, that put it together, I just told them where you were and met them at the gate to get them here."

"It's great to see you, Dad," and he hugged his father.

Peter was standing up by then, and it was obvious that everyone was very happy about that. They really didn't know what to expect. He walked around the room for a few minutes just hugging everybody, except the captain.

"Orin's filled us in on things, son, but we weren't expecting seeing you doing this well. What are the doctors saying?"

"Same as last time. Cerebral concussion. My brain is just too big. What can I say, Dad."

"Don't joke," said his mother. "Now what exactly are they telling you?"

"Everything they're telling me is stuff that they're expecting to go away. Headaches, dizziness, blurred vision, that kind of stuff."

"They must be saying more than that, Peter," said Jackie in a mother-like tone.

"Yeah, they said don't stand too close to bombs again."

"I don't even want to know anything about that stuff," was Jackie's reply.

The captain had disappeared for a few minutes while they were talking and when he came back he had two large pizzas with him.

"It pays to be a Green Beret captain on a military base," he said with a big smile.

He had paper plates, forks, knives, and plenty of napkins. "Enjoy. I'll catch up with you all later."

"No way. Don't you dare leave me alone with these people," said Peter.

"Thank you Orin, that is so nice of you, but we can't accept this unless you share it with us," added Tom as he grabbed Orin's sleeve.

"You're right, Pete. He is tough."

They all laughed and had some pizza. While they ate Cap gave the Contis all the particulars on where he had them staying. There was a nice hotel right on the base. Everything was already taken care of, but he didn't tell them that.

After they ate Peter's mom said, "I don't want to leave, son, but they did tell us not to overdo it and I think we have."

"I'm all right, Mom."

"No, son. We're going to stay a couple of days. You'll see plenty of us," said his dad.

"OK, I am a wee bit tired."

"I've taken care of things buddy. No worries."

"Cap."

"You're welcome," he responded before Peter had a chance to say anything

"I mean it."

"You're welcome. 'Nuff said."

Peter turned to Jackie and said, "Honey Just seeing you has healed me. If they would let me leave."

"Peter." She walked over the two steps kissed him and whispered. "I love you."

Everyone walked out. Pete's dad was last to leave and just as he was ready to head out he turned and asked, "Hey son, what is this Po Pete thing?"

"Nothing Dad. I'll tell you about it sometime," answered Peter and right then, reality hit him, that nickname was going to stay with him. Forever.

The next morning Jackie and the Contis went to the hospital early. They had coffee and a light breakfast in the cafeteria and went up to Peter's room. Peter already had his breakfast as they walked in.

"Good morning, son," said Tom entering the room.

"Hi Dad, hi Mom, hi Honey. Damn it's good to see you."

"You just saw us last night," said his mother.

"Mom, I don't think I can explain it, so I won't try."

Jackie kissed him and sat on the arm of his chair.

"Did you see the doctor this morning?" she asked.

"Yes I did and he said nothing in so many words. The bottom line is it's going to take time. Rest and time."

Teresa said, "Yes honey, we know that. I guess what we're hoping to hear is, when that time comes, you'll be back to normal?"

"Mom, I'm not really sure I'll ever be back to normal again."

"What do you mean by that?"

"Nothing. How was the hotel?"

Tom answered. "Very, very nice. Only one small problem. Your friend the captain prepaid for everything and there is nothing I can do about it."

"Dad, that's exactly right. There is nothing you can do about it. That's the captain. You'll just waste your breath trying. I've told you about my team in my letters. Captain Olsen was its heart as well as its brain. He's a good man. He's one of the bravest men on this planet. They don't come any better. I was lucky to have served under and with him. And I'm sure I owe my life to him."

"Did you two rehearse saying that because that's exactly what he said about you?"

"Well, All I'm saying is all you can do is thank him."

"OK, son. You have a hell of a friend there."

"Tell us about your team, son," said his mother.

"Nothing to tell, Mom. Orin Olsen was the leader, Nigel Burk was my roomy, he was an explosives expert, Joe Lavaca, Tom Tully, and me. Mom they are all Green Berets. In the army that says it all. Can we just leave it at that?"

"Sure Peter. I was just wondering."

"No problem Mom. Army stuff is just army stuff." Peter walked over to his dad and asked, "How are Russ and Marie?"

"Happy you're back, that's for sure."

"How's your parents, Jack?"

"Worried about you, that's how."

"No worries. I do have a small bit of news, I asked the doctor if I could go out for lunch today with my family and he said I could go to the cafeteria. Jackie, how about a date? My mom and dad can be chaperones."

"Sorry Peter. I'm busy. But I guess I could wash my hair some other time."

"Are you sure, son?"

"Yes, Mother."

"We'll leave now and give you a chance to rest and come back at say eleven thirty."

"Sounds great. Only Jackie will you stay a little while longer?"

"Not too long, OK Jackie."

"OK, Mom."

"You call her mom now?"

"She asked me to, so I do."

"I'm dead meat."

The stay was great for Peter's morale. They stayed two days and went back feeling positive that Peter was going to be just fine. They were as happy as parents and a fiancée could be, and why? They were assured Peter had seen his last day in Viet Nam.

Two weeks went by and Peter's progress was stellar. The ringing was gone and after a couple of days the headaches were gone, well, they were infrequent at best. He had no vision problems whatsoever, and he only got dizzy if he got up too fast from sitting. He was moving around the hospital like he worked there and he knew his time there was getting short.

Finally the day came when he was to be released. Dr. Brato came into his room with some paperwork and was reading some of it when he said, "Sergeant Conti, Pete, after going over your records and also conferring with Dr. Reynolds, our residing neurosurgeon, frankly we're surprised you were ever inducted into the military. Your civilian records show a cerebral concussion suffered in 1966 that should have kept you out."

"Yes Sir. What does that have to do with me now?"

"Peter, we believe your condition is ongoing, and any trauma to that head of yours could be extremely serious."

"Fatal serious?"

"It's possible."

"Is there anything I can do about it?"

"I'm not trying to be funny at all when I say this, but it's sort of like the doctor asking the patient does it hurt when you do this, if it does then don't do that, kind of a thing but simply put, don't hit your head. Protect it at all times. When you're in a position or doing something that has a chance of injuring it, wear a hard hat. You're vulnerable. I can't say it any other way. Another episode like this last one could be fatal."

"What about my time in the army? How's that gonna work?"

"That's what I'm trying to tell you. Doctor Reynolds and I have put you in for an early out. You service to the military has been fulfilled. You're going to be discharged, Peter."

"When?"

"All the paperwork has been approved. So soon. Right now your immediate superior officer in camp is Captain Olsen. He will inform you of the times and procedures. After we sign you out here you'll report to him at the administration building. Someone from here will take you there. Captain Olsen will give you more information then.

"Sergeant Conti, your record as a soldier, I've had the privilege of reading some of it, is exemplary. The army is losing a hell of a man."

"Wow. Wow Thank you Sir I'm a little taken back. Wow."

"Let's get this paperwork signed and get you out of here."

The ride over to the administration building was confusing to Peter; it took a little while for what was happening to sink in. His life as he knew it was the army. He was Sergeant Peter Conti Special Forces Green Beret. He couldn't remember anything else. The thought of life as a civilian was alien to him. His skills were honed to such a fine edge that he had become one of the most dangerous men in the armed forces. How was that going to play out as a civilian? He was scared. Through all those campaigns, when his life was balancing on a string, he had no fear. He just went forward with reckless abandonment and did his job. Now he was afraid, afraid he wouldn't be able to fit in again. It was Jackie, the thought of being together with Jackie that snapped him out of those thoughts. He realized that whatever life had in store for him as long as he was with her it didn't matter. That's when it really struck him. "I'm going home."

He met Cap at his office. After the salutes a warm handshake took place. Orin read Peter his final orders. He was going to be discharged at the parade grounds in one week, at the graduation for the men who just completed their basic training. Orin told him he might want his parents to come down to pick him up and not take a plane home.

"They might want to be there to watch you get your commendations," said the captain. "I told you the major put us up for some. I was told we both would be honored. Joe, Nigel, and Tom are being honored too, over there."

"What were we up for?"

"The Tong River Bridge thing and the Fong Lo Peak thing."

"Damn man, I guess I really didn't think about that."

"Well, the major did."

"You're up for that Po Jing thing too, Peter. I never told you but the day you joined the team, just before we met, we all heard about Po Jing, it was going around the camp like wildfire; we were all impressed. We always kidded you about it, but it was something else."

"That's funny. That's really funny. That's like Mohamed Ali telling Joe Frazier he thought he was tough."

"I mean it, kid. The army doesn't give out medals like they're giving out candy bars. This is a big deal for both of us. My family is coming and you'll get a chance to meet the best part of my life, my wife."

"That's great. I can't wait to meet Betty and your parents. I will absolutely tell my folks and Jackie. My dad wouldn't forgive me if I didn't. I hope we can work out the timing so that we all can have dinner together. Cap, this is all pretty unbelievable."

"Man, it's funny how things turned out," he answered.

"No kidding. I can't believe I'm going home. One thing though. I'm not supposed to take any more shots to the head. So I'm asking you right now, please, please, don't make me fight you over the bill for the dinner. I mean it Cap. Please.

"We'll see."

"Cap."

"OK, but I'm ordering lobster and a bottle of scotch."

"I hope you do, I'll drink it with you." They both laughed.

CHAPTER FOURTEEN

Jackie was ravishing as always when she stepped out of the car. Peter hugged his mom and dad and lifted Jackie off her feet and hugged her like there was no tomorrow.

"It is so great to see you, honey!"

"We just saw each other."

"Sort of," he said smiling. "How was the drive, Dad?"

"Fine son. Just excited about all this. Thought about it the whole way. Your mother and I are so proud of you, Peter."

"Thanks Dad. Mom I swear, you get better looking every time I see you."

"Thank you honey, now don't change the subject, Peter. We are proud. This is a wonderful thing that's going on," she said and with that she started to tear up.

"Mom, don't even think about crying. I am happy to be recognized by the army. I'm proud, I'm proud that I lived and right after this, I'm coming home, home for good. I can just smell the spaghetti sauce cooking on the stove right now. I'm gonna get a nice job. Find a nice girl and settle down," Peter said waiting for the usual slap on the shoulder, which didn't take long, in fact it was immediate.

"You made great time, Dad. Have you guys eaten anything lately?" asked Peter.

"No, I figured if we could make it before nineteen hundred hours we'd catch you for a bite."

"That's funny Dad. But from now on that's seven o'clock to me. Good deal, I was hoping you guys hadn't eaten yet. I haven't either and I'm starved."

They had a nice meal and a wonderful time talking. Questions were asked of course but Peter didn't answer many questions that pertained to the ceremony except verifying when it was, which was Saturday at noon. He did tell them that he was told that after the dedications there were a few planned events, publicity wise, and that they would easily carry into Sunday. He also told them about Cap's family coming and there were plans to have dinner with Captain Olsen and his wife Betty and his folks on Friday night. When they asked him about his commendations he just skirted the issue saying it's just Army stuff. His father knew better but didn't press. They had a lovely evening and went back to the hotel. They were all tired.

The dinner Friday night went off without a hitch and the families jelled like they've known each other for years. The two sets of parents became immediate friends. Betty and Jackie acted like they were sisters-in-law. After a wonderful dinner Cap made an attempt to grab the check but Peter wouldn't even hear of it. Bob Olsen, Orin's dad, said sorry boys, I'm the oldest so that settles that, I've got this. Tom just smiled. He had edged all three men out earlier that evening knowing this would happen so he gave the waitress his credit card before they even sat down. No way he was going to give the Olsens even a chance at that tab.

Saturday came and it was a beautiful sun shining day. The Contis, Jackie, Betty and the Olsens sat in the grandstands in readiness waiting for Peter and Orin to receive their commendations. They were talking and laughing and had already accepted each other as one big happy family. It would be impossible to explain the pride they all felt. They had no idea what their sons were being honored for because neither of the men liked to talk about things that went on over there, but just the fact that they were being honored was enough.

The time came for the awards. Colonel Jorgenson the base commander stood in front of the two soon to be decorated soldiers and read:

"For their courage under fire above and beyond the call of duty while engaging the enemy and executing to completion the complete and utter destruction of the Tong River Bridge, and the troop transport on that bridge, ultimately saving countless American soldiers' lives. The United States of America is proud to award Special Forces Green Beret Captain Orin Olsen and Special Forces Green Beret Sergeant Peter Conti, for Heroic and Meritorious Achievement, the Bronze Star."

He pinned them on the men's' chests and saluted, they returned his salute and he took three steps back and read again:

"The Purple Heart for Military Merit is awarded to Special Forces Green Beret Sergeant Peter Conti for injuries obtained while engaging the enemy during the execution of his duties at The Tong River Bridge."

He pinned it on the Peter's chest and saluted, he returned his salute and the colonel took three steps back and read again:

"For their courage under fire above and beyond the call of duty while engaged in the elimination of the defenses protecting Fong Lo Peak, which lead to a complete victory in the capturing of Fong Lo Peak Observation Camp, again saving the lives of countless American soldiers, the United States of America is proud to award Special Forces Green Beret Captain Orin Olsen and Special Forces Green Beret Sergeant Peter Conti, for Gallantry in Action, the Silver Star."

Again he pinned them on the men's' chests and saluted, and again they returned his salute, he took three steps back and read again:

"For courage under fire above and beyond the call of duty while transporting supplies from the base Camp at Da Nang to the base Camp at Po Jing. In order to defend and protect the lives of his men, he single-handedly, without regard to his own safety and life dispatched to elimination an entire patrol of enemy soldiers. The United States of America is proud to award Special Forces Green Beret Sergeant Peter Conti, For Valor, the Distinguished Service Cross."

He pinned the second highest award the country gives, second only to the Congressional Medal of Honor, on Peter's chest and saluted; Peter one more time returned his salute.

The Colonel stepped back saluted both men, congratulated them, and dismissed them. When they started to walk away, the people and soldiers in attendance cheered like they were at a football game and their team just scored. It was a proud moment for both men.

Thomas Conti stood and as he applauded a tear of complete and utter pride slid down his face. As he sat there and listened to the pure acts of bravery, the undeniable courage, the selflessness, all he could think of was, that was his son down there getting those medals. That was his son that had earned the respect and admiration of his peers. That was his son who was simply stated a hero.

The rest of that day and the next were days of celebration. There were pictures and interviews strictly for Army propaganda and a couple of just fun parties for the men and their families, but it finally came to an end. It was time to go. The Olsens and Contis checked out of the hotel and after all the hugging and hand shaking both families headed to their cars. Peter was going home. Home for good. The Contis loaded everything in the trunk and just before they pulled out Peter excused himself. He had to say good-bye to someone first.

"Captain."

"It's Orin now, Pete."

"Not to me. I have no words."

"None needed. You know sometimes men are just meant to be in the same place at the same time. It's called destiny. That's what happened to us five."

"Yeah, I know exactly what you mean. Couldn't explain it if we tried. I know I don't need to say this but I'm going to, if you ever need me, no matter what it is, no matter when, I'll be there."

"You're right; you didn't have to say it. Just like I know I don't need to say that goes the same here. A man is lucky if in his lifetime he has a friend like you, me I hit the jackpot, I got four all at once."

"We all did. Good luck, Cap." Peter hesitated a moment and then said. "Orin, thanks for everything and I mean everything. This is not good-bye, I promise you we'll always be in touch."

"See ya, buddy. And if you think of it, maybe you could invite us guys to your wedding," added Orin.

"Fuck you, that's for friends only."

They shook hands and then hugged. Peter Conti, Special Forces Green Beret, was going home. He had to get a job.

They pulled into Peter's house about six thirty Tuesday morning. Got out of the car, went into the kitchen and Teresa immediately put a pot of coffee on the stove. Peter dropped his stuff in his room down in the basement and when he came up his baby sister who wasn't a baby anymore was in his arms and hugging him like there was no tomorrow.

"Welcome home, Pete. I missed you so much."

"I missed you too, Marie. More than you could imagine."

"Will you look at this? When is the last time you've been up at this hour Russ?" said Peter.

His brother Russell didn't say a word. He just hugged Peter.

"Good to see you, Bro," said Peter.

"I was scared the whole time you were gone. I'm so happy you're home, Pete."

"Me too, Russy."

That night was a night of celebration for the four friends. Peter was home from the war. It was going to get mighty drunk out that night.

"Jake keep 'em coming," said Ray.

"You got it Ray," said Bobby. He gave up a long time ago correcting the guys with his name.

"Pete, you're a celebrity. Did you see yourself in the paper today? said Ray.

"Ray, don't believe everything you read."

"Peter, this is big stuff, man. You're a fucking hero."

"Guys, ask Al, when you're there you just do what you gotta do. Really, don't make a big deal out of it," responded Peter.

"Peter," voiced Al. "Man, what you did is way different. I know what you're saying but, a Bronze Star, a Silver Star, a Distinguished Service Cross, Peter it says in the paper that you're the most decorated Viet Nam soldier in the state. You got a handle. They're calling you Po Pete. I can read, Pete, there's a whole page dedicated to what you did over there. It ain't no big deal my ass. It is, Peter. It's a big fucking deal."

"Sonny will you tell him?" asked Peter.

"Yes, I'll explain. Guys, Peter is being a complete fucking idiot. He's a fucking hero and won't let us celebrate it."

As they were talking at least three maybe four guys walked by and raised their glasses all of them welcoming Peter home and all of them using the nickname Po Pete. They read the paper too, plus in a little town like Tonawanda, news travels pretty fast. Instead of being proud of it Peter was getting aggravated.

Then out of nowhere, something happened. Some guy who didn't know Peter from a bag of apples picked up on the Po Pete thing and to show off in front of a couple of girls he was hitting on, said to Peter,

"Po Pete, Po Pete, what's that—Little Po Pete has lost his sheep," and he laughed and laughed

Peter stood up. Pissed off. Sonny reached for him and grabbed his arm. Bobby leaned over the bar and immediately using just a few words like Green Beret and War hero and Po Jing killed them all, said enough for the guy to almost yell, "I am sorry man. I am really sorry. I was just trying to be cool. I am really sorry. Please forgive me."

Peter didn't say a word. He just sat down. Then out of nowhere he said, "You see? You see what I mean now?"

Before the dust even cleared, Bobby put a round on their table and said, "Timmy is sorry, he's an idiot and he hopes you can forgive his stupidity. He bought you all a round and he said welcome home."

"Tell him thanks," said Ray.

"I'm sorry, guys," admitted Peter. "I guess I just don't know how to handle everything. Stuff is just hitting me and I'm just not ready for it."

"Ready for what Pete, ready to come home?" asked Sonny.

"I'm not ready to be a fucking hero. I never thought of myself like that and I still don't."

Sonny responded with, "Well tough shit 'cause you're just gonna have to. Pete, you're news. You might not want to be special but you are."

"Special, Sonny? Special, those medals, you wanna know how I got those medals. I killed guys. I killed a bunch of people. They're dead, gone forever. Dead. I killed some of them with my bare hands. I choked some of them and felt them jerk their last jerk. I stabbed them in their backs. I cut some of their throats. Ray, I broke a guys fuckin' neck with my bare hands and felt him exhale his last breath. Ah fuck it. Never mind."

"Guys we need to get out of here," said Al "OK, Peter? Let's just grab a little food someplace quiet."

"Yeah, OK. I'm sorry."

Peter was apologetic as they sat and ate chicken wings, a Buffalo specialty, at Yogi's House of Wings. Peter was telling the guys how his life changed in what seemed a blink of an eye. He didn't know what he was going to do. Go back to school or get a job. Jackie already wanted to get married and he wasn't in a financial position for any of that right then. And then there's all this fucking hero stuff.

"OK. I've heard enough. Peter. Take a look around, man. Your life changed in a blink of an eye. I ain't got an eye. The war sucks but life goes on. I got a job. I'm doing fine. So will you. You are who you are. You're a war hero. Use it. Somebody's gonna love to have you work for them. Publicity man. You can almost pick what you want.

"I listened to you tonight. I understand what you're saying. But, you need to understand something, you know that gook whose neck you broke, if he saw you first, he would have gutted you from your ass to your elbow. If not you the next American soldier he met. All of them would have. Think about all the men you saved. I read the paper. When I read it I almost fucking cried. You are a fucking hero. Period. I saw piles of dead American soldiers. You stopped that from happening. You don't want to be proud. Then I'll be proud for you.

"I don't mean to preach, buddy, but your head ain't on right. A Bonze Star, a Silver Star, Jesus man. A fucking Distinguished Service Medal. Sonny, Ray, that's right under the Congressional Medal of Honor. You don't have to talk about it Pete, you've never bragged about your accomplishments all your life. I know, I've watched you, I've watched you hit home runs, run for touchdowns, score winning baskets; it was great, you never bragged once. But that didn't stop people from knowing how good you were. That's how this is gonna be. You don't have to talk about it. People know. You are going to be respected. You are a hero. A mother fucking hero and that's it. Live with it."

"I swear to God Al, that's the most I've ever heard you say all at once," said Sonny. "And every word absolutely true."

"He is right, Pete," confirmed Ray.

"Al, I deserved every bit of that, and I needed it. Thanks I truly missed you, guy."

"Welcome home, Pete," Al said with a smile.

Peter's new life started that very second. He really was home. For him, the war was over. It was time to make a plan, and soon.

The guys filled Pete in with what had happened in their lives while he was gone. Ray had graduated from junior college with his associate's degree in accounting and got a job at Midland Bank. Al got his old job back at Chevy and all was well, Sonny, he was doing terrific, married life was great, and he was running two of the family cleaners. One more thing Sonny added to the conversation.

"Oh yeah. Rosey's pregnant."

"You waited this long to tell me that?"

"You were being too much of a pain in the ass to tell you sooner. I waited till you were Pete again."

"Congratulations, buddy. When?"

"About two months."

"Is it yours?"

"I think so." Everybody laughed.

"Sonny, do you have any idea the pressure you continually add to my life?" said Peter.

"Just set the date fast and stop whining."

"With that said, I have got to go. She's waiting for me as we speak."

They said their goodbyes and left. Peter headed to Jackie's and Sonny went home. Al and Ray went back to Jake's.

When Pete pulled up to Jackie's, she came right out; she'd been looking out the window and waiting. Pete didn't need to go in; he had already stopped and met with her parents earlier that day.

"Hi, Babe. What do you think of Sonny's good news?"

"Great news. I couldn't be happier for them."

"Give you any ideas?"

"Jackie!"

"I think we need to make a plan. I've waited Peter, just like you asked."

"Jackie, give me a few days to get my feet back on the ground. I'm not sure of anything right now."

"You're not sure of what?"

"School, job, I don't think I want to live at my folks, I need to figure out shit."

"I know what you're saying honey, I just want to be with you. Maybe we can get a place and just move in together?"

"I don't think that's a good idea at all. Your parents would go wild.

"Jackie, Al said something tonight that made a whole lot of sense. Use the publicity from the paper as a springboard. He thinks I should make hay while the sun shines and he's right. If it don't work out, screw it, I'll use the G.I. bill and let the army pay for the rest of my college. I can always get a job doing something. Everything will work out. It will just take a little time, that's all."

"If it's money. I have been saving like crazy and the hospital pays well. That's why I'm still living home. I have money, Peter. I have plenty of money. We can afford to get an apartment, really."

"Jackie you are acting like I don't want to. That's not it, honey. Your parents, I just don't think the apartment thing is a good idea. I love you Jack, and believe me I want to marry you more than anything. Things are just moving a little fast and I need them to slow down. I've been home one day. Let's wait just a little time before we start throwing dates around."

"You're right. But don't take too long."

It didn't take long before things changed again. The very next morning Peter got a call from a Mr. Paul Williams, the national sales manager of American Fastener, a manufacturer of paper-fastening products for the office supply and stationery industry. After a brief introduction he asked Peter if he had made any plans for the future and said if he hadn't, would he be interested in talking with American Fastener about a position they had open in the western New York area. Peter didn't hesitate for a second.

"Mr. Williams, I have not made any plans as yet. I just returned home from the service and haven't even unpacked yet. What you're saying is very interesting to me, I am familiar with your products, sir, and I would like very much to talk to you about your opening. When would you like to get together?"

"Peter, you don't mind if I call you Peter, I'm aware that you just arrived home. I read about you in the newspaper and quite honestly I was very impressed, enough so that I made this call. I am going to be in the Buffalo area for two more days. I'm staying at the Hilton in downtown Buffalo. I am fairly open this afternoon. How would two o'clock work for you?"

"Two is no problem, sir."

"Perfect. I'll meet you in the lobby. I won't have any trouble spotting you. I have your picture from the paper. I'm looking forward to meeting you, Peter."

"Thank you, sir. I'll see you at two then."

The meeting went perfectly. Paul Williams had full authority to hire on the spot. He usually didn't act impulsively but with Peter he just didn't see where he was taking a chance. The most decorated American soldier fighting in Viet Nam from New York State selling in New York State for a company with a name that starts with American. Just didn't seem like any kind of a stretch at all.

Peter handled himself well in the interview. Showed a nice command of the English language, was personable, nice looking, and did something that every person who ever interviews for a job should do at the end of the interview, he asked for the job. Mr. Williams hired him on the spot. Peter walked into that lobby not knowing what direction his future would take. When he walked out he did. He was the newest employee of American Fastener. He was brought in as the Territory Manager covering Western New York.

Paul told him that he would send him a packet of information and a schedule including a trip to their headquarters in Dallas, Texas, where he would be attending an extensive two-week training program. He told Peter to take a little time to get his affairs in order. He said that the first of the month would work out fine for the company if that would work out for him. Peter said that would be plenty of time for him to wrap up what he needed to do. He thanked Mr. Williams, told him how excited he was about the opportunity and assured him he would never regret the decision. They shook hands and Peter left.

He went from there right to Kenmore Mercy Hospital. He knew that Jackie's shift was over at five and he couldn't wait to tell her the news. He was pacing in the parking lot when she walked up to the car. She was very surprised when she saw him and immediately said, "What happened? What's the matter?"

He answered with a big smile, "Jackie, we're on our way."

CHAPTER FIFTEEN

Peter took to sales like Betty Crocker took to baking. He absorbed the training like a sponge. They told him that product knowledge was the main key so he studied the product descriptions and pricing like there was no tomorrow. When training was over he knew their product line as well as many of the veterans. The company had three new reps attending this training program. Mike Rickets was hired for Kansas City, Peter would cover Western New York from Rochester to Eire Pennsylvania, and Dick Lutz was their new guy in Indianapolis. They were all greenhorns so basic sales skills took a large portion of the time. Paul Williams would normally attend the last couple of days and usually the very last afternoon addressed the trainees. This group was no exception.

"Welcome, Gentlemen! How do you like us so far?" Paul asked rhetorically. "My job is to put the tools in your hands that let you work efficiently and profitably. We know you're the lifeblood of this company; me, I'm just the guy who takes all the credit when you do well and none of the blame when you don't. My personal goal is that someday one of you gentleman will take my job. Why, you ask? Because I desperately want my boss's job. Man, talk about a cake job! Just don't tell anybody I said that.

"Now as you are aware, or at least I hope you are aware by now, distributors are the keys to our success.

They supply the small end users, not us. Yes, we sell to the big end users direct, as per our contracts with our distributors, but the wholesaler and distributor will make or break your quotas.

"So how do I get to distributors or office supply houses we don't do business with? I am so glad you asked," he said with a smile. "Sales are a numbers game. The more calls you make the more sales you'll get. The harder you work the luckier you get. It's as simple as that, along with a few basic rules that I like to call the three Qs.

"What are the three Qs Boss, you ask? Wow you guys ask great questions without saying a word, impressive. Well here they are:

"Qualify. Don't waste your time calling on the wrong person. Make sure the person you're talking to can place an order. It does you no good to make a long presentation to a person who at the end of it says that they have to ask Mary first. Call on Mary. Ask questions and find out that it's Mary who you need to talk to. What's the first question you ask Mary?

"Quantify. Mary, how much of our kind of products do you use in a year? If you don't ask that question and at the end she say they only use twenty dollars of staples, fasteners, paper clips, and paper clamps, a year. What have you accomplished except losing the time you could have spent pitching to a prospective customer that actually uses our products. Quantify. How much do you buy?

"The third Q Ask OK, it doesn't start with a Q but question does and to me it's the most important Q 'Question'. What is that question, Boss? I cannot believe how many questions you guys are coming up with without speaking. I'll tell you what that question is.

"Q. Ask for the order. 'How many would you like to order?' Do not make a long presentation and then at the end tell them we have plenty of them in stock. Ask for the order right then.

"How many staplers do you need today? How many cases of staples would you like to order to go with them? Let's check your supply of paperclips and clamps to see how many we need to order today as well? Ask for the order.

"OK, team you've just heard my spiel but I am not completely done with you yet. There is one more task you'll have to put up with. What's that, Boss you might ask? I would like to take you all to dinner tonight. You're training is complete. Go home, kiss your wives or girlfriends or whomever you would like to kiss, give yourselves a few days to let the smoke clear and get ready to go to work. Thursday of next week, one of us, Virgil, Ray, or I, will work with you in your area for two days. We'll make calls together, some cold calls, and some end user calls, but mainly we'll call on your major accounts so you can be introduced as their new territory managers. After those two days, you are on your own."

"Guys, welcome to American Fastener. See you in your lobby at six."

Jackie was waiting at the airport when Peter landed. She was excited when he got off the plane. They kissed and hugged hello. She was happy to see him and hear all about the new job.

"Well?" She asked excited to hear his answer.

"I loved it. I can't wait to hit the streets. The products are great and so is the company. The people who put on the meeting really knew their stuff. The only way to describe the people and the company is to say they are totally professional in every way."

"When do you actually start work?"

"Well, I'm on the books now but I won't hit the streets till next Thursday when one of the guys who trained us comes into town for my indoctrination into sales, I can't wait."

"I am so happy for you sweetheart. I mean for us." Jackie said with a wry smile.

"Are you going to start again? Honey, I haven't gotten a paycheck yet. I live in my parents' basement, it's not time to set a date."

"Why?"

"Money, place to live, don't have an idea how I'm going to do in this job, just got home, I don't know, do you think I'm wrong?"

"YES You're going to do great at the job like you always do, I have money, we can find a place in a matter of days, and it doesn't matter how long you've been home. Peter Conti, you are stalling."

"OK, OK, you win, but not soon. We can set a date but not too soon."

"Am I supposed to be happy about that answer? Well, I am," she said excitedly. "It takes time to arrange everything. I'll start right away, checking things out. Will that suit you, your majesty?"

"I know you. I mean it. It better not be a week from Saturday. I don't care what you find. I need a little time to get on my feet please. I love you and I want to marry you but I need a little time. Is that too much to ask?"

"You are taking all the fun out of this, mister."

"You are something else, lady. I mean it."

"If that's a compliment, thank you. If that is sarcasm—" She made a fist and shook it in the air.

Peter responded with, "I'm not afraid of you one bit."

She shook her fist even harder and tried to make a mean face but she's so pretty she couldn't really do that.

"OK, I guess I am a little afraid. Check things out and we'll pick a date."

Jackie wrapped her arms around her future husband and kissed him. It was finally going to happen.

Peter took the next few days studying. His nose never left the company and product information. He wanted to be armed and ready. He was taking a break when the phone rang.

"Honey, let's go out to eat tonight. I'm off at five. I'll grab you right after. How's that?"

"Sounds good. What are you in the mood for?" he asked.

"Well, I think you know? I mean food you pig. You are really something else. How about Cunneto's. I'm in the mood for their ravioli."

"OK, sounds good. See you a little after five. I'll wash under my arms so I won't smell so bad," joked Peter.

"Thanks, you usually smell like Tonto's loin cloth."

"That is sick. You're a sick puppy, you know that, Jackie."

"Takes one to know one. See you soon. Love you."

"Love you too babe. Bye."

Jackie showed up right on time; that was unusual.

"OK, what's up? Something's going on. Spit it out."

Jackie was bursting to say, "We got Crestwood Country Club for September fifteenth. You said pick a date. I did more than that. We're getting married September fifteenth. Aren't you excited?"

"Of course I'm excited. But I said we'll pick a date. It's just sooner than I thought. New job, we need to get a place to live, and I've only really been home such a short time."

"Yes Peter, I know. You said not too soon. This is just a little soon. I thought you would be a little more excited."

"Excited? I'm absolutely elated. You just surprised me, that's all. How'd you pull this off so fast? Six months, wow."

"Just luck, Mary Burney, a friend from work, is dating the guy who runs the club. She found out they had a cancellation and she, in her own way, convinced him to move us in. We got it. I am so happy, Peter."

"Me too, honey. But that doesn't give us all that much time to put everything together."

"My mom and I have already started. We've already coordinated some things with your mom and with a little luck everything should turn out perfect. I know it's not a ton of time but there's enough. Peter I do want everything to be perfect but for me only one thing is really important, at the end of the day we'll be husband and wife. That's all that matters."

"I know what you're saying, Jackie, I feel the same way. I'm just spinning a little here, sweetheart. My mind is in two places at once. I don't want you to think I'm not excited. I am Jackie. Just give me a minute to get my bearings."

"I'm sorry Peter, I am just so excited about getting that place and how lucky we were to get it. We'll make a plan we can follow to get everything done. I know what your new job means to our life and I know your focus is on that. It needs to be. I just want to be your wife."

"Me too. Jackie, nothing else matters."

Peter stood in the driveway staring at his parent's house, feeling overwhelmed. Less than a year ago he was crawling around the jungles of Viet Nam like he wasn't even human. He was for all intents a well-oiled killing machine. He couldn't even attempt to count the number of men he had killed over there. Now he found himself in a different jungle. The jungle we all face as we fight our way through life. Home, job, family, and of course, money. He stood there realizing he was actually ready to face this challenge. Eager to start his life with the woman he loved, no, adored. Peter looked up to the heaven and in his mind said to God, "Thank you God for everything you have given me! I know sometimes I complain but when it comes to important things you've always showered me with your blessings. I never say it enough but I'm saying it now. Thank you, Lord!"

The next few days were spent studying his product line and at the same time looking for a place to live. Again luck was running good for the couple and they found a nice house close, but not too close mind you, to their parents. It was a lease with the option to buy and they jumped all over it. What was even better was the owners were doing some rehab on the place so it wouldn't be ready for possession for three to six months, again working perfectly into their timetable. It was a three-bedroom ranch with a two-car garage and a beautifully landscaped yard. They would have attempted to purchase the home right off the bat, Jackie sure wanted to, but after some conversation they decided to rent for a year and then decide.

"What do you mean you found a place and rented it? Already?" said Tom. "And you might buy it. Did I hear you right?"

"Yes Dad, we love the place. We got a terrific deal on a lease/buy option situation. It's perfect."

"Jesus Christ, Peter. You're making me a nervous wreck. You just got home and already you're getting married, you've got a new job, and now you're committing to a house, I can't keep up with you, son."

"Don't worry, Dad, I know what I'm doing. Everything is perfect, trust me."

"What did Jackie's folks say?"

"About the same as you."

"Doesn't that confirm what your mom and I have been saying about you kids moving way too fast?"

"Dad, everything we're doing is part of our plan. We are not kids. Everything is going to be fine. Stop worrying."

"Stop worrying? You haven't worked a single day yet. How do you know if this new job will work out? You don't. But you're already spending money. I don't get it."

"OK, I'm not talking about this anymore. I told you I know what I'm doing and I do. And as far as my job, I know I'll be good at it. You'll see. "

"You're driving me crazy, Peter."

"Dad!"

"OK, I've said my spiel. You know I'm only saying these things 'cause I love you."

"I know, Dad, and I love you too. Now I need to go study, OK?"

Just then the phone rang and it was Paul Williams.

"Hi Peter," he said. "I guess you drew the short straw and ended up with me for your on the job training."

"I quit then," replied Peter laughing as he said it.

"I don't blame you. I wouldn't want to work with me either. But what the hell it's only two days."

"What do you want me to do, Sir? Pick you up from the airport Thursday morning?"

"No Peter. I plan on coming into Buffalo late Wednesday afternoon. You don't have to pick me up; I'll grab the shuttle to the Hilton. But thanks for the offer. Why don't you plan on having dinner with me Wednesday evening, though? Say seven. We can talk a little and plan our itinerary."

"Sounds great, Sir. I'll be there."

"One thing, Pete. From now on call me Paul; you're not in the army anymore."

"Yes Sir, I mean Paul."

Peter was excited as he pulled up to the Buffalo Hilton to meet with his new boss. A brand new career was waiting for him there. He walked into the restaurant and saw Paul sitting, sipping a cocktail and reading the newspaper.

"Hi Paul, good to see you."

"Hello Pete, same here. You all ready to hit the streets tomorrow?"

"Ready as I'll ever be."

"You'll be fine. I am sure of that. How did—it's Jackie isn't it?—react when you got home? Positive, I hope."

"Are you kidding? She's more excited about this opportunity than I am. She's running around like a chicken with her head cut off planning our wedding."

"Congratulation Peter, did you guys set the date?"

"Not we, Paul, she. September fifteenth. Do you think you and Jill could make it?"

"Sorry, I have to go to a wake that day," he said laughing "Of course, but will the invitation still stand if I turn out to be a pain in the ass as a boss?"

"Have you ever had the feeling when you first meet someone that you instantly know you're going to get along really well? I had that feeling about you. As long as I don't stink at my job."

"Have you ever had the feeling when you hire someone you're a hundred percent sure they'll be great? I had that feeling about you. Now that we're done buttering each other up, sit down, order a drink, and let's eat. I'm starving. We can go over our two-day plan and get you jump-started. I'm excited to see you in action."

They had a nice meal along with comfortable conversation and Peter was chomping at the bit to make a call. He always took things head on and this was no exception. Working with Paul was just the topping on the cake. Pete was picking up Paul in the morning at seven for coffee and then on to BS Adams, Peter's third biggest account.

He was excited and nervous at the same time as he left the hotel. The unknown faced him but he was ready. Of course he'd rather fight a street gang armed with only a popsicle stick because he knew how to do that, but he wasn't absolutely sure he knew how to sell. He was about to find out.

"Good morning, Paul Williams and Peter Conti with American Fastener to see Jim Jones. We have an eight thirty appointment," said Paul to the receptionist outside Mr. Jones office.

Paul said as they walked into the man's office "Mr. Jones, Paul Williams, with American Fastener, we met at the Office Supply Show in Chicago earlier this year. And this gentlemen is Peter Conti, he'll be handling your account for us."

"I remember you, Paul; I loved your booth at the show. Whose idea was it to have those phenomenal-looking women luring customers in?"

"I have to plead the fifth on that, Jim. But we did have a marvelous turnout."

"Peter Conti. Are you the war hero Peter Conti?"

"I don't know about war hero but I was recently employed by Uncle Sam."

"It's a pleasure to meet you, Peter. I read all about your exploits over there. Please except my humble thanks. Men like you make our country what it is."

"Thank you, Sir," Peter responded, with a handshake.

Jim changed the subject and said, "Now, getting right down to business, I hate to start this out with a problem but here's the deal. I bought six dozen of your A-1 staplers for a trial. They stink. I sold a dozen to my best customer and I've gotten every single one back. I've got five dozen left that I've already pulled from stock and to be honest with you if I didn't need your fasteners I wouldn't even be talking to you guys right now. I want the staplers gone and for that matter you can take the staples back, too."

Peter to the surprise of Paul spoke up. "Jim, we totally understand, that batch of staplers from the show came from our first manufactured run, we rushed to get them out just so we could introduce them at the show and you're one hundred percent right. They were definitely defective. They stunk. The push springs didn't work. The springs were way too strong and they jammed every time.

"But we corrected the problem and now we have what we think is the best stapler on the market. Of course we'll take the staplers back. We planned on going over that with you this morning. How's this sound, I'll replace the seventy-two with eighty-four AND when you see how much better they are than the

Bosak or the Swing you're going to order more. When you do, I'll give you an additional twenty-five percent off your cost.

"That's not all Jim. I'd like to send a half-dozen staplers as a gift from American Fastener and BS Adams to your customer with an explanation. They can try them again against the Bosak or Swing. I guarantee you the next time they order they'll order American. What do you say?"

"Who is this guy, Paul? I like him."

Peter handled himself like a seasoned veteran the entire call. Paul just sat back and watched. Peter asked for on-hand quantities of the other American Fastener products they stock and wrote the fill in orders. After a signature on the purchase order Peter thanked Jim, told him he would be back in a month unless he was needed sooner and he and Paul left.

Walking out to the car Paul said. "Best first call I have ever seen. Absolutely the best first call I have ever seen, and I've been doing this a long time. Do you know what you just did? I'll tell you what you just did. You took a customer that was ready to throw our line out and not only did he not—he bought more. I am thoroughly impressed Peter. I don't know what else to say."

"Thanks, Paul. I feel good about it too. I was a little nervous but it just seemed like the thing to do."

"How did you know about the spring tension on the staplers?"

"I read about that in the literature."

"You read about it in the literature? Jesus, Peter."

"Now where we going, Paul?"

"We're going for a cup of coffee. I want to talk about this a little more. I usually critique a new guy's first call but you didn't give me anything to correct. It was perfect. Even the twenty-five percent off thing, that's our deal right now. You made it sound like you were doing him a favor. Hell—I wanted to buy a gross. I'm impressed. I'm very impressed."

The rest of the day went as well and went very fast for Peter. He was in his element and he didn't even know it. Paul said flowery things all day and meant every word. Peter was good. Peter was very good and Paul let him know it. When Peter dropped Paul off at his hotel Paul asked Peter to join him for dinner but with a catch, he was hoping that Jackie could join them, he was anxious to meet her.

Peter and Jackie walked into the restaurant at the Hilton right on time. Paul was seated at a table but when he saw the couple walk in, he stood.

"Hello Jackie, I'm Paul. What a pleasure it is to meet you. Peter said you were a pretty woman but he lied to me. You are way past pretty. Peter's a lucky man. Please have a seat."

"Peter, did I say that exactly the way you wanted me to?"

Peter and Jackie laughed and were seated.

"I'm sorry Jackie, I hope I wasn't out of turn. I meant that to be a compliment."

"It was a marvelous compliment, and thank you, Mister Williams."

"Oh please, call me Paul. Peter told me about your upcoming nuptials and I would like to congratulate you both."

"Thank you again, Paul. I have been waiting a long time for this big galoot."

"Hey, I can hear you, you know."

"Well I hope you like the wine I ordered. I was told Tuesday was a good year." Paul said as he poured each of them a glass. "To Peter and Jackie, may your lives be filled with health, laughter, and success."

They both thanked him and they all drank.

"You're sure in a good mood," said Peter.

"Peter, Jackie, I am in a good mood. This will be the only business talk of the evening but it needs to be said. I'm just going to say it and get this out of the way. Peter you are a natural. I was thoroughly impressed with your sales ability, your knowledge of our products, your overall comfort level, and your obvious confidence. I have been at this game along time and I am not easily impressed but I was today." Paul lifted his glass once again and said. "Welcome both of you to the American Fastener family."

Paul continued with. "Now, what are you guys in the mood for? Tonight we celebrate."

As Peter sat there reading the menu he felt a tap on his shoulder.

"Oh my God. Hello Sir," said a surprised Peter. "It's been a long time."

"Hello, my young friend. It certainly has. I hope I'm not interrupting, I just wanted to say hello."

"I'm glad you did, Sir. Let me introduce you. Vito Bansano, this is my fiancée Jacqueline Millen and my boss Paul Williams."

Vito Bansano signaled the extremely burly men who accompanied him to step back with just a flick of his hand and they immediately did. He took Jackie's hand in his, kissed it, and said, "It's a pleasure to meet you my dear. And you, Sir. Peter I really stopped because I wanted to tell you how proud I am of you. You made my year, kid. I even saved the damn paper, excuse me miss, I mean I saved the newspaper for crying out loud. Impressive, my young friend, impressive. I had to tell you that."

"Thank you, Sir. I appreciate it."

"I have to go now, it was nice meeting you both, enjoy your meal. Peter, I've taken care of your bill. Everything is on me. No need to say thanks, it's my pleasure."

Peter stood shook his hand and quietly said, "Thank you, Sir." Mr. Bansano nodded and left with his entourage.

As soon as they were out of sight Paul asked. "Peter, is that the Vito Bansano?"

Jackie looked straight into Peter's eyes awaiting an answer. Peter, trying to act like it wasn't a big deal and not like he was talking about the head of the Mafia, simply said, "Yes."

CHAPTER SIXTEEN

Paul and Peter had another good workday together. Peter met his top accounts and they made a few cold calls as well. Paul was more than satisfied with Peter and left Buffalo with a feeling of confidence and satisfaction. He never questioned Peter about Vito Bansano. Peter did explain his brief interactions with the man when he was but a kid in college but that's all that was said. Paul left it alone.

Jackie on the other hand grilled Peter like Elliot Ness was interrogating Al Capone the second they got in the car after their dinner with Paul.

"I don't understand what you mean. He must know you better than you're saying. I want to know how you know the most notorious man in the country, Peter."

"Honey, I just finished telling you. I met him in the restaurant near work when I was going to Buff State. He was a pleasant older gentleman. I had no idea at that time who he was. I liked him, he was very nice to me and we had a number of pleasant conversations. I didn't find out until later what his line of work was. Now stop."

"I see. You made friends with the head of the Mafia and I'm supposed to just say OK."

"Yes. Now, don't make a big deal out of this."

"Well I won't stop. This is a big deal. Peter, he kissed my hand. He bought our dinner. How good of friends are you?"

"Jackie. I wish you could hear yourself. You're way off base. I ate at his restaurant. We talked about things. He was a very nice man. That's all."

"Oh Peter—I'm so proud of you—I am so proud that I saved the fucking newspaper!' Are you kidding? Do you think I'm stupid? He's the head of the Mafia, Peter."

"OK, I can see you're not rational about this. I will tell you one more time. We met, he was a nice man. I liked him so we talked. He never for a second gave me any reason to think he was anything other than a kind and generous restaurant owner. I respected him. We talked about being Italian. We talked about Italy, because he was born close to where my grandparents were born. You know stuff like the weather there. Small talk. One day he said that he didn't think it was a good idea for me to go there anymore and I didn't. This is the first time we've seen each other since that conversation. What do you want me to say?"

"I don't know but I'm not happy. Why don't you understand that?"

"I promise you, Jackie, I barely know the man."

"You know what? I have eyes, OK. You don't want to tell me, then don't."

"I give up. You don't want to believe me, then don't believe me."

The ride home after that conversation was very quiet. Peter dropped Jackie off at her house without even a kiss good bye. She stormed up the driveway and rushed into the house. Peter started to get out of the car but after a moment of thought, just drove off. He thought about seeing the old guy again with mixed feelings. Maybe many people feared this man. Peter didn't. To Peter, he is just Vito, a friend from his past.

What Peter didn't realize is that when you become a friend of Vito Bansano, you have a friend for life. Vito Bansano doesn't give his friendship out easily. It has to be earned. Obviously Peter left a mark on this man and Jackie was right, it was a big deal. Jackie was crying as she entered the doorway. Her mother was at her side in an instant.

"What happened? What's the matter? Is there a problem with Peter's boss or the job?" She asked.

"No, nothing like that."

"OK, then this must be about Peter. What did he do to make you cry like this?"

"Nothing, it's nothing. I'm the one that's stupid."

"Do you want to talk about it honey or not?"

"No, well, yes ok, here's what happened Mom, tonight at dinner some man came to our table and out of the blue gave Peter numerous accolades and then bought our dinner."

"Honey, Peter is a hero here in Buffalo, he's famous right now but that will wear off soon enough. Just go with the flow. I don't know why you're so upset about this."

"Mother, I have known Peter since we were little kids. I have loved him almost as long as I can remember. The fact that we're only months away from being married is something I have dreamed about. He tells me he feels the same about me. We talk about everything. We have no secrets. I trust and will trust Peter about everything and anything for as long as we live. Every relationship is built on trust and truth."

"What's your point Jackie? What happened?"

"It's probably nothing, Mom. I'm crying because I found myself not believing Peter tonight. What's wrong with me? He's never lied to me about anything ever. Why did I disbelieve him tonight? He left mad and he should have. I just couldn't stop."

"What in the hell are you talking about?"

"Nothing."

"Nothing, my foot. Is he fooling around on you?"

"NO! It's nothing like that."

"Well it must be something."

"He said he met him when he was younger and he didn't know who he was then. I know that was true but I was just so scared."

"Jackie. Met who—you haven't made any sense since you walk in the door."

"The man that bought our dinner, Mom, the man was Vito Bansano."

"The gangster Vito Bansano? OK wait, start again from the beginning."

Jackie explained exactly what happened and exactly the conversation she and Peter had driving home.

"If that's what he said, then that's what happened. You said it yourself a second ago. Every relationship is built on trust. Daughter, you are making a mountain out of a molehill. People will be coming out of the woodwork right now because of what he did over there in Viet Nam. Let this go. I've known Peter a long time too, honey. You're wrong."

"I know Mom. That's why I'm crying."

When he walked into the kitchen at home his mother was there to greet him.

"Peter, Sonny has called three times. He's at Tonawanda General. Rose Marie is having the baby."

"Thanks, Mom. See you later," Peter replied snatching up the car keys he just put on the table and rushing back out.

He got to the hospital just in time to see Sonny hugging his mom and dad in the waiting room. When Sonny saw Peter he quickly turned and hugged him.

"I've got a son, buddy. I've got a son."

"Congratulations, Sonny. I'm so happy for you guys. How's Rosey?"

"Great. She had a really easy time for a first baby they said. I almost went in there when she was having him but I couldn't do it. Now I'm pissed at myself."

"That doesn't matter, man. You've got a son." They hugged again and this time with tears.

Peter stayed with Sonny until the nurse told them Rose was resting comfortably and the baby was fine. She suggested Sonny go home and get some rest. They left the hospital about ten. Peter knew he was working with Paul the next day but that just didn't matter. It was about to get very drunk out. The four friends met at Jake's at 10:30. They walked in, Sonny bought a round of drinks for the entire bar, about twenty people, and the four of them started. They closed the joint down about 3:00 a.m.

Peter and Jackie made up on the telephone first thing the next morning. They both said they were sorry so many times it was almost sickening. It was a short conversation though; Peter had to meet Paul and go to work. At the end of the day Peter dropped Paul off at the airport and picked Jackie up so they could go to the hospital together to see Sonny and Rosey's baby. When they walked in Sonny still had that perpetual smile on. He hugged Jackie and said, "Do you want to meet my son?"

They walk together to the nursery and peered into the window. The nurse in charge rolled the small bundle of joy to the front. Jackie gave out the appropriate "Ohhhh."

Peter laughed out loud.

"What are you laughing at?" She asked with anger in her voice.

"Look at his name tag. It says Mister Lippa." He laughed again.

"Yeah, we haven't named him yet, so they put that down."

"He's magnificent, buddy."

"He's perfect," said Jackie.

"Thank you, guys. I've been blessed in every way. Beautiful wife and now a healthy baby."

"Yeah, and one other way, too," added Peter. "The kid didn't get that tremendous honker of a nose that you carry around."

"I was just about to say that," retorted Sonny and both men laughed and hugged again.

Jackie and Peter left the hospital hand in hand. Jackie looked at Peter with a shy grin on her face and was just about to say something when Peter beat her to the punch.

"Do not and I repeat do not start. I love you and yes I want to have children with you but that cannot be in our plan at all right now. We're not even married yet. Please Jackie."

"I was just going to say how happy I am for Rosey and Sonny and how beautiful the baby is. That's all. Geez."

"Oh."

"But now that you brought it up," she said laughingly.

Peter knew that line of conversation needed to stop right then and there and quickly said, "Let's grab something fast for dinner and head over to my parents' for coffee. Mom is anxious to hear all about the baby."

They stopped for a burger and headed to Pete's house. Peter was quite aware that after they answered all his mother's questions about Sonny and Rosey's baby, grandbaby innuendos would be part of the conversation. It was a very happy time in their lives in every way. That is until they turned the corner and saw the ambulance parked in Peter's driveway.

Peter dashed from the car and was in the house in a flash. His mom was hysterical as the paramedics were in the process of lifting Peter's dad onto a gurney.

"Oh my God. What happened? What's going on," screamed Peter just as his mother flung herself into his arms.

"It's a heart attack Peter. It's a heart attack. Oh dear God help us," she said with panic streaming through her voice. She of course was crying and was taking small breaths in between each word.

Peter handed his mother over to Jackie so he could somehow get information from the paramedics. Both woman were now crying and holding on to each other.

"How bad is it? Is he going to be ok? I don't know what to do. What should we do?"

"Who are you?" asked the paramedic holding a clipboard while the other two were frantically working on his father.

"Peter, Peter Conti. I'm his son."

"Sorry Mister Conti. Your dad has suffered a coronary and unfortunately not a mild one. He is alive and is breathing on his own. We are doing all that we can do for him here and as soon as we have him stabilized we will be taking him to Tonawanda General. That's all the information I can give you at the moment. We don't have the equipment to do any further testing here and with him being unconscious we can't even question him concerning severity. It's not good though, I recommend you get your mother and follow us to the hospital."

"Of course. But can one of us ride in the ambulance with him?"

"I'm sorry Sir, but no. We're pretty busy in there. Just follow us."

The next thing they knew Peter, his mom, Jackie, Peter's brother Russell and their sister Marie were sitting in the waiting room area of the emergency room, searching for any information they could get. It was long in coming. Finally the doctor in charge, Dr. Scott Ridley, addressed the awaiting family.

"We have done all we can do. Mr. Conti has had a massive heart attack. We did a coronary angiogram to monitor the blockage of the blood flow to his heart. The blockage is extensive. He needs what is called a quadruple bypass. That is a severe and complicated procedure in which small sections of arteries are removed from the leg area and inserted into the heart to replace the clogged arteries. In order to do so the rib cage must be separated to enable that process to occur.

"There are only a handful of doctors in the country that can perform such an extensive operation and unfortunately there isn't one in the Buffalo area. We have put out calls in hopes that we could find one. But the odds are not good and Mister Conti is not in any condition to travel, even by helicopter. We have however bought him some time by inserting a stent, an artificial splice if you will, that will only temporarily keep blood flowing to and from his heart. If we are unable to secure a heart specialist to perform the quadruple bypass you may have to prepare for the worst. I'm so sorry."

Teresa Conti melted into her son's arms with the news. Peter gently sat his mother down passing her to his brother Russ and started questioning Dr. Ridley.

"I don't understand what you're saying. Can't someone here try?"

"Sir, this procedure is so new and so complicated there are only half a dozen surgeons in the world who could perform this type of operation. If this were a few years ago there would be no hope at all. We have calls out in hopes but as I have mentioned these doctors are in such high demand. I don't know what else we can say other than we will try as hard as we can."

"Is there anything we can do? Anything."

"Pray!"

As the doctor walked away total dread swarmed over the entire Conti family. All just sat there in tears. Teresa was crying so hard Peter was worried that she could stroke out. There was no consoling her and to be honest there wasn't anyone who had the strength to try. They were all close to catatonic, just sitting there in disbelief. Even Peter, who had faced death as a daily occurrence, was shaken to his core. All they could do was wait and pray for a miracle.

They sat there in the waiting room throughout the night, just hoping that their prayers would be answered. That someone, a doctor or a nurse, would come bursting in and tell them that one of the doctors they contacted had called and was on their way. But let's be real, that was a pipe dream.

Peter told Jackie to go home and get some rest. He knew that it would be pointless to suggest that to his mom or siblings but saw no reason for Jackie to sit and wait for the sad news they were all totally expecting. Jackie hugged Peter with all her might and just simply said, "No way honey. My place is right here by your side." With that Peter hugged her back and just cried.

Moments later the ER nurse, Nurse Sorrell, rushed in and informed the family that Dr. H.T. Swartz, the foremost surgeon in the field, just called back and said as luck would have it he was traveling to Niagara

Falls with his family and would be here later this afternoon to perform the procedure.

A miracle. The elation that exuded from the family was so uplifting it filled the room with warmth. Disbelief was the only word that would come to mind. Thankfulness and disbelief.

After the family got their composure and the jubilation of the news sunk in, the reality of the severity of the operation was at the forefront. The odds were better but still not good. They knew the chances of losing him were still high but at least now he had a chance.

He was in surgery for many hours. The entire family just waited and prayed. Dr. Swartz emerged from the OR with a smile on his face.

"I am so happy to say the operation was a complete success. He is in recovery with full blood flow surging through his heart. It will be a long recovery but if he follows all the post op instructions I see no reason why he can't live a long and healthy life."

Tears of fear turned to tears of joy. Teresa first thanked God and then the doctor. Happiness and relief filled the air. Everyone hugged everyone, even other people who were in the room, strangers, were hugged. "Thank God" was said by all.

Peter was the last to shake the doctor's hand and as he did he said, "There is no way I can thank you enough for saving my father's life. The fact that you were coming here when you did is unbelievable to me. I don't know what to say."

"Well, Peter. To be honest with you I really wasn't suppose to come until next week but I got a call from a friend and he asked me if I could move my trip up a week. He said it would be a personal favor to him if I would. I told him that wouldn't be a problem. So here I am. He also wanted me to tell you something." He said to say, "You're welcome . . . my young friend."

"Oh my God, Oh my God, Oh my God!" thought Peter as the doctor walked away.

Jackie overheard the entire conversation and watched as the doctor left the waiting room. When he did she rushed to Peter's side immediately and said, "Did he say you're welcome . . . my young friend? Did he Peter? 'Cause Peter that's what Vito Bansano called you when he talked to us at the dinner. Jesus, Peter."

"Jackie, if you're looking for an argument right now, you just came to the wrong guy. I don't care what his reason for making that call was. It doesn't matter to me. I'm going to see Mr. Bansano right now and I am going to thank him for saving my father's life."

"No, you're not, Peter."

"Yes. Yes, I am. Please, Jackie!"

"Do you know what can happen to our lives right now? Do you realize what you're doing?"

"Not really. I just know I owe this man for my father's life and not you or anybody else can stop me from thanking him. No matter what the cost."

"I don't know what to say."

"Try good luck. More important is what I don't want you to say, don't say a word, not a word of this to anyone, ever. Not a word. I don't ask you for much Jackie but I am asking for this. I have to go. I have to go right now. I'm sorry honey but I just have to do this."

"Peter."

"Jackie. Please."

"Good luck, Peter," she said with tears rolling down her face. She knew this was her moment of truth about believing in Peter. She believed.

Peter left the family in the capable hands of his brother. Told them he had to handle something but would be back soon. He kissed everyone, including Russell, and headed out. He was heading to a restaurant called the Delaware Grill.

He walked in with purpose. Tony Sotto and Joe Gatta, two of Vito's henchmen, stood up from their table but slowly sat down when they recognized the guy who just walked in. He was the guy at the dinner the other night and they knew better than to make Vito angry by saying something.

"Is Mr. Bansano here?" Peter asked.

"Hang on a second. I'll check," said Tony and he walked to the back offices.

"Hello, my young friend," said Vito as he stepped from the back and sat at his table. "Sit down. What can I do for you?"

"Sir. I don't know how you knew about my father but I can never thank you enough for what you've done for my family and me today. It was the nicest most generous thing anyone has ever done for me and I rushed over to personally thank you from the bottom of my heart!" Peter had a lump in his throat when he continued full knowing what he was about to say next could change his life forever.

"Sir, if there is anything I can do for you. Anything. Please just say the word."

"First. How is your father? Second I have eyes and ears all over the city. That's my job."

"Thanks to you, Sir, my father is alive and well."

"That's great news. I'm happy for you. Understand this Peter, I told you many years ago that you made a good friend. I meant that. All I want from you is for you to be happy. This has nothing to do with my business, nothing. All I ever wanted from you you've already given me, your friendship. Not because of my position in life but because of the beautiful conversations and respect you always showed me, as a man not because of my job. That has always meant a lot to me. You owe me nothing. Absolutely nothing. I did what friends do. That's all I did. Now get out of here and go be with your family."

Peter got up to leave and said, "God bless you, sir."

The response, "Call me Vito!"

CHAPTER SEVENTEEN

The next few months seemed like minutes to Peter. His job was everything he hoped it would be, Jackie, along with her mom and Peter's mother, had the wedding arrangements nearly completed, except for a few minor details, and on top of that their house was now vacant and ready for their stuff to be moved in.

The morning of the move Peter, Sonny, Ray, and Al sat drinking coffee at Your Host, a popular Tonawanda restaurant, discussing the moving plans.

"Pillows and lamp shades, that's it," said Ray "My back is so bad my doctor told me that I have to pee sitting on the toilet."

"What the hell are you talking about? Why?" asked Sonny.

"He told me I shouldn't lift anything over five pounds."

"You're sick in the head, you know that Ray," said Peter as they all laughed.

Peter showed his friends the house inside and out. As they walked outside and rounded the far back corner Peter saw a small window he hadn't seen from the inside.

"What the hell," he said and immediately went back in to investigate. He knew it was in the small bedroom with the bookcases. He went into the room and the window wasn't there. He then pulled on the corner bookcase and it swung out, it was on a hinge.

"Look at this shit, guys. There's a small room behind this bookcase. Why?"

Al said. "It's the closet. They must have used this room for an office, thus the bookcases. I guess they wanted a place to hide things. What's the difference? Take the bookcases down and you got your closet back."

"Why? It's cool. A secret room, I like it. I can have some fun with this."

The guys finished the move without a problem, and just like that, Peter and Jackie had a house. They didn't have a lot of furniture but they did have enough to get started. The wedding shower the moms gave Jackie supplied many of the kitchen needs and Jackie spent the last few evenings buying the rest. Peter moved in that night, alone. Jackie really wanted to join him but after a small discussion they decided it would be better to wait the two weeks until they were married. They both thought it would be more romantic that way, plus the whole parent thing would have made it more uncomfortable than it was worth. Especially with Peter's dad still in full-fledged recovery mode Peter didn't want to upset him. Thomas Conti worked very hard making sure he was plenty strong enough to go to the wedding. Two weeks? So what.

The following Saturday night was Jackie's bachelorette party. Jackie and her girlfriends went out on the town. Since Jackie was a lady in every way, it was going to be quite subdued. She wasn't about to do anything that was against her moral fiber. However as the night wore on, she got plowed out of her mind. Rip roaring drunk. Male strippers and the whole nine yards. It turns out that even demure women know how to party when the situation fits. The next morning said it all. She was hung over, hung over bad, and I mean for the first time in her life. After numerous aspirin and cups of coffee she swore the mantra of every person suffering from a hangover. "I'll never do that again."

Peter's bachelor party wasn't going to happen until Thursday, just two days before the wedding, and this party had no choice, it was going to be an out and out blow out. Why you might ask are they waiting until Thursday? That's the day Peter's army buddies were getting into town. Joe and Tell were still doing their thing in Nam but Orin and Nitro were coming. Look out Buffalo New York.

Nitro's plane from New Jersey hit the ground first. He had just returned stateside three weeks earlier and was now stationed at Fort Dix. If the war continued he'd probably do another tour but for now he was happy working with the higher ups passing on some of his knowledge at Dix. Orin, who was still in intelligence at Bragg, came in about an hour later. Joe and Tell did send a very nice letter to Peter and Jackie, along with their deepest regrets. The first part of the letter was filled with best wishes for the two of them, but the rest was not fit for human consumption for anyone else on earth except for Peter, Nitro, and the captain. Peter just read the first part to Jackie.

The reunion at the airport was heartwarming. There is no bond that can equal a bond formed when men fight for their lives together. Such was the case here. They left the airport and headed to Peter's house. A dozen guys met them there and the party began.

Sonny, Al, and Ray headed up the festivities. There was a keg of beer and three bottles of Crown Royal to start things off.

"Gentleman my name is Orin Olsen, this is Peter's and my friend Nigel Burk, please feel free to call him Nitro. It is our great pleasure to be here with all of you to celebrate the upcoming nuptials of our friend and hope that you do not feel like we are intruding.

"Peter has told us many things about some of you and we're happy to finally meet you. I'd like to start things off with a toast. To Pete and Jackie, we wish you a long and happy marriage." And they all drank.

"Thanks, Cap," said Peter "But you coming here has completely changed these guys' image of both of you. I told them that you were animals living in human bodies and you show up sounding like nice guys. Come on." Everybody laughed.

"Animals?" said Nitro. "I resemble that remark, I mean I resent that remark." Everybody laughed again.

They all talked and drank for a few hours until the bus Sonny ordered showed up. They loaded up and away they went. First stop, Jake's of course. Bobby knew they were coming and as they entered made an announcement to the other patrons in his place.

"People. Listen up. These guys are here for Pete Conti's bachelor party. Please for your sake and the sake of my place do not confront any of them for any reason. They are not humans. Pete himself is not completely sane. I fear for my bar." Bobby lifted up his glass and said. "Congratulations Pete, the first round is on me." Everyone in the bar lifted their glass and drank.

"You ever been in here before?" Asked Nitro sarcastically.

"Yes, twice," answered Pete.

The drinking continued at Jake's for a few hours before there was any trouble whatsoever but anytime you have a bunch of guys drinking and partying and things get a little loud someone is going to say something to the wrong somebody.

"Hey, why don't you guys quiet down? You're bothering us," said a leather-jacketed guy from one of three tables full of his clones.

"You talking to me?" said Al.

"Yeah, One-eye. I'm talking to you."

Jake's went from riotous to quiet in seconds. Three guys immediately stood up. Peter signaled everyone else to sit. Orin, Nitro, and Peter slowly pushed their chairs back. Orin told Peter to sit down but Peter didn't. Instead Peter took the lead.

"Hey look we're sorry if we're a little loud, we're having a party over here and minding our own business. Why don't I just forget about the insult you just laid on my friend and we'll just call this a misunderstanding?" said Peter.

"I've got an idea. Why don't you shut your fucking mouth and take your party somewhere else?"

"See, that's where we're having a small disagreement. I don't want to. I have a better idea. I see you have a bunch of friends with you and so do I. I'm thinking you're thinking it would be fun to fight us. It wouldn't be. So here's my idea. Why don't I come over there and just you and me, we have a little fight. The thing is I'll only use my thumb." Peter said as he stuck his thumb up in the air.

Orin and Nitro laughed as Peter started towards the guy, in the mean time they slid into a position to assist if necessary.

The burly guy stood up as Peter approached. When Peter was in reach, the guy threw a punch. Peter ducked it and with his thumb outstretched poked the guy solidly in the throat. The big mouth went down like he was shot. Some of the big mouth's friends started to stand up. Peter just calmly said, "I learned that when I was a Green Beret. As a matter of fact I've got some friends with me who are still Green Berets. If you would like some more instructions I'm sure they will be happy to oblige. Oh look. They're already standing. Your friend will be OK in a minute or two and you can tell him this, we didn't start this but you can bet your ass we'll finish it. Stay or go that's your choice and feel lucky I'm the one that came over here. If it were my friends, we'd be answering questions from the police right now and you'd all be lying on the ground writhing in pain. Have a nice night. Sorry, Bobby."

"What the fuck, Pete?" said Nitro. "That was gonna be fun."

"Would have interrupted our party," answered Peter. "Maybe you can beat someone up later."

All of Peter's friends laughed but make no mistake, they saw what just happened; it's one thing to read that your friend's a dangerous man and another to see it firsthand. Peter handled that like it was nothing. Bada bing, bada boom, it's over. After an hour or so they all took off again, and this time there would be naked women involved.

The rest of the night was uneventful. The bus took everyone back to Peter's and the guys who couldn't walk home either took a cab or slept right where they fell. Sonny, Ray, and Al stayed up and were fascinated with the conversations between Pete and his army buddies. They were all definitely inebriated and because of that some war stories were coming out. Pete, Orin, and Nitro laughed about things that were absolutely terrifying to Sonny and Ray. Al just listened and understood. When Sonny, Ray and Al left the reality of what Peter did while he was fighting in Viet Nam became etched in their minds forever. Peter never did nor would he ever talk about it. All they knew is what they read in the newspaper. They didn't realize that the article barely touched the surface. It wasn't something they would talk about either, even amongst themselves. They felt privileged to be in the same room with those brave men no less listen to their tales. Peter Conti, their lifelong friend, wow. When Sonny, Ray, and Al left to go their separate ways one word was running through each of their heads. That word was respect.

CHAPTER EIGHTEEN
The Finger Man

Jackie looked like a goddess in her flowing white wedding gown. To say she looked beautiful would not do her justice. She was exquisite. The smile on her father Mike's face as he walked her down the aisle spoke volumes. The man could not be happier for his daughter. But nothing could compare to the smile Peter had, it was so big his face was starting to hurt.

As she approached the altar you could feel the culmination of two people's dreams coming to fruition. When their eyes met and their hands touched as far as they were concerned they were married that second. The rest of the ceremony was just formality. Russell, Peter's best man, much to the chagrin of Sonny, Ray, and Al, beamed with pride as he handed his brother the ring he was about to place on the ever-awaiting finger of Jackie's left hand. The three friends were groomsman and Peter loved them all like brothers, but Russell was his brother. Same thing with the maid of honor—Jill, Jackie's sister held that honor. The two ushers Orin and Nigel (Nitro) looked like the war heroes they were in their dress uniforms complete with medals. Peter's mom and dad felt such a sense of pride to be escorted to their seats by the obvious friends and comrades of their son. The two men were honored to do so. If there is such a thing as a perfect wedding, it just happened.

Just before the bride and groom took the walk back down the aisle to the cheers of all who attended, a solo figure of a man who entered late and was leaving early got up to go.

Vito Bansano told Peter when Peter personally handed him the invitation that although he really wanted to attend, he respectfully refused, he just didn't want his presence and reputation to be a topic of conversation at all. Not on this special occasion. But he just couldn't resist. You see, even a man of his stature, a feared man, seldom has friends, but when he does, enough said.

The food, the drink, the entire reception went off as planned. Wonderful. The only down side of the whole thing was that Tom Conti could not drink. He wanted to but doctor's orders. He still had a sip of champagne when his son Russell proposed the toast. He said to Teresa, "If I die I die!"

What a fun wedding!

. . . .

Five years flew by like a lightning strike. Peter was now the Regional Sales Manager of American Fastener and Jackie was one of the happiest people on earth. Well, maybe that is a little overstated. You see, the joyous couple was lacking something. Try as they may there were still only two people in their family. No pitter-patter of little feet. Jackie was feeling incomplete, but hope springs eternal and her never say die attitude never took her spirit away.

"Hi, sweetheart. How was Cleveland?" asked Jackie as Peter walked in with his suitcase in hand.

"Cleveland? Is that where I was? I'm traveling so much now, I'm starting to look at the phone book in the rooms to remember what city I'm in."

"Wah, wah, wah," she said pretending to wipe tears from her eyes.

"You are looking for a beating there, Mrs. Conti."

"You and what Army."

"I'm not afraid of you," he said as they kissed a passionate kiss.

"I'm glad your plane came in on time. Your mother hoped we could go over for dinner. She made sauce."

"Come on. I'm tired. Why didn't you say we were busy?"

"Pete, you're not here to hear how often she asks. Is it too much for you to make her happy every now and then?"

"You know, now I know why I married you. I needed someone to nag me until I can't stand it anymore," he said lifting his shoulder for the slap that was about to come. It came.

Peter came back with, "OK, I give up. It's just that I wanted to spend quiet time with you. That's all. I love my mom's sauce, you know that."

"We will. I promise I plan on throwing you on the bed when we get home."

"Do we have time now?" Another slap.

Teresa Conti could flat cook. That's no secret. The table was set for six. Mike and Patti Millen were invited as well.

"Oh, what a great surprise!" said Jackie walking in the back kitchen door and seeing her parents.

"Hi, everybody," said Peter. "What's up?"

"Nothing special. It's just you guys are so busy Patti and I thought we could kill two birds with one stone and all have dinner together."

Peter whispered in Jackie's ear, "This ain't good. I can feel it."

The dinner was great and the conversation was pretty much small talk, that is until Teresa and Patti started talking about grandchildren.

"Of course we want children, Mom. Sometimes God decides these things. I've read everything I can about the subject and talked to numerous doctors and other nurses at work. We truly are following all the rules," answered Jackie to what she felt was a grilling.

"We know that, sweetheart. But we have been talking a little and just thought we should mention that there is a fertility clinic on Elmwood that people are saying is performing miracles for couples. We just thought you might want to hear what they say," retorted Patti.

"Mom, both moms, I know about places like that. There are too many risks involved concerning the children. Multiple births and birth defects and like that. We want natural. Is that hard for you to understand?" said Jackie with a tear forming in her eye.

"Enough!" said Tom. "These are not children were talking to. It's their lives and they will handle it. All we're doing is making it worse."

Peter stepped in and said, "We know you want grandchildren but maybe it's God's will that Russell,

Marie, and Jill will supply all you need," Peter paused a few seconds and said, "Thanks for dinner, it was great mom, but we have to go."

"Peter, wait," said Mike. "Please don't leave mad. You know your mothers are just anxious."

"We know, don't you think we are?" With that said Peter and Jackie got up to leave.

"We're not mad mom, just sad," said Jackie.

Tom said, "That's it, kids. The last time we will talk about this. You're right, God will decide. Don't stay away from all of us now because we stuck our noses in your business. We all love you both and that's the bottom line. Your mothers said what they wanted to say and that's it. Agreed." The entire table nodded their heads in agreement.

"OK dad, thanks, we understand, but Peter just got home from a business trip and truly is tired. We're not leaving mad but we do have to go."

"No coffee?" asked Teresa.

"I'm tired, Mom, We're just going to go," replied Peter.

"You're not mad at us stupid old people are you, son?" said Teresa.

"No. Just tired Mom," said Peter.

"I'll call you both tomorrow, ok," said Jackie.

They kissed everyone and left.

As they got in the car Peter said, "Are you OK, sweetheart?"

"Yes and no," she replied.

"What do you mean?"

"I mean maybe we should talk about a fertility clinic," she begrudgingly said.

"Anything concerning your body is completely up to you. I want children almost as much as you. I say almost because I know how exasperated and disappointed you are that it hasn't happened yet. We'll just keep trying."

"I know, honey. Of course we will. But maybe going to a fertility place will give us some answers. Answers we haven't be able to get from our doctors. They all say we're fine. I just don't know what to do."

"If you want to explore that avenue, we will. Make an appointment and I'll work my schedule around it."

"That's not necessary, Peter."

"Yes, yes it is. I'm every bit as anxious as you are to find out what the procedures are and what the consequences could be as well."

"OK, I'll do it." she replied as she leaned over and kissed Peter on the cheek. "By the way," she added. "That kiss was the start of a hundred more."

"I love you, Jackie."

Jackie struggled over the decision to go to the fertility clinic. She so desperately wanted to start a family. She tried in vain to get Peter to make the decision but Peter knew it was Jackie's decision and Jackie's decision alone. It was her body that would be at risk. Along with the life of their would-be child. But to be honest, Peter wasn't really willing to put Jackie's life in danger. The thought of losing her would be too much for him to bear. He wanted to say that but just couldn't find it in his heart to squash her dreams. What a dilemma.

"Peter, I think I have come to a decision." Jackie said as they ate dinner out on the patio. "I want a baby. I've done as much research as humanly possible and I think the end result is well worth the risks involved. I want to go to the fertility clinic our moms were talking about."

"Look Jackie, I want a baby too. But . . ."

"No buts, Pete. I don't feel whole. I love you more than I can express and I tell myself every day it's enough but I see our friends with their kids and it breaks my heart the way they look at us. Pity. I see pity."

"Stop right there. Just stop and listen to yourself."

Jackie broke into a full-fledged cry as she laid her head on her arms on the table.

Peter jumped from his chair, squatted down next to his loving wife, put his arms around her and just hugged her. He had no words.

After a few moments he said, "OK, if that's what you want, make an appointment."

Peter left to go to work the next morning but was hesitant to leave his wife alone. He knew she was distraught but there really wasn't anything he could do about it. He figured she would make an appointment and together they would find out all they needed to know. He cancelled his flight to Chicago and was only driving to Rochester a couple of hours away to work with one of his sales guys just in case she was able to get in sooner than later, he absolutely wanted to be there for his wife.

Jackie phoned the Life Fertility Clinic that morning to set an appointment, not knowing what to expect but expected a fairly long waiting time. Normally she would have been right, their lead time was usually five to six weeks but as luck would have it they just had a cancellation and asked Jackie if she could make it in tomorrow at eleven a.m. Jackie did not hesitate. She did have second thoughts about Peter going with her. She was nervous enough and Peter there was going to make her even more anxious about the whole situation. After a few moments she realized he needed to be there. He was every bit as tense about it as she was and besides that she could use the support. So, tomorrow it was.

The hesitant but determined couple left early the next morning. Peter thought a nice breakfast out would calm his anxious wife and thought it would be a good time for them to discuss different options that possibly could occur after the appointment. He didn't want to curb her enthusiasm but also wanted her to realize this was not life or death. They did have options.

"Jackie, I want you to know that I agree with your decision about this a hundred percent. I know this is exactly what we need to do. I feel in my soul everything is going to work out. But no matter what happens we will have a child. There is no reason to discus adoption right now because this clinic is going to help us. But just realize adoption is a real option to me." Peter said hoping to ease the growing anxiety he could see in his wife's eyes.

"Honey, of course I have bounced that idea around in my head hundreds of times. First I want to exhaust every effort to have a baby the natural way. Thank you for saying that because it worried me that you wouldn't be happy even talking about adoption."

"Sweetheart, the only thing that really makes me happy in this life is your happiness. Whatever you decide is what I want. I promise you we will be raising a child together. Now let's go. All the answers we're looking for are a half hour away."

They headed to their appointment and arrived right on time. After a short wait they were in seeing the doctor.

"Good morning Jacqueline, I'm Doctor Davis. I know you're a little nervous, totally expected. Most women in your shoes are, but there are a number of different options we offer here that help our patients and the conception rate is very high."

"Before we can even discuss those options we have to do an evaluation on both you and your husband. We have all the facilities here to do our testing and that's how we'll start.

"Peter, if you would, please follow my assistant and he'll show you where to go so we can get a sample from you. Jacqueline, please follow me. This will only take a short time. After the evaluation we will meet back here to discuss options and make a plan."

"Thank you, Doctor," answered Jackie.

Jackie looked into Peter's eyes with great hope and aspirations. Peter returned the look with eyes that said I love you.

After an hour or so the couple found themselves back in Dr. Davis's office.

"OK, we have your results."

Jackie and Peter waited patiently for what they were about to hear.

The doctor started out with, "Well, I have good news and bad news. Which one do you want to hear first?"

Jackie held her breath and said, "I guess give us the bad news first."

"The bad news is we cannot help you."

"And the good news," said Peter as their hearts sank.

"Mrs. Conti, you're pregnant. Congratulations!"

CHAPTER NINETEEN

There are two factions of organized crime in America. The Italian Mafia was the main one and had been in charge for a very long time, but in recent years the Russian mob had been trying to move in on the action. A small war had been brewing for some time in the northeast, and Vito Bansano wasn't very happy about it.

Ivan Terski headed up a small army of Russians who had already stepped on a number of Bansano's deals and the Godfather wasn't going to let that happen again. Boris Meco was Terski's right hand man and Milas "the Butcher" Vukavich was Meco's main man in Buffalo. These men and their rag tag crew of undesirables were making life more complicated than Vito wanted.

"I don't like it. I don't like it at all. Time to do something about these assholes." Vito said to Tony Sotto, his enforcer and right hand man.

"What do you want me to do, Boss?" he asked.

"I want to know what those Russian bastards are up to. Put some men on their tails. Get some fucking bugs planted somewhere. Terski is up to something. Get Tiny and Joe Gatta on it. I want to know every move Terski, his guy Boris, and that patsy jerkoff, Milas make. I want to know when and where they take a shit."

"OK, Vito. I'll take care of it."

A few weeks later Sotto reported to Vito. "Terski has an arms deal in the works and he's expecting it to go down Saturday night."

Tony's informant told him, under extreme duress I might add, that Terski's guys waylaid a truckload of Uzis, small easy to handle semi-automatic machine guns, and were delivering them at the old tire warehouse at the foot of Ferry St. Saturday night, but he didn't know what time or who the buyers were.

"I want the guns and if I know Terski his buyers are gonna be there too. Grab the guns and the fucking money. I want it all and I especially want Terski to know I've had it with his shit. This is my town; tell him to get the fuck out. Bring a big crew. Terski's no fool. If anything goes wrong. Kill them all. Understand?"

"Yes, Sir. I got it. You know, this is going to start a fucking war."

"Don't tell me what to do!" he screamed. "Just do what I tell you. Now get outta here. If they want a war they'll get a fucking war and when it's done, they'll be done! Finito."

Saturday night the warehouse on West Ferry was not a happy place for the Russians. Tony Sotto's plan worked to perfection. He and his hooded men ripped off everything, the guns and all the money, all without a shot being fired.

Ivan Terski screamed, "Tell Vito he just made the biggest mistake of his life. The biggest. Tell him he has no idea who he's fucking with. What do you think, you're fooling us with those fucking hoods. You tell your boss, this ain't over. It ain't over by a long shot. You sons a bitches."

"Fuck you," came the response.

And so it began.

Terski was out of his mind with hatred as he addressed a group of his guys.

"Anybody recognize any of those assholes? I know they were Bansano's guys. Who else could it be? You guys know any of those motherfuckers?"

"I know who one of them was for sure, Boss," answers Boris Meco. "The big guy with the tattoo of a barbell on his hand was Tiny Gatta."

"Gatta, Tiny Gatta, I want that mother fucker dead!" screamed Terski, spit flying from his mouth as he yelled every word. "Dead! If those mother fuckin' dagos want a war they got one.

"Vukavich, I want that fucking Gatta dead," ordered Terski.

Milas Vukavich, a born killer who was also known as the butcher, actually enjoyed his role as a ruthless brutal killer and Terski used him whenever he wanted to make a statement. He could use any of his guys to just shoot someone but this was statement time and Terski wanted Bansano to know this was war. Bansano started it but Terski planned on ending it.

It was a beautiful morning. Sun shining, birds singing, and Peter was whistling a happy tune when his lovely wife came out of the house to hop in the car. They were heading to her obstetricians' for a routine check-up.

Jackie opened the car door to a very nice surprise; Peter had a beautiful bouquet of a dozen long stem white roses perched on her seat waiting for her.

"Peter, you never cease to amaze me. You know how much I love white roses; they are the happiest flowers in the world."

"Jackie, in case you didn't know, you are my white rose."

"I love you, Peter!"

"Ditto."

"Ditto. Ditto, God you're so romantic."

"Let me rephrase that. Jackie I love you more every single day so much that I can't wait until tomorrow. I love you sweetheart."

Without saying a word she leaned in and kissed Peter like he just returned from the war.

"Thank you darling, thank you so much. You are so thoughtful. I think you just might be the best husband in the entire world."

"Aw shucks ma'am, it weren't nothing," he said in a southern accent.

"Yes it was, but you know what would top off this wonderful morning? A Dutch Crunch bagel, I have got this overwhelming urge for one."

"A Dutch Crunch bagel aye, anything for you, you pain in the ass." Peter replied knowing full well he had absolutely no choice in the matter. He knew that wasn't a request...it was an order. They had to pass the Bagel's R Us on Niagara Falls Blvd right on the way anyway. So off they went.

Entering the bagel shop Peter noticed a semi-familiar face sitting at the first table beside the door. It was one of the guys he'd seen a number of times at the Delaware grill. He didn't know his name. The guy recognized Peter as well and nodded as he and his wife walked in. Peter gave a polite nod back and then reached for Jackie's hand. They ordered the Dutch Crunch bagel Jackie was craving and Peter ordered a cinnamon roll. They grabbed their order and sat in the back of the store far from the gentleman Peter knew as one of Vito's men.

Tony Gatta, who was known to his partners in crime as Tiny because he was as big as a house, stopped every morning at ten a.m. like clockwork at the Bagel's R Us for a sesame bagel and two strong cups of black coffee. This day was no different.

After enjoying her bagel, Jackie looked at her watch and said, "Honey, we have to leave shortly or we'll be late but first I have to go to the ladies room, OK. So why don't you finish up your coffee and we'll go when you're done."

"Yes, dear," he replied as he slugged down his hot drink.

When she came back he grabbed her hand and they walked to the front door. Gatta stood up just as they got there, he was leaving too, and as they approached he politely opened the door for them. Jackie stepped through the door and as she did she turned to Peter.

"Sweetheart, I left my sweater on the chair would you get it for me please."

"Sure, Jackie."

Jackie walked out the door and Gatta followed. As Peter pulled his wife's sweater from the back of the chair. He heard a sound he would never forget for the rest of his life.

BANG BANG BANG BANG BANG BANG BANG BANG BANG BANG.

Peter rushed past the now squatting patrons in the shop who were ducking from the flying glass coming from the front window and the glass door. He stepped over a young couple that had obviously been hit by the barrage of bullets coming from machine gun fire. He jumped over the mutilated body of Tiny Gatta and slid to his knees beside the still body of his bleeding wife. She was hit twice, once in the shoulder and once in the chest. Peter's life flashed before his eyes. He did all he could to stop the bleeding all the while pleading to his unconscious wife. "Please don't leave me! Please don't leave me. I love you Jackie, I love you."

She moaned as Peter held her in his arms. A sign she was still alive, but barely.

The ambulance arrived seconds after the police. Peter informed the officers that he knew and saw nothing. He told them that he was all the way at the other end of the store when the attack happened. He spoke with them but wasn't really paying much attention. He was infinitely more interested in the condition and welfare of his wife who was being frantically attended to by the paramedics.

In minutes the paramedics had her on a gurney and were rolling her into the ambulance. Peter jumped into the ambulance right behind them. He didn't ask and he wasn't leaving, no matter what they said. He never let go of Jackie's hand the entire ride to the hospital. As soon as they arrived Jackie was rushed to an operating room. All Peter could do was wait. And pray.

He called his parents and told them where they were but didn't give them particulars, only that they needed to call Jackie's parents and get to the hospital as fast as they could.

Tom and Teresa ran through the emergency doors to a sight that broke their hearts. Peter sat there looking catatonic. Staring at nothing. He looked up at his mother. This is a man that faced death so many times you couldn't count them. But this time everything was different. So when Peter saw his mother, he burst out in such a loud sob you could hear it throughout the hospital. It could not be considered a cry it was so much more than that. He placed his head on her shoulder and uncontrollably sobbed. Teresa wrapped her arms around her son and at that moment he was able to choke out, "She's dying, Mom. They're doing all they can but she's dying. What am I going to do? What am I going to do?"

"You're going to wait and let the doctors do what they have to do. All we can do is pray. What have they told you so far?"

"They said that one of the bullets is so close to her heart that they are waiting for a specialist before they try to remove it. They said prepare for the worst because they are not sure they can remove it."

"Bullets?" screamed Tom.

Mike and Patti rushed in minutes after the Contis. Peter couldn't even look at them. He was not capable of even talking. All the parents hugged and Tom explained what he could from the information he received from the nurses. He grilled everyone he could while Teresa was trying to console her inconsolable son.

The five of them suffered together as they waited for any information they could get. Peter's tears turned to unconscionable thoughts. He wasn't thinking about anything other than Jackie's condition but thoughts, bad thoughts, kept creeping into his mind. He kept going over and over the circumstances of the morning. But the sadness had simply engrossed his thoughts. He was oblivious to his surrounding and the people with him. Only thoughts of Jackie Jackie Jackie ran through his head. He cried periodically and prayed in between the tears. Finally a doctor came out to speak to the anxiously awaiting family.

"Are you the Conti family?"

"Yes, Doctor, yes. How is she?" replied Peter almost in a begging tone.

"The news is not good. The surgery went well for the circumstances but the damage she incurred is life threatening. The next few hours will tell the story. I wish I had better news but the main wound is so close to her heart, we just don't know."

"Will she live?" asked her sorrowful father.

"That's what I'm saying. She is in recovery at the moment and we just don't know. I'm so sorry!"

Jackie's mom, Patti, fainted right in her husband's arms. Teresa and Tom helped Mike with his wife but they were crying as they did. Peter stood there stupefied. This was surreal to him. He couldn't accept what was going on. There had to be something he could do. "I'm her husband, Doctor. Can I see her?" asked a weary Peter.

"Not just yet Mr. Conti. We'll let you in as soon as we finish with her in the recovery area. That shouldn't be much longer. We've done and are doing all we can for her right now."

Peter just flopped back down in his chair, heartbroken. Within the next half hour Peter's brother and sister arrived, followed by Sonny and Rosey. The tears were flowing from all. Peter was no longer crying; he was definitely in shock. Sonny went over and sat by his lifelong friend but said nothing. There wasn't anything to say. He just sat there just to be with him.

Dr. Michalko came out two hours later. Everyone stood up expecting the worst. He walked over to Peter and said, "She opened her eyes for a brief moment but she is not lucid at all. I think you should go in there now, Mister Conti."

Peter pushed himself up out of his chair, visibly weakened by the ordeal. Everyone watched as Peter followed the doctor through the ER doors. No one spoke. The only sound you could hear was the crying from all of them. He entered the room where she lay. Her eyes were closed and she looked angelic. Peter sat next to her bed and simply held her hand. His mantra was simple, "I love you, Jackie," over and over again.

He sat there for what seemed hours but was only minutes when her hand started to slip from his. He called out frantically but it was too late. A team rushed in but to no avail. Dr. Michalko turned to Peter and said. "I'm sorry Mr. Conti. She's gone."

"NOOOOOOOOOOOOOOOOO," screamed Peter, and he dropped to his knees.

CHAPTER TWENTY

Peter sat on a chair in his living room staring at the television. The thing is, the television wasn't turned on. He was so lost he didn't know what to do next. His grief was so deep he could feel pain in his heart and it wasn't medical. A piece of it was missing. He turned the TV on just to end the dead silence. The channel two news was on.

This morning in Kenmore, a suburb just outside of the city limits of Buffalo, a person or persons unknown but alleged to be part of a Russian crime syndicate, perpetrated a execution style assassination. The suspicion that the Russian syndicate is somehow involved in this despicable act is predicated on the fact that the assumed victim, forty-three year old Anthony J. Gatta, is allegedly part of another crime syndicate commonly known as the Italian Mafia. The drive by shooting occurred at 10:24 a.m. just as Gatta was exiting the building. Three bystanders were fatally wounded as machine gun bullets riddled the entire entranceway of the building just behind me at Bagels R US, located on the corner of Niagara Falls Blvd and Delaware Ave. The names and identities of the other victims are being withheld until their families can be notified. More detail should be upcoming and we will keep you informed every step of the way. Buffalo police fear we may have a mob war on our hands and they intend to nip this in the bud before it gets out of hand. Tell that to the families of the three innocent bystanders who lost their lives this morning.

This is Mary Motta, reporting live from the Bagels R US in Kenmore.

Peter's expression turned from grief to hatred. The killing machine persona he left in Viet Nam started building back up inside Peter until it hit a crescendo. Thoughts of his life flashed through his head. His love for her was so deep and so intense that it has engrossed his being. The Peter that left the house this morning whistling a happy tune, holding hands with his pregnant wife, and looking forward to knowing if they were going to have a son or a daughter, was gone. Totally and unconditionally, gone.

A new Peter arose and now sat in this now empty house, depleted of Jackie's laughter, beauty, charm, and more importantly her undying love for him. The raw emotion that surged through his body was directed to one unstoppable goal. His life was over, as he knew it. He wasn't interested in any other life. Only one thing was left for him until he left this earth.

Revenge. Cold-hearted revenge. The Russian scum that just took Jackie's life were about to face an enemy that would be their worst nightmare. A cold-hearted killing machine with nothing but revenge on his mind. A man that was more dangerous than any man they have ever faced before and for one simple reason. This man had no fear because he didn't care if he lived or died. This enemy would hunt them down like dogs until he or the last one standing was dead.

Peter stood up, the blood rushing to his face from sheer adrenalin, stared into the television set and screamed at the top of his lungs.

"I"LL KILL THEM ALL, EVERY SINGLE FUCKING ONE. I"LL KILL THEM ALL."

Meanwhile at the Delaware Grill, a half crazy Joe Gatta, Tony's brother and one of Vito's strong arms, was stomping around uncontrollably.

"Vito, please, I know who it was, we all do, it was that motherfucking Vukavich. I want to tear his fuckin' head off and stick it up his ass. Then I'll throw his mutilated carcass right at Terski's feet, just before I kill that cocksucker. Please Vito, just say the word."

Vito responded in a calm and cool voice, the kind of tone that one uses when they are so mad they are beyond yelling, a tone far more threatening and dangerous, said evenly, "Joseph, Vuckavich is a walking dead man, of that there is no doubt. But the cops will be all over us over this thing for a while. We have to be patient.

"When the time is right I'll give you the nod. You can kill and eat the motherfucker if you want. I want more than just that piece of shit. Tony was a good man and a good earner. We will all feel his loss. I know, not like you. I get it. But I need you to keep your cool. You will have a cop on your every step for a good long time. Vengeance is a meal better served cold. Let those fuckin' Russians look over their shoulders for a while. Let them shit in their pants, waiting. Then there will be a blood bath in this town like it's never seen before. Patience, I'll tell you when. And when we come they won't be able to stop us."

The wake for Jackie was unbelievably sad, all wakes and funerals are, but this one seemed even more so. The big room at The Viviano Funeral Parlor was filled with Jackie's friends, family, and co-workers. There were small groups of people huddled in sections throughout. Most were crying. Jackie's parents sat on the side of her coffin and greeted all who approached. Patti was nearly cried out by the end. Mike was weak from the ordeal. Peter sat with his family across from it so the people who had just paid their final respects to his wife could stop. He nodded a thank you to all but he did not speak to many. His close friends and family all sat close to him in his support. It was a heartbreaking sight. An Army officer walked in, wearing his full dress uniform, walked to the coffin, kneeled and said a prayer. He then turned to see his friend sitting there with his head down almost oblivious to what was happening but going through the motions.

"Oh my God, Orin," Peter said as he stood up. The two men hugged.

Newly promoted Major Orin Olsen whispered to his brother in arms, "I don't know what to say and I didn't know what to do."

"You did both just by being here. Thanks for coming. You're staying with me of course so we'll talk later."

"Whatever you need my friend!" responded the stoic man.

Orin joined the family group that sat supporting Peter, which included Sonny, Ray, Al, and their families of course. For Peter, this entire episode was a living hell.

The final act of the ordeal came the next morning. The funeral. Peter arrived at the funeral parlor early. He sat looking at the garden of flowers that surrounded the room. The notes and messages written on the cards spoke volumes about the love people had for Jackie...and for Peter. Peter strolled the room reading many of the heart-felt sympathies written on each bouquet. He stopped at the one that was simply signed, Your Friend. There was an envelope attached to the giant bouquet of flowers. The note was addressed to Peter. It was marked personal. It was short but said it all.

My young friend, the sorrow I feel for you is overwhelming. I know I can say nothing that could ease your pain. All I can tell you is, the scum responsible for this will pay. That does not bring her back. This fact I know. It will not help how you feel right now but I hope knowing this can give you some peace.

My door is always open.

Vito

Peter read the card and disposed of it before anyone else saw it. Not meanly. He did not blame Vito in any way. It wasn't him or his men that pulled the trigger. He only blamed the cowards that caused his pain. But it did tell him one thing. He needed to act fast before Vito and his men did. To Peter there was only going to be one person to end the life of the people that killed Jackie. So he didn't have time to grieve. He needed to formulate a plan now. He was about to bury his beloved wife today but he vowed from deep in his heart that there would be more graves dug before he was done. Many more.

The final goodbye was a tearjerker. Just looking at Peter was heartbreaking. After the service the crowd of mourners solemnly exited the grave site area. There was to be a gathering for the attendees at the nearby Willow Restaurant just around the corner.

Peter left last; he stopped in front of the box holding his wife and nearly collapsed as he choked out his last words, "I love you, Jackie. Goodbye, my love."

He faced the coffin as one man but when he turned around to walk to the limo, he was another. The mood in the limo, already occupied by his parents, was somber, of course. Peter just sat there and said nothing. Silence filled the air. Peter was quiet to the point of worry. His mother Teresa wanted to say something but thought before she acted and decided to just let him be. She knew it would be best to just give him his space. Nothing she could have said would have comforted him. She just held his hand.

After the breakfast, Peter rose from his chair to say something to everyone. He tried to ease a few minds by announcing that he was fine and was grateful for their concern, concern that was written on most of their faces. He politely expressed that he really didn't need anyone making meals or bringing anything over to the house. Company is not what he wanted for a while. He just wanted to be left alone. He needed some time to heal. He hoped they understood where he was coming from. He also wanted to tell them how grateful he was for the support they were showing him during this terrible ordeal and for that matter have always shown him his entire life. Most importantly he just wanted to tell them how much he loved them all. He just needed time. After his brief announcement he went back to his family table and sat down.

He did stop along the way to whisper into Orin's ear. "That wasn't meant for you. You're with me until you leave."

Peter, Orin, Sonny, Ray, and Al went to Peter's directly afterwards. Small talk mostly. Sonny asked Orin about his promotion and wondered if he was reassigned. He answered all their questions by simply stating that the only thing that changed was the insignia on his uniform. He went from two bars to a gold leaf. Everything else was just about the same. Anything concerning Jackie was not mentioned. That subject was taboo, naturally. After a short while the boys, seeing that Peter was worn out from the day's activities, and knowing that Orin was only in for another day, left the men alone. They hugged Peter like it was going to be the last time they were going to see each other. It was a touching scene. These men were in pain. They felt for Peter with every fiber of their being but knew there was nothing they could say at that moment. Nothing needed to be said. They all lost a little piece of themselves that day and life would never be the same. Especially for Peter.

They left, and as soon as they did Orin said, "I know you and I know what happened. No matter what or how you proceed, count on me. Just use your head. You going to the electric chair doesn't bring her back."

"The man that pulled that trigger will die by my hands," proclaimed Peter.

"Peter, you need to take some deep breaths here and think about the consequences."

"The man that pulled that trigger will die by my hands. Period. Fuck the consequences, Orin."

"Look, buddy. You want to kill the son of a bitch, I got it. I'll stand next to you and laugh when he takes his final breath. But you don't even know who it is."

"I know who it is, Orin. I saw the bastard on the tube being questioned by police. He was so smug with his answers it made me sick to my stomach listening to him. It's him all right. There wasn't enough evidence to hold or arrest the piece of shit, so they had to let him go. But it was him."

"Who is he?"

"A two-bit criminal who works for the Russian syndicate. His name is Milas Vukavich. He has been a suspect in a number of homicides but he's beaten every charge. He's described as an enforcer for the Russians. But the police just haven't been able to pin anything on him yet. His nickname is "the Butcher."

"Whatever you want me to do I'll do. Do you understand? Whatever! You've saved my life many times, my friend. I'm here for you. But prudence needs to be taken into consideration. A plan."

"I've got a plan, Orin and for Christ sakes you owe me nothing. You've saved my life many times too.

That was a different war. This war is mine. But I do need something from you before my plan can work."

"Name it."

"I only know the names of a few guys connected with this son of a bitch. I don't know if he was alone when it happened but I think I have a way of finding out. I think I have a way of finding out all the names I need and that's where you come in."

"Pete, I don't know shit about these people. How can I help?"

"Being in intelligence you have access to people throughout the world. These sources of yours can find people anywhere. Maybe not based on who belongs to a civilian gang or anything like that but just normal people, right? Well this is what I need. I know this Vuckavich has family. Maybe not here is the USA but for sure in Russia. His wife, if he's has one, his mother, his father, brothers, sisters, any children or grandchildren he has, anyone I can use. I need their names and where they live."

"Jesus Christ Peter, what are you going to do?"

"Nothing to them, Orin, you think I'm an animal? But with those names I can get the information I need from Vuckavich."

"This is suicide."

"What would you do if this were Betty?"

"I'll have your info by the end of the week."

CHAPTER TWENTY-ONE

Orin had to leave the next day. He was deeply saddened for Peter on many levels and a nagging thought kept running through his mind; was this the last time he would see his friend? Just before they left for the airport, full knowing what he was offering, Orin made another attempt to join Peter in his quest. Peter hugged his brother in arms and told him that the information was all he needed for now. He added that if things really got out of hand he knew where to go. They left the house and before you knew it Orin was gone.

Peter knew he had to come up with some kind of alibi for himself through all of this. He had been thinking about it ever since his transformation, the conversion that started him on the path of revenge. He had a good idea on where he would go to set it up. He called Sonny and asked him if he could get away for lunch. Sonny's response was any place any time. They met at the Anchor Bar on Main Street, the birthplace of Buffalo style chicken wings.

"Sonny, I need to ask you for a favor."

"Anything."

"I need time to be alone. I mean totally alone. It's not that I want to hide from everyone, wait, yes it is, that's exactly what I want to do. I need solitude. I need to heal."

"What can I do? You know I'll do anything."

"Can I stay at your place on the lake? I just want to be alone and your place in Angola is perfect for me. Peace and quiet, the lake, and it's only twenty minutes from home, it's just what I need right now. "

"What kind of question is that? I'll give you the God damn house if you want it."

"I know that, Sonny. Thank you. I'm hurting, buddy. I just called Dallas and took a leave of absence from my job. I told them I couldn't do it right now, and they understood. They told me I could have all the time I needed, no matter how long. They were adamant about one thing though, they said just don't quit. I'm just lost and want to be alone. I'm devastated, buddy."

"Who wouldn't be? Of course you can stay there, buddy. We don't go there hardly at all anymore anyways, too busy. We haven't been out there in a month of Sundays and won't be. No problem, you won't be bothered by a soul. Just promise me you'll call me if you need someone to talk to. And, I cannot believe I'm even saying this, but if you have any and I mean any suicidal thoughts you call me immediately. I mean it, Peter. I swear if you don't I'll kill you myself."

"Don't worry, pal. That's not what Jackie would want. I just need time."

"You know where the key is. When you get there all you have to do is turn on the water and the hot water tank. You know the short cut to the marina so when you go their walk; it's easier than parking. It takes about five minutes by foot. The boat is in slip one ten, you know all this but I'm just refreshing your memory. The key for the boat is hanging next to the back door on the duck key holder. It has a red floater attached to it. Everything you need for the boat is in the lock box in the front of the boat, and the key for that is on the boat key ring. The utilities are always on. Buy some food. There isn't shit in the place and you're all set. You've seen me do everything a million times."

"Sonny, I've told you a billion times. Don't exaggerate!"

That was the first time in a week that either of them smiled. They both needed it.

"Thank you, pal! No way I can repay you."

"No thanks necessary. Come on Pete, you know that. Stay as long as you like. Move there if you want. But, and this is a must, you are paying for lunch, and I mean it."

When they stood up to leave, they hugged. Sonny's love for his friend was so intense that he would do anything for him, anything but trade places. He simply wouldn't know what he would do if the shoe was on the other foot. Peter had a different feeling for his closest friend, one of sadness because with what Peter was about to undertake, this could be the last time they would be together. Peter could almost feel the pain Sonny would have to endure if Peter died too. Peter was near tears when Sonny walked away. Peter had a momentary relapse in thinking when he considered all the loved ones he had and the added grief that would ensue if he died. But that thought was just momentary. His anger and hatred was still raging and overtook all other thoughts. His heart and mind were focused on one thing and one thing only. Revenge, cold-blooded and brutal revenge.

* * *

He moved into the cabin the next morning. Calling it a cabin was an understatement; it would be better described as a beautiful log home. The place was gorgeous, spacious, and spoke volumes about Rosey's taste and the couple's success. They were doing well financially and it showed. Peter stayed in the bedroom he usually stayed in when visiting. Sonny had the guys over often for let's call it one of their fishing expeditions. At least that's what they would tell their wives. Most of the time they were drinking and just being boys but they did fish a little too. The place held many memories for all of them. What a great spot. Peter stopped on his way there for groceries and was pretty well all settled in by lunchtime.

Now it was time to start his plan. Item one, an alibi. He would walk over to the Angola Marina and Restaurant, a place he had been many times before with Sonny and the guys. He needed to mingle and make friends with some of the locals. The restaurant served a great lunch so it had a vast number of regulars. Their customers included residents in the area, fisherman, plus folks just on their lunch hour. A good many came in daily. Peter was going to be one of them.

As Peter walked in he heard, "Pete, Pete Conti, you're one of Sonny's friends, right?" blurted out one of the marina's regulars.

"You got it. Jesus, man, you've got a good memory."

"Not really, I was over there in Nam, too. The guys like me who were there when you were definitely know who you are, buddy. I'm Gary Neer, met you here a couple of times before when you were with Sonny and a couple of your friends. You guys were busy so I just said hello. I was happy to just shake your hand. Wow, Po Pete."

"Gary, really nice to see you again. Now I remember you." (even though he didn't). "Thanks for the compliment, but if you don't mind could you do me a favor, and keep that whole Viet Nam, Po Pete thing to yourself. That was a hundred years ago and it's something I'm really trying to forget. It sucked in that hellhole and the memories are just not good for me. I know you know what I'm talking about."

"I do, buddy. I really do. No worries. Where's Sonny?"

"He's not coming. I'm staying at his place alone for a little stretch. Just needed some peace and quiet and some alone time."

"Woman trouble?"

"Yeah, something like that."

"I'm just sitting down for lunch. Wanna join me?" asked Gary

"Sounds good. But Gary, no talk about Nam, the thought of that place and even the thought of violence sickens me now. I'm a lover not a fighter."

"Enough said. What do you do for a living?"

"Sales guy. But I'm taking some time off. How about you."

"Handy man. Kind of a jack of all trades. If anything breaks down around here you can bet your ass my phone will ring. I like it because my time is my own."

"I'll keep that in mind. You come here often I take it."

"Every friggin' day and I love it. Best food around and I drum up business almost on a daily basis. I kind of kill two birds with one stone. Life is good."

"Sounds good to me. Looks like we'll be seeing a lot of each other then. I'm only a few minutes away and this place is perfect. I think I'll be eating lunch here every day myself."

"Conti, this could be the beginning of a beautiful friendship."

"Could be Gary. Could be."

They made small talk over lunch and then Peter left. Phase one accomplished. He had a place that could verify his whereabouts when needed and a guy who would vouch for him. Now he needed another source to go to for timing. Again the marina came into play, fishing. Peter left the restaurant and walked over to the marina side of the establishment. Sitting behind the counter was the owner and operator of the joint, Mark Stevens.

"Hey Mark, Peter Conti, Sonny Lippa's friend. You remember me?"

"Yeah, sure Peter, I remember you and your trouble-making friends," Mark said laughingly while sticking his hand out to shake Pete's hand. "Good to see you. What can I do for you?"

"I'm going to be around for a little while and need your expertise on fishing Lake Erie. I'm fishing out of Sonny's boat, slip one ten. You're familiar with it I assume. So let me start out by asking what the limitations are on his boat for wave heights?"

"Easy, stay off the lake if you see any white caps, period. It's dangerous out there in any size boat. What kind of fish are you after?"

"Small mouth mostly but I like the perch too."

"If you want to fish live bait, minnows. Otherwise, crank baits, spinner baits, and old faithful a plastic worm. You just got every bit of my fishing knowledge in one fell swoop."

"Great, thanks, that's about what we have always used but of course that was based on Sonny's knowledge of fishing. I love the guy but his fishing talents leave something to be desired."

"I know Sonny's boat, it has two live wells," said Mark. "One for the fish you catch and one for live bait. Minnows are three dollars a dozen for large and two dollars for mediums. The mediums are fine. As far as how many you need, that depends on how the fish are biting. Start out with a couple dozen. If you run out, good for you, we're open till dark."

"Where would you go if you were me?"

"I would go something a little bit different than you, I'd go and sit at the bar for the afternoon but if I were going fishing I'd fish the backs of coves and points. Use the minnows on a number six gold hook with a split shot about a foot up from the hook, no bobber. You need to feel the bite."

"Thanks Mark, I have no idea why Sonny says you're so dumb. I think you are kind of smart," laughed Peter. "That's for the troublemaking-friends line."

"Touché," was Mark's comeback.

"What does touché mean?" Peter asked with a giant smile.

"I think it's a hair piece but I'm not sure," said Mark.

Both men laughed out loud, shook hands, and Peter turned to leave. "See you tomorrow Mark, thanks again. You have helped me more than you know."

Peter left the Angola Marina feeling good about his plan. Mission accomplished, he thought to himself. Now I need to start following that piece of shit Vukavich. I need to see if he has any habit that puts him at the right place and at the right time to fit my plan.

While walking back to the cabin Peter said out loud through clenched teeth, "That's right, Vukavich, get ready to take your last breath."

CHAPTER TWENTY-TWO

Peter sat outside an Erie Street warehouse early the next morning eager to see if he was in the right place to start the surveillance on his intended victim, the notorious Milas Vukavich. He knew Vukavich's face from a number of newspaper articles he found in the library when doing research on the guy. He used hearsay to locate the possible locations he might frequent and through that he discovered the most likely place, a warehouse building generally known to the police as the headquarters for the Russian crime syndicate. The storehouse was on Erie Street. Peter naturally started his search there.

The place was located just off the shores of Lake Erie right under the skyway bridge on the edge of downtown. The main contents stored there was Russian vodka. It was a distribution point for the booze but many other pieces of contraband traveled through there, illegal things of course. The police had raided the place numerous times without finding a single thing. The Russians were a crafty group.

Vukavich showed up and Peter was excited that his resourcefulness paid off. He arrived in a black Lincoln Town Car around eighty thirty a.m. and exited the vehicle acting like he was someone important. He had a driver and traveled with what seemed to be a bodyguard. Both the driver and the bodyguard were very large men. Peter was fairly close; close enough to hear the driver complaining about wearing the chauffeur's hat.

"Why do I have to wear this God damn hat," spouted Anton Dupraven, one of Terski's henchmen who worked under Vukavich as a bodyguard/driver.

"Because it's your turn you dumb asshole," came an answer from Artur Savarov, Vukavich's other driver/bodyguard.

Anton turned to Vukavich and said, "Milas, isn't having us drive you around enough for you? Is this hat thing really necessary?" he asked cautiously.

"Just wear the fucking hat and shut your fucking mouth Anton, or I'll shut it for you, permanently," yelled Vukavich. And that was that.

The three men went into the warehouse but were out again in less than fifteen minutes. They got back into the Lincoln and off they went. Peter followed closely behind but kept a safe distance so as not to be detected.

They made stops at a number of businesses. Peter watched closely as they exited each location. Vukavich came out of every one carrying what looked like a bag of money. Peter assumed it was protection money. The three musketeers visited three or four places that morning, which took about an hour, hour and a half. Afterwards they dropped the money off at a pawnshop on Grant Street near Auburn. Peter figured it must be a Russian collection depot. Terski was smart and wouldn't use the warehouse. No way he wanted to bring unwanted attention to himself or to his organization.

Peter followed the sleaze bags for five days and it was exactly the same thing each day. Different businesses but the money drop off was always at the same place and about the same time, between 11:00 and 11:15 give or take five or ten minutes. Vukavich and one of his henchmen, the one who wasn't driving that day, would be in and out within fifteen minutes. They always parked in the alleyway alongside the pawnshop. If Anton did the driving that day he would sit and wait in the limo but if it were Artur's shift he would walk around and smoke. After the criminals left the pawnshop they would head over to the Ivanho Restaurant for lunch. This was a daily occurrence and it was like clockwork. Peter had the place and the time he needed to execute his plan and I do mean execute.

Now was the time he needed the information from Orin. When he was sure he knew when and where Vukavich would be, Peter called his friend.

"Orin, Peter. Were you able to get the information I asked you for on Vukavich?"

"Yes, Peter, I've got what you need," responded his friend. "The guy has some family in Moscow. He's still married but kind of in name only and the only connection they have is that he sends her money every month. The money is for the wife and his mother. The two of them are living together in the mothers' house. It's the same house that Vukavich grew up in. His father was two-bit gangster who worked for the mob while Milas was growing up. He was shot dead on the front porch of that same house. His wife's name is Natalya. His mother's name is Marina. He has a daughter who lives in Saint Petersburg. Her name is Anna Markavona. She's married and has one kid, a fourteen-year-old daughter named Arina. His son Yuri lives minutes from his sister. He's single and works as a bartender in a swank hotel called the Saint Petersburg Inn. You need any more than that?"

"No, I think that's all the information I need. Thank you, buddy."

"Anytime for anything. You know that."

"Orin, if you are wondering if these people are in any way shape or form a target, they're not. I just need the information for tactical reasons."

"I don't want to know a thing about anything. The less I know the better, but I am glad to hear that."

"Thank you my friend."

"Good luck. I'm here if you need me. One call and the team will be back together before you can say Jack Robinson. One more thing and I know I don't have to tell you this; everything said between us stays between us."

Peter replied, "I know that and I know what you're offering but what I have to do I have to do alone. I hope you understand."

"Of course, Peter. Of course. Good bye, my friend."

"Goodbye, brother."

Orin hung up the phone knowing there was nothing he could do or say to stop the onslaught that was about to begin. He was sorry it had to be but he knew nothing was going to stop his friend from avenging his wife. Nothing or no one on earth could.

Peter would go for lunch at the marina every day directly after leaving his vantage point near the pawnshop. He tried to make it between 11:30 and 12:15

so he could set up a pattern and an alibi. He didn't eat every day with his new friend Gary but often times he did. Now it was fishing alibi time too. The next morning he started that routine. He walked into the boat side of the marina where Mark spent most of his time behind the counter.

"Mark, let me have two dozen of your finest minnows. The kind fish simply can't resist."

"Peter you are lucky this morning. I have got minnows that can talk. All they say is 'breakfast is here come and get it.'"

"Great. Just what the doctor ordered," exclaimed Peter as he handed Mark a minnow bucket. "Backs of coves and points, right?"

"You are correct, sir," Mark answered using his best Ed McMahan impersonation.

Peter laughed, took the minnows, jumped into Sonny's boat, and away he went. He fished but all he was really was doing was setting up his whereabouts from somewhere around eight a.m. until he came back for lunch, every day. He continued the pattern for well over a week. Enough times so he felt that Mark would swear Peter was fishing in the morning and Gary would swear he was eating lunch around noon. All was set.

There were only two things on Peter's mind the morning it was going down. His loving wife Jackie and the scum that took her from him. His hatred had not subsided in the least for those responsible for her death and his goal had not changed. There were going to be many graves dug before he was done. Probably even his.

He went to the marina for minnows like he had been doing for a while, made sure he had a nice conversation with Mark, and left in Sonny's boat as usual. He caught a few fish, put them in the live well and then drove the boat to where he had his car parked. He then beached the boat on shore to await his return. In the car was his service .45 complete with silencer. The same gun he used many times when he was overseas. He brought a number of things back from Nam as memorabilia but most importantly his weapons; they were personal to him and acted as a reminder of the times.

He changed to old clothes and drove to the pawnshop on Grant, parked a little ways away and waited. The limo pulled up and Artur parked it in the alley as usual. Anton and Milas went in. Artur got out for a smoke and noticed a homeless guy sleeping against the wall too near the limo to suit him so he walked over to him and kicked him.

"Wake up you piece of shit and get moving."

Peter stood up and in one quick movement grabbed Artur and snapped his neck like he was killing a chicken for dinner. He picked him up, threw him in the trunk, grabbed his chauffeur's hat and jumped in the driver's seat. He then pulled the hat over his face a little, pretending he was napping, and waited. The two unsuspecting criminals returned five minutes later and jumped into the back seat.

"Wake up Artur, you fucking bum," yelled Anton.

Peter spun around gun in hand and put a bullet right between Anton's eyes. He fell forward dead as a doornail. Peter slung the gun towards Milas and put bullets in both of Vukavich's shoulders and one in his knee, incapacitating the killer of his wife.

Vukavich racked in pain, spit out, "You mother fucker. Who are you?"

"I'm the man who is about to end your miserable life."

"Who sent you, Vito?"

"Shut up, I'll ask the questions. First who was with you when you killed Gatta?"

"Fuck you. Just pull the trigger and get this over with."

Bang, Peter shot him in his other knee.

"Not the answer I wanted to hear," he said with a sinister smile.

He continued with, "I want to know who was with you on the Gatta hit and I want the names of all the guys in Terski's organization."

"Go fuck yourself. I give you nothing. You're going to kill me anyways."

Peter laughed and said, "You right. I'm going to put one in your throat and watch you choke to death on your own blood. And do you know why. You killed my wife that morning. She was in the doorway with Gatta."

"Good!"

"Good," Peter said as he smashed the barrel of his gun across Milas's face. "Here's the deal you piece of shit. You're already dead, that's a given. So you can tell me who was with you and give me the names of the other guys in Terski's gang or right after I kill you I'm

Roses are White

going to Moscow. I will go to the house you grew up in because your wife and mother still live there. First I kill your mother Marina while your wife Natalya watches. Then I'll kill her. You want to hear more. Next stop Saint Petersburg. I will wait for your son Yuri outside the Saint Petersburg Inn where he works and when he leaves to go home I'll put a bullet in his head. More you say. OK, Anna and your granddaughter Arina die next. More?"

"Stop. Please."

"Who was with you that morning?"

"Anton, Artur, and Dimitri Stepenov. Please don't kill my family."

"They live if you give me the rest of the names. You can save your friends or save you family. It's your choice."

"They're not my friends. I don't give a fuck about them. But please, my family."

"Names."

"Ivan Terski, Boris Meco, Yuri Antipenko, Alexy Makarski, Nicoli Pentrenko, Stanislav Stepko, Victor Benko, Mikhail Chekho, Nikita Sayko, Konstantine Yankovsky, Mikal Stavro, Anton Dupreven, Dimitri Stepinov, Klaus Lasski, Nikoli Domogarov, Oleg Chekhov, and some young fat kid I don't know his name but I think he's Terski's nephew. That's all of them. I swear. Please, my family."

Peter wrote the names down on a little pad he was holding but he would remember each of their names even if he didn't. When he was finished writing, he said, "My wife sends her regards!"

Then he shot Vukavich in the face twice and watched him as his last breath left his body.

Before he left the brutal scene he had one final and meaningful act that he wanted to perform. He threw a long stem white rose on each of their dead bodies, symbolic to Peter but meaningless to anyone else.

He walked away unseen but not satisfied. The rage inside him was not gone. He was not finished, not by a long shot. Next to die: Dimitri Stepenov.

CHAPTER TWENTY-THREE

The police were at the crime scene in minutes. There were no witnesses. The assumption of course was that Vito Bansano had something to do with it. Dean Dillion was assigned lead investigator on the case and immediately headed over to the Delaware Grill to question Bansano.

"Where were you this morning about eleven thirty or so?"

"Right here. I was hosting a luncheon for a number of business associates. We put together an organization that sponsors charity events here in the city with all the proceeds going to charities for children. Many of my associates as well as myself belong. It's a wonderful thing and I'm proud to be part of it. Why are you asking me this?"

"Milas Vukavich and two of his cohorts were just found murdered. We know you had a dislike for this guy and his friends. Do you have anyone who can verify your story?"

"What are you talking about? Many of them are still here and are very prominent men in our city. Ask any of them. The mayor even stopped by to say hello. They will tell you I've been here all morning. Just ask. Plus I have no idea what you're talking about. I have no animosity towards anyone. I'm just a restaurant owner and I resent the allegations."

"OK Mr. Bansano. But if you hear anything about this I would appreciate a call. Here's my card."

"Sure officer, Dillion is it?"

"That's right."

"If I hear anything I'll be sure to call. Now would you and your men please leave you are interrupting a very nice meeting and embarrassing me in front of my friends."

"Yes, of course. These men have backed up what you've said. Sorry to have bothered you."

Vito apologized to the men who remained and explained how he is always accused in every case of wrong doing in the city based on no facts at all. They all nodded in unison and that was that. As soon as the place emptied out he screamed at Tony Sotto,

"Where is Joe Gatta? Find him. I want him here now!"

"He's in New York City Boss. You sent him there yourself."

"Get a hold of him. I want proof he's there. If he did this, I'll kill him myself. I don't need this shit. I told him to lay off. I really don't need this shit."

About a half hour later Sotto walked into Vito's office. "He's with Gino Telesco at Titto's restaurant in the Bronx. It wasn't him. He said he had nothing to do with it."

"Who the fuck did it, then?"

"The Russians have many enemies, Boss. I have no idea."

"We need to back off this even more now. The cops will be on us more than ever and I didn't think that was possible. Put your ear to the ground and find out what you can. I don't know if we have a new ally or a new enemy but we need to find out."

Peter returned to the boat about 11:15 and was back at the marina by noon.

"Mark, I have a few small mouth bass in the live well. If you want them for the restaurant you can have them. If not I'll throw them back."

"Thanks Peter. I'll send one of the cooks down and clean them up. Appreciate it buddy."

"No worries, mate. That's Australian for you're welcome."

They both laughed and Peter went over to the restaurant side for lunch. He was happy to see Gary there.

"Hey, Gar, did you eat yet?"

"Nope, just got here. You been here long?"

"Not real long, a little bit though. I was talking with Mark and gave him my catch for the day. You know, brownie points."

"You brown noser."

"Maybe but he never even counts when I get minnows in the morning. He just gets close and says there you go. He's a good man."

The men ate together and Peter left. Walked to where he parked his car and drove back to the cabin. Everything went perfect. He walked into the family room, sat down on the couch, and thought about the morning's happenings. He had absolutely no remorse.

There wasn't joy. What he did wasn't going to bring Jackie back. But there was the feeling of satisfaction. The satisfaction that the scum that ended the life of the person he loved most in his world were dead. Well almost all, there was one more man in the car. Dimitri Stepenov. He was the next to die, but not the last.

* * *

Terski was livid. He called for Meco to come into his office.

"Those fuckin' dagos are going to pay. I know it was them. Boris, see if you can find Joe Gatta. Dollars to donuts it was that prick."

"OK Boss. You want I should just kill the guy?"

"No, bring him to me. I want to talk to him before we kill the son of bitch."

"OK Boss, I'm on it."

Two hours later Meco reported to Terski. "It wasn't Joe Gatta Boss. The guy is over in New York City. He's been there a couple of days."

"Who then? Bansano wouldn't let anybody else at Vukavich. Bansano is up to something but I don't know what. The entire police force is all over both of us like stink. The guy is not that stupid. Something is up, definitely up. This doesn't make any sense."

"He wants us to counter. I bet that's what he wants. Well we're not. I won't play into his hands. Let's sit on this and see what his next move is."

The next day in the paper there was an article describing the murders. The reporter dubbed the killer "The Flower Man" because of the white roses left on the bodies. The name stuck and every newscast and every article written or reported referred to the killer using that nickname. Soon the entire city was talking about it.

"Who the fuck is this Flower Man?" screamed Terski. "Does anybody know if Bansano has a guy that they call the Flower Man?"

"Boss, I know most of Bansano's guys. There isn't anyone called the Flower Man, unless they got a new hitter in from out of town," answered Dimitri Stepenov.

"Somebody better find out something. I want to know who this guy is and I want him dead. Dead do you hear me? You don't kill my men and live. I want him dead."

Stepenov left the warehouse in a hurry. He was going to find out who that Flower guy was and he was going to find out fast. He headed to the shipyard where they had a couple of snitches working hoping to find out something, anything. He hopped into his black Cadillac convertible and took off. He had no idea that he had a tail following close behind. Peter followed Dimitri the same way he followed Vukavich. He was looking for a pattern.

After several days Peter didn't have a plan. The guy was all over the place. He needed Dimitri to be at the same place around 11:00 a.m. every day so that Peter's alibi would fit.

Stepenov did eat lunch twice at The Paramount Restaurant on Canal Street that week. He parked in the parking lot across the street from the place and the lot was fairly secluded. Peter decided that was his best bet so he went there three days in a row without a glimpse of Stepenov. Dimitri was a smart cookie and was suspicious of everything and everybody. He knew someone was hunting the Russians and he wasn't going to be the Flower guy's next victim. Well that's at least what he thought. He was wrong. The police found his body lying next to his car in the parking lot across the street from the Paramount Restaurant. He had been shot in the back of the head twice and a white rose was thrown on his carcass.

On the channel two evening news that evening came this report:

> *This afternoon another fatal shooting occurred in a parking lot on Canal Street. Thirty-eight-year-old Dimitri Stepenov was gunned down apparently on his way to lunch at the Paramount Restaurant across the street. There are no suspects at this time but a white rose was laid next to the victim's body. Police fear we have a serial killer on our hands. Detective Dean Dillion has not ruled out a mob-related execution due to the fact that Stepenov was a known member of the Russian crime syndicate. More news at ten.*
>
> *This is Mary Motta reporting from Canal Street.*

"MOTHER FUCKER," screamed a half-crazed Terski. "They want a war, I'll give them a fucking war. Don't tell me Bansano's not behind this. I know he is. Someone is going to die over this. One of Bansano's guys is going to die. I don't give a fuck who. Someone is going to die."

"How Boss?" answered Meco. "We can't even take a shit without one of Dillion's men asking to wipe our ass. How?"

"I don't give a fuck. Somebody is going to pay."

"Yes, sir. I understand. But this will not be easy," retorted Boris Meco.

"Boris, one of Bansano's guys dies or you do," said an overly angry Terski as he pulled a gun from the top drawer of his desk and pointed it at Meco.

"I got it Boss. Consider it done. Just give me a little time."

"We don't have time. If this keeps up we won't have an organization left."

"I'll take care of this, Boss."

"You better."

In the mean time, Vito pulled his men in for a meeting.

"Look, we're being set up. I wouldn't put it past Terski killing his own men just so we have the cops all over us. If it ain't him, we have another player in this game. Who or why, I have no idea. But you better watch your asses. Terski is coming and he has blood on his mind. Consider yourself at war and this ain't a war we can afford to lose."

Peter ate lunch with Gary like nothing had happened at all. He went about his routine and was back at the marina by noon again. The difference was, he just got through putting two slugs into the back of a guy's head. It was like killing a squirrel to Peter now. He had no conscience about it and no remorse. It was what he planned on doing and was going to keep doing it until they kill him. Period. After lunch Peter went back to the cabin and when he did he walked into a surprise.

"Hi Peter, I've been worried about you so I decided to drop by and see how you are. So, how are you?" asked Sonny.

"I'm good, pal," Peter replied as he hugged his lifelong friend. "I'm actually happy to see you."

"What have you been doing?" asked his concerned friend.

"Soul searching and fishing."

"How you doing with both?"

"I'd say I'm doing a lot better with the fishing. I'm sad, Sonny."

"I was thinking maybe being alone is not what you need any more Pete. You have a lot of people who want to support you at home."

"Are you evicting me?"

"Shut your pie hole. You know you can stay here as long as you want. It's just that everybody is worried about you. What do you say about coming home for a little while and start getting back to your life?"

"You might be right. I just don't want to face the world without Jackie."

"What choice do you have? You think wallowing in self pity is the answer? I'm here for you buddy but you have to help. Help yourself through this terrible ordeal."

"I know you're right. I just miss her so much."

"Is this what you think Jackie would want you to do? Come on Pete, you know she would be pissed off if she looked down and saw you like this."

"I guess you're right."

"You can bet your sweet ass I'm right. Now what do you say. You want to come back to my house for a while and be around friends?"

"How about this? We call the guys and we have us a good time right here tonight and maybe go fishing in the morning like we use to?"

"That sounds great. Hold on a second," said Sonny as he walked to the front of the house and yelled out the door.

"Ray, Al, come on in."

CHAPTER TWENTY-FOUR

Ray and Al walked into the cabin not knowing what to expect from their brother-like friend. They felt so sorry for Peter that they were hesitant even talking to him. That lasted about five seconds. Peter hugged his friends and said, "Thank you guys for coming. You have no idea how happy I am to see all three of you. It's been a long hard ordeal for me and I can tell you it isn't over. I'm saddened to the core."

Al spoke first, "We've almost come ten times since you starting staying here but we all knew you needed some time."

Ray interrupted with, "But here we are now. How you doing, Peter?"

"Good days and bad days, my friend. This is one, well it's one of the good ones."

Sonny added, "Well, get ready to make it even better. We got booze and steaks and plenty of both."

"I really missed you guys!"

The boys bellied up to the bar and the drinking commenced. No talk of Jackie. Not a word. Mostly talk about sports, the weather, and such. The conversation soon turned to fishing.

"I've been slaying them," boasted Peter.

"What are you using?" asked Ray.

"Nothing but minnows."

"What size minnows, where are you catching them, and most importantly how's the boat running?" questioned Sonny.

"Mediums, in the backs of coves and on points. I've got four or five spots that I have been nailing the piss out of them. And Sonny, the boat's running like a champ. No problems whatsoever. Except for the fire, of course."

"What the hell did you do to my boat?"

"Ha, got ya. Boat's tip top and ready for tomorrow. Thank you, Sonny. You have no idea what that boat has done for me. No idea at all."

"Why do you have to pull that shit on me? You almost gave me a heart attack. You know my mom gave me that just before she died."

"Your mom's alive, Sonny,"

"Do not bring my mother into this, Why would you bring my mother into this."

All three laughed out loud.

"To my mother. I love that woman," toasted Sonny as he raised his shot glass full of Crown Royal.

They all drank and said in unison, "To Sonny's mom."

"Now back to the important question, have you caught any big ones?" asked Al

"Al, be ready to put one on the wall. They are biting like there's no tomorrow."

"OK, that's what I wanted to hear. Now back to drinking."

The boys over-indulged and naturally the drunk talk started. Even under those circumstances there was no talk of Jackie. They all knew that would change the entire mood. But 'I love you like a brother' was said so many times it was getting sickening. Then out of the blue Peter said something that caught all their attention.

"Guys, I want to tell you something and it requires no response. My life is not the same anymore. I don't know what I'm going to do with it. But it's not going to be the same and I'm afraid I don't know who the new Peter is going to be."

"Peter, don't make any rash decisions. As much as I hate even saying this, time heals all wounds," said a saddened Sonny, who was sorry to hear his friend's remarks.

"It's so much more than that, my friends. And I really don't want to talk about it. Just mark my words. Life has consequences and circumstances change people. I will say this and this will be the last word on this subject, if you guys don't mind. Our friendship is one of the most important things in my life and I thank God for it. I do not know what the future has in store for me; just know that I love you guys."

"Pete," started Ray.

Peter interrupted before another word was said, "No more talk about it. I needed to say this and it's said. I know you guys are worried about me. I'm not suicidal. It's not even a thought. I just don't know what's going to happen in my life. I'm different. Just accept that."

Sonny started to say something but Peter stopped him.

"Let me finish and this is definitely the last word on any of this. It's the most important thing I have ever said to you guys and please as I said let it be the last word on this, no matter what happens I want you to know this.... I am truly sorry."

"What the fuck are you talking about?" asked Al emphatically.

"I'm just sorry, OK. Can't we leave it at that." Pete said as a tear rolled down his face.

"OK, you just got way too serious," interjected Sonny. "But it's my turn to say something and I'm talking for all three of us. Whatever the future holds we will be there for you. Period. Thirty years of friendship doesn't grow on trees."

Peter hesitated when he realized he was about to confess to his friends about the Flower Man. He stopped himself before he said another word. There was no reason to involve them in any way. Even knowing could put them in danger.

"I loved Jackie with all my heart," was all he said.

All four guys cried. The drinking was over.

Sonny simply said, "We all did!"

After a few solemn moments together they gathered themselves. Sonny made a motion to hit the sack so they could get an early start in the morning. Fishing became the topic of conversation before they all went to bed.

The next morning came sooner than any of them wanted. They fought through their hangovers because honestly they wanted to fish. They were at the boat, not quite as early as planned but early enough. The weather was perfect. The fishing was excellent and all present had a wonderful time, mostly because they were all together. All in all it was a great day. They cleaned enough fish to take back to the cabin for a fish fry and ate like kings. After a while it was time to leave. They had families they had to get back to.

"Peter, I asked before and I'll ask again. No, I think I'll beg this time. Please come home with me and stay with us for a while. If I go home without you Rosey will kill me."

"Sonny, staying here, away from everyone is making things right for me. Rose and you are making that possible and I can't thank you enough. I know staying here will come to an end soon. Can I stay a little while longer?"

"You son of a bitch. You're going to get me killed. How many times do I have to tell you that you can stay as long as you want? You're making me mad now."

"Tell Rose I love her," Peter said as he hugged his friend. He hugged them all like it was the last time he would ever see them.

Why, because it could be? This wasn't over. The Flower man wasn't finished yet!

CHAPTER TWENTY-FIVE

"Who in the hell does that fucking Bansano think he's dealing with? First he kills Vukavich, Anton, Artur, and now Dimitri; fuck Bansano. He throws a fucking flower on their bodies and all of a sudden he's innocent. Bullshit. The Flower Man my ass," yelled Ivan Terski. "And, and, all the while we can't make a fucking move or leave this fucking warehouse without a cop sitting in our back seats for Christ sakes. How is he getting away with this shit?"

"Boss, the cops are all over them just like us. The guy and his men have covered their asses in every case. I don't know what you want me to do." answered Boris Meco.

"Kill somebody!"

"How Boss, you said yourself we can't go anywhere without a tail. How do you expect us to get away with killing anyone right now no less one of his guys?"

"I don't give a shit. That fucking Bansano is doing it somehow. He's trying to wipe us out and you expect me to just sit here?"

"Boss, maybe that's his plan? Maybe he wants us to strike back knowing full well the cops got eyes on every one of us and every move we make. We get a man caught and we're done."

"Are you deaf, Meco? I don't give a God damn what that dago wants, I want one of his men in the morgue right fucking now!"

"This is a mistake, Boss."

Terski said, "One of his guys dies or you do. Do I make myself clear?"

"Jesus Christ Ivan, get a hold of yourself, man. We'll strike back. I'm with you on this, but we got to be smart about it. Let me figure out a way that we can make him pay and make a big statement while doing it."

"I want it done fast. Before that bastard kills another one of us. If this keeps happening there won't be any of us left for him to kill."

"I'm on it, Boss. I'll take care of it. Don't I always?"

"You better. I'm up to here with his shit," Terski said placing his hand under his chin.

Peter continued his routine at the marina. He wanted to let things settle down for a while before continuing his rampage on the Russians and knew he needed his makeshift alibi to stay in place. Eventually the cops would get around to questioning him. Look at the facts, the Italians and the Russians have been watched like hawks and the Flower Man Murders keep coming. They eventually will research other avenues and Peter, a war hero with serious skills, who lost his wife in one of the mob's skirmishes, would definitely be worth questioning. He was right. It wasn't long before Detective Dean Dillon showed up at his door.

"Peter Conti?"

"Yes."

"I'm Detective Dillon from the Buffalo Police. I'd like to ask you a few questions."

"I've already told a number of the police that I was on the other side of the building when the shooting started. I didn't see a thing."

"Yes sir. I have all that information. This is about something else."

"What can I help you with?"

"Where were you on the morning of June eleventh around noon?"

"When? June eleventh? I don't know. Let me think a minute."

"Take your time; I'm not in a hurry."

"Well sir, after I lost my Jackie," Peter hesitated a moment as he did anytime he said her name, "I asked a friend if I could stay here at his cabin. I needed to get away from the memories. That was the first or second of June. Since then I have been pretty much alone. But if you're talking about noontime, I ate at the Angola Marina then and have every day since I got here, give or take a few minutes. I can guarantee you, there are plenty of people who can verify that. Can I ask why you're asking?"

"Routine, questioning sir. We search out every angle."

"Every angle about what?"

"The flower murders, Mr. Conti."

"The flower murders? You think I have something to do with them? Is that what this is all about?"

"Sir, we have to question anyone who might have some skin in the game and Mister Conti, you do have motive."

"Wait. Are you saying the Flower Murders have something to do with my Jackie? Are these guys the perpetrators of her death? If they are, when you catch the Flower Man who ever it is, please give him my thanks. But it ain't me."

"We are not accusing you, Mr. Conti. Just following up on any lead or leads you can give us."

"I don't know a thing. All I know is my wife is dead and no one has been accused of her death or is in custody. I know that. Look Officer, I'm not blaming you and to be honest whoever did it I hope rots in hell for eternity but it won't bring my wife back. That I do know. Other than that I can't help you."

"OK, Mister Conti. I'll check out your story at the marina. If it all checks out you won't be hearing from me again."

"Sorry I couldn't help you, Officer. But I hope when you catch the son of a bitch that killed my wife you don't bring him in alive. If that's bad saying that, sue me."

"I understand sir and I truly hope this is the last time we'll be talking."

The detective left and headed straight to the marina. Peter's story checked out in spades. It wasn't just Gary Near who verified Peter's whereabouts. Mark, the owner of the operation, confirmed it, as well as many others. Dillon was convinced that he was barking up the wrong tree. He left to continue the investigation on the suspects he thought it was all along, the Italian Mafia. He knew it had to be them.

Boris Meco had come to the conclusion that even though Joe Gatta was supposedly out of town when Vukavich and his guys were hit, it was Joe's brother that they gangland styled murdered at the bagel joint and Meco knew that Joe Gatta was sure it was them. Joe was definitely in town for Stepenov's killing so Meco didn't believe the bullshit New York alibi at all. Joe was likely the killer. Meco decided that he was not going to just murder Joe Gatta, he was going to make a spectacle of his death and show Bansano that they were not going to stand for anymore of this bullshit. Business is business.

Meco's plan was to disguise himself so he could somehow sneak out from under the cop's watchful eye and without being followed plant himself in Joe Gatta's house. He was going to kill the guy right where he lived.

Joe walked in to his palatial apartment without a bit of suspicion and threw his keys on the coffee table. Turned on the tube and plopped in his easy chair. Moments later a sinister character appeared at the entrance of the kitchen pointing a gun at Joe's head.

"Hi Joe," said Meco.

"What the fuck do you want?" he said trying to reach for the gun he just placed next to his keys.

"No no," said Boris. "With your left hand push that gun off the table towards me."

Joe realized if he didn't do what Boris said he was dead. He slid the gun off the table onto the floor between the two men and said, "Wait a minute Boris, don't do anything rash. What is it you want?"

"I want to know who the Flower guy is. Is it you?"

"Fuck no. We have nothing to do with the guy. I don't know who he is. Even Bansano doesn't know. We are not killing your men."

"That's funny. I guess they're just killing themselves. Is that what you want us to believe?"

"I don't know what to tell you, Boris. But I had nothing to do with any of that. Nothing."

"Well we'll see about that. Let's take a ride. I think Terski might want to ask you a few questions. Stand up and put your hands behind your back. Don't try anything funny or you'll force me to put a bullet in your head," Boris commanded with no intention of taking him anywhere.

Gatta stood up and slung his hands behind him. Meco grabbed Joe from behind and with his arm around his neck stuck a knife in between his shoulder blades. He hung on to Joe until he was dead. He laid him down on the floor and grabbed a section of rope he brought with him. He flung the rope over the chandelier that decorated the middle of the room and tested it for support by hanging on it. When he was sure it would support Joe's weight he tied the rope around Joe's neck and hung him from it with the knife still sticking in his back. Before Meco left he went to the pantry and grabbed a box of spaghetti. He pulled a couple of small handfuls and placed some sticking out of each pocket.

"That ought to tell Bansano he's fucking with the wrong people," he said out loud as he slithered out of the place.

The next day on channel two news, Mary Motta reported:

Another murder related to the crime war between the Russian and Italian mob took place last night on Allen Street at the home of known gangster forty-seven-year-old Joseph Gatta. He was found hanging from the chandelier in his uptown apartment with a knife sticking out of his back. Joseph Gatta is the brother of previously slain gagster Anthony Gatta. The police now are convinced that we are in the middle of a syndicate war.

The reason they are so confident that the Russian mob is the prime suspect, was the message the killer left on the body. It wasn't a written message but it spoke volumes. The police found uncooked spaghetti sticking out of the victim's pockets. Sending an obvious message to the Italians that the Russians were definitely involved. There was no hard evidence left at the scene but all indication point to the Russian crime syndicate. This is the sixth murder of known gangster from these crime organizations in the last two months. The police feel that both sides are ramping up even more and fear this war has no end in sight. The police do not think this is part of the Flower Man Murders but are not counting out anything. We here at channel two are asking people to stay inside at night and keep your children close. The streets are no longer safe, and until the police can get a handle on this, they won't be.

Peter watched the news report with great interest. He realized he was the instigator of this so-called war. Maybe not the instigator but he definitely escalated it and now he was the sole reason for Vito's man to be killed. He had to do something. This was not at all what he intended. Maybe it was inevitable but not what he wanted. He put himself in the middle of something that he didn't know how to get out of. Vito was the key. Peter knew he had to do something.

But what?

CHAPTER TWENTY-SIX

Vito called his men into the office. Things were seriously getting out of hand. It turned from a business situation into a personal one. He knew he had to take the appropriate action. Retaliation was the key but it had to be done right. He had to think before they took any action. If the cops were all over them before, he knew that was just the start. They would be out in full force now. He was sure that if he or any of his associates would sneeze a cop would say God bless you.

Tony Sotto was the first to walk into Vito's office, followed by Alberto Nazzi, Vittorio Sordi, Vic Desica, Nino Torisi, Franco Andolina, Gino Paladino, and Frankie Nero who stood guard at the door between Vito's office and the restaurant.

Vito started by saying, "We all know those fuckin' Russians did in Joey Gatta. I know you guys and I know you want revenge and you want revenge right fucking now. Believe me that will happen, they will pay, in spades. I think I might pull the trigger on Terski myself. But, I told you before and I'll say it again we have to be patient, especially now. The cops are going to turn up the heat big time. We make a move too soon and we could lose everything. I need to put something together. Just hold off. No John Wayne shit. You hear me? When this is done we'll all piss on their graves. But for now—" Vito was interrupted when Frankie Nero turned to walk out of the office.

Someone just walked in to the restaurant at an inopportune time.

"I'm looking for Vito," announced Peter. "Tell him Peter Conti needs to see him."

"He's busy. Get the fuck out."

Peter kept walking towards Frankie without even slowing down. By the time Peter reached Frankie a number of Vito's men were already entering the restaurant from the back office including Tony Sotto. When Peter was but a foot from Frankie Nero, Frankie pulled out his gun. With the speed and sleight of hand of a magician Peter snatched the gun right out of his hand and pointed it right back at him. Five or six men reached for their guns and as soon as they did, Tony Sotto yelled out, "Everybody stop. What the fuck's going on, Conti?"

"Sotto, I need to see Vito, right now."

Vito Bansano, the Don, walked from behind the door, pushed a number of his guys' gun hands down, and came front and center.

"My young friend, this is not a good time. I'm in an important meeting. What's so important that you came in here like this? I'm not very happy with you right now."

Before Vito even started talking Peter spun Frankie's gun around and handed it him. As soon as Vito was finished spouting his little spiel Peter answered, "Vito, no not just you Vito, all you guys, I put you in danger. I'm sorry Vito. Can we talk?"

"You can say what you need to say in front of these guys. What are you talking about Peter? Wait a second before you start talking, let me talk to my guys for a minute.

"Gentleman, I think most of you know this man, he's a friend of mine, and his name is Peter Conti. He's been coming in here for more than ten years now so I know most of you have seen him. He's a good guy, so don't get antsy. I want to hear him out. If anyone does anything stupid you'll answer to me. Capisci? Now, what's this, you say, about putting us in danger?"

"Before I spit this out, I want you to know Vito if you decide to put me down right here and now I understand and wouldn't blame you. But here it is, I'm the guy that got Joe Gatta killed."

"Jesus Christ Peter, what the fuck are you talking about?" responded Vito.

"I'm talking about what the press is calling the Flower Man Murders. You see, I'm the Flower Man. I killed those fucking Russians. I killed Vukavich, Anton Dupraven, Suverov, and Dimitri Stepenov. That's not all, because unless you stop me, I'm plan on killing as many of those sons of bitches as I can."

Vito shook his head and hesitated a minute before he spoke, "Nino, lock the door and everybody sit down. I think we all need to hear more from Mister Conti."

Vito paused a second and then continued. "Hold it Peter, before you say another word I think it would be a good idea for my guys to know just who you are and even more important than that, just what you're capable of doing."

Vito turned to face his entire crew and said, "A lot of you guys know who this guy is but for those who don't, let me tell you about Peter Conti. He's a big time war hero. He's a Green Beret, he's Special Forces and a highly decorated killing machine, and one of the deadliest men that our army has ever seen. So before I make any decisions about anything I want to hear what this man has to say. This is no guy off the street claiming he's a bad ass. He is a bad ass, so I plan on listening and I think it would be a good idea for you guys to do the same."

"OK Vito, here's what I have to say and I'll lay it out straight. I know you're in the middle of what they're calling a gang war. And I am all too aware that I unwittingly escalated the thing but I didn't start it. It started when those fucking Russians put a hit on Tony Gatta. This you all know. What you might not know is those two bit Russian punks killed my wife who was standing near Gatta when it happened. You understand what I'm saying. They killed my wife.

"Revenge, revenge is the most powerful motivation a man can have. Make no mistake I have it running through my veins. You guys are thinking retaliation but I'm thinking revenge. Vito is right. I know how to kill. I'm good at it. Real good. You think you're bad. I could kill three of you before you could blink an eye using a dull spoon. I say this not in a threatening way at all. Vito's not my enemy, he's my friend, he's more than a friend to me. I'm telling you this 'cause it's just fact. I telling you this so you know I'm not spinning some kind of bullshit yarn. Those motherfuckers killed my wife. They will all pay with their lives, I swear it; so, Vito, it's up to you. Either kill me now for what I've done or let me go and I'll kill more of those sons of bitches."

"Jesus Christ, Conti. Jesus Christ. You know what you've got yourself in the middle of my young friend?" said the saddened Mafia boss.

"Yes I do Vito, and more than that. I've got a plan."

"You're in this so damn deep now my young friend, all I can say is let's hear it."

"Terski and his boys are waiting, hoping you will avenge. They want you to. They know the cops are all over you like stink and as soon as you make your move, the cops grab you and they end up with it all. Well fuck 'em. Here's what I propose. An air tight alibi and some dead Russians."

All ears were on Peter now but Peter spoke directly to Vito, "You take all your guys here on a little trip. Maybe Atlantic City or Vegas or, hell it doesn't matter where. Just as long as there are plenty of witnesses around who can verify you were there. When you buy the plane tickets, buy one in my name. I'll bet one of your men has a trusted friend or a cousin or somebody that resembles me, bring him with you as me, in my place. Now, I've got an alibi. The police have already questioned me. They know I have motive so I need an alibi myself. Then I'll kill more of those bastards while you're gone and throw a flower on their rotting carcasses. Who gets the blame? The Flower Man."

"How you plan on getting close to those pricks?" asked a now very interested Tony Sotto.

"Look, those Russian pigs know every move you guys make. They'll know you're out of town. When they see that, I think they'll let their guard down and when they do I'll put some bullets in a few of their heads. The trick is to be close enough so I can drop the white roses."

"Can you take out that fucking Terski?" was Vito's question.

"That's up to you, Boss," answered Peter. "I wouldn't, but that's your decision. Here's why Vito, we take him down and somebody will just take his place in a New York minute. We kill the men around him and Terski might turn tail and get the fuck out of here. Isn't that what you really want? I'll kill that fucker later. He's the one that pointed, Vukavich was only the gun he used. Terski will die, that you can take to the bank."

"Jesus Mary, and Joseph, Conti! I need a second here. This is something my friend."

"Are you in?"

"When do you want this to go down?"

"Vito, you're the boss. I'm just glad I'm still standing here upright."

Vito laughed out loud followed by his whole crew. He didn't hesitate a second before saying, "I love every word you just said. It's smart. It's more than smart. It's genius. They die and we come out, excuse the expression, smelling like a rose. But before I give you my final word on this, let me say one thing, and saying this is very important to me. Peter I am truly sorry about your wife. I wish you knew how deeply I mean that. I want you to know my plan has always included avenging her.

"I was going to kill Vukavich myself. I want you to know that. Yes, I was mad when they killed Tony but his death did not hurt me like your Jackie's. You know how I feel about you. So, go, you kill them bastards. One more thing, you just called me boss, there's no need for that, it's still just Vito. This is your caper; you're the one calling the shots on this. Let me just answer you by saying, we're in. All in, all of us."

"Give me a day or two to do a little scouting. I'll be back."

As Peter turned to walk away, every guy in the place recognized that, in the world they lived in, this was a man to be reckoned with, a man to be respected, more than respected, a man to be feared. Vito had a different emotion going, pride. If it were anybody else who would have challenged his authority right in front of his men the way Peter just did he would have put a bullet in the guy in a second. But it wasn't just any guy. It was Peter Conti and Vito Bansano, the Godfather, the Don, loved this man like he was his own son. He never said it, but he has felt that way about Peter for a very long time. He was sorry that Peter came into his world but understood why and was going to back his play all the way.

CHAPTER TWENTY-SEVEN

Peter started his watch early the next morning back at the warehouse on Erie Street. Peter knew someone had to take Vukavich's place in Terski's protection racket scheme. No way they would let that kind of money go. He was right. Around 9:30 Boris Meco, Terski's right hand man, walked out of the building followed by Yuri Antipenko. They jumped into what looked like a brand new silver Ford Bronco. Peter was on their tail as soon as they took off. Again he was right. They stopped at five businesses. Meco walked out of each holding a bag. Then sometime around noon ended their little trip at the pawnshop on Grant Street. The same place Peter had his first taste of revenge.

They repeated the routine three days in a row, only difference was the places they stopped at to collect their extortion money. Wherever they went, Peter followed. One constant, they always ended up at the pawnshop, and it was always around the same time. Peter knew what he was going to do, he was ready, and he had his strategy. He left his vantage point at the Grant Street location and headed to the Delaware Grill.

He walked into the place to a chorus of, "Hey Conti," ... "Conti," ... "Hey Pete," ... "Conti, how you doin'?" from the men sitting around. He headed straight back to Vito's office.

"Hello, my young friend," said Vito with a smile.

"Hi, Vito."

"What do you have for me, Mister Conti?"

"I'm going to take out Terski's right hand man Boris Meco and one of his henchmen Yuri Antipenko the day after tomorrow in the same place I snuffed Vukavich."

"Is that smart? The cops are watching that place."

"I don't think they are. I've scoped it out for three days. I haven't seen hide nor hair of any police. They're thinned out right now, watching you guys."

"Meco. That will get Terski's attention, big time," sneered Vito.

"That's what I was thinking. We keep this up, two at a time and we'll send Terski limping home to mother Russia in no time. Remember, I don't really care where Terski goes. I'll kill that son of a bitch no matter where he goes."

"I think you got this covered, my friend."

"You ready to go on a trip?" asked Peter.

"Sounds like tomorrow would be a nice time to see Vegas."

"Let's see, tomorrow is Thursday, I'll do the deed Friday around noontime. I think it would be a good idea if I got together with you as soon as you land. Mingle with the crowd at the airport keeping out of sight and then slip into your entourage to join you and the guys. That way we will be seen leaving the airport together. If it's early enough, maybe have dinner. You can fill me in on details. After all I was with you, right. Just tell me the day and time you land."

"You'll be informed of our every move there. There are flights in and out of Vegas daily. I'll book our trip so we get back Saturday afternoon. Then you won't have to hide any longer than needed."

"Good. Good luck in Vegas, Vito."

"Don't get yourself killed. You hear me, boy?" Vito hugged Peter as he said it.

Vito and his men headed to Las Vegas. Peter, who now sported a three-day growth of beard that he let grow ever since he decided to utilize his initial disguise of a homeless guy, took a position in the alley next to the pawnshop Friday morning. It worked the first time, why not use it again. Meco and Antipenko arrived about fifteen minutes later than they had been arriving but close enough. Peter sat knees up and head down like he was trying to sleep. He wore a baseball cap which he had doctored up to look grungy, waiting for his prey. The Russians pulled up, got out of the car and started walking towards the back entrance of the building. Yuri noticed the apparent homeless man, Peter, and meandered over to where he sat.

Meco was just about in the door when he turned to Yuri and said, "Leave that fucking bum alone. We're late and I'm hungry. I want to get this done and get the hell out of here."

Yuri spun around and they both went in. Peter was lucky. He could have disposed of Yuri without a problem but Meco was almost out of his sight. Peter needed both men together or his plan wouldn't work.

The hoodlums came out and as they did Peter stood holding a dirty rag and walked to their car like he was going to wash their windshield.

Yuri said to Boris, "I should have shooed this piece of shit away when we got here."

Boris stuck his head out the passenger window and yelled at the vagrant, "We don't need our window cleaned. Get the fuck out of the way."

He wasn't finished screaming his rant when Peter pulled out his silenced .45 and put a bullet through Meco's head. Yuri reached for his gun, but way too slow. His reward was two shots so close together they almost touched each other right between his eyes. Peter threw a long stem white rose on each of them and disappeared without making a sound.

Vukavich, Dupraven, Suvorov, Stepenov, now Antipenko, and Meco, all dead by Peter's hand and Peter wasn't through yet. Not by a long shot.

Vito read the newspaper with a smile, while having breakfast in the palatial Caesar's Palace dining room the next morning. He then read the article out loud to his guys who were seated with him at a large conference-like table situated in a private seating area. They laughed in unison when he finished the article, which read:

The city of Buffalo New York is reeling this morning. The so-called Flower Man Murders are in full bloom, according to Buffalo police. They have no clues to the identity of this person they call the Flower Man who struck again. Two more of his victims lie in the morgue this morning. These men, suspected members of the organized gang referred to as the Russian Syndicate, are fifty-five-year-old Boris Meco and thirty-seven-year-old Yuri Antipenko. They are the latest to receive the feared long stem white rose which was found lying across their bodies, the trademark of the killer. The police fear this is all part of the mob wars that are plaguing the city and at this point seemingly have no end. They are asking all residents in the area known as the west side, site of five of these related murders, to come forward with any information that can lead to the capture of this cold-hearted serial killer. The main suspects who are under the constant surveillance of the police are not currently in the state, adding more confusion to this baffling case. Any information at all would help the stumped instigators in their pursuit.

"Conti, Conti, Conti, this man is a dangerous man," whispered Tony Sotto to Vito. "I'm glad he's your friend, Boss."

"He's more than a friend, Tony. Always keep that in mind."

"What do you think Terski's next move will be now, Godfather?" continued Tony.

"If he's smart, he'll do nothing for a bit. I know he's going to want to kill someone but he doesn't know who. HAA HAA HAA," laughed Vito.

All the guys laughed. But make no bones about it Terski would not take the loss of Boris Meco well. Not well at all. Vito was right. Terski couldn't retaliate against the Italians without putting his organization at total risk, especially when he doesn't exactly know who's at fault.

"That mother fucking Bansano, that mother fucker! I don't want to hear he's not in town one more time from any of you. He's behind this. He's got some super hit man from out of town or something. I know it's him. Somebody find out something. God damn it. And I mean now!"

"How, Boss? Where do we even start? Every guy he's got is with him in Vegas. What do you want us to do?" asked Meco's heir apparent replacement as Terski's right hand guy, Mikal Stavro.

"I don't know. I don't fucking know. But do something!"

Peter slithered into the crew at the airport and exited the terminal like he was with them the entire time, as planned. Numerous eyes were on them as they got into two limousines and left and headed to Antonio's, the best Italian restaurant that Buffalo has to offer, and owned by one of Vito's lifelong friends.

"Vito, my friend. Welcome," said Antonio Scavazzo the owner, as he hugged the Don.

"I have your private dining room all set up. Come, follow me."

"Thank you my friend. Antonio, I want you to meet someone very special to me. This is Peter Conti. I want you to consider him like he's family to me when he comes here, capisci?"

"Nice to meet you Mr. Conti," said Antonio with his hand sticking out.

'The pleasure is mine," responded Peter, grasping Antonio's hand.

"Are you the soldier, my friend?" he asked.

"Yes sir. I was."

"Then the pleasure is certainly all mine. Vito has mentioned you to me many times. He always speaks with pride when he does. You're welcome here anytime. Just like Vito. No reservation is ever needed. Follow me, gentlemen."

They ate and drank like they were at a wedding. Every man there knew what kind of coup Peter pulled off. The Russians were hurt at their core, reeling from the Meco loss. Peter's plan worked to perfection and they all knew it.

Peter spoke. "Laugh and enjoy this now my friends, but these Russians will still blame you. They will be coming. Watch your backs. Don't go anywhere alone and keep an eye on your partners' six, I mean back. They are coming. Mark my words. Oh God, Sorry Vito, I apologize, I need to keep my mouth closed when you're present. It's not my place."

"No, No, Peter. I like what you have to say. You are one smart cookie my friend and one dangerous man. Am I right, my friends?"

Every man at the table nodded their heads in agreement and lifted their glasses to Peter.

"I told you this is your show, Mister Conti. What do you have planned for an encore?"

"OK, this is what I think, let's sit tight and watch our backs. Terski is steaming hot right now. This is when mistakes are made. We wait. Trouble is he is going to want to kill someone and probably someone sitting at this table. He's going to try and stick it up Vito's ass like he's Vito's equal when he ain't shit. We'll bide our time. But soon, the Flower Man will return. You can count on that."

CHAPTER TWENTY-EIGHT

All was quiet for weeks. The police surveillance was steady; both sides were being watched on a minute-to-minute basis. Peter spent more and more time at the restaurant, making sure he was seen with Vito regularly. He knew if he was planning on using Vito for an alibi again, like for Meco, he needed to be seen with them a good number of times. That would certainly verify his vacationing with them. Any time he was around these men they all walked a little softly. Peter had an air about him. Call it out of respect or call it out of fear but he was looked up to by the entire crew. Make no mistake Vito was the boss man, the Don, the Godfather. Peter never infringed on this powerful man's authority in any way. Peter acted different than the rest for good reason. He wasn't one of them. He had an agenda and this was the best way to meet his goal.

Terski was chomping at the bit to retaliate against his enemy. He had eyes and could see the constant vigilance bestowed upon him and his men by the police so he too had to be patient. But his patience was running thin. The death of Boris Meco was tearing at his soul. His friend, his right hand, being cut down by that son of a bitch Bansano was pushing him to the brink. He had to do something.

He came up with a plan, a way to kill two birds with one stone. Mikal Stavro was a good earner for Terski but not the man he wanted by his side as his number two. He really didn't have a man that could replace what Meco did for him. But back years and years ago, when Terski was just starting his life of crime in Russia, he had a partner, Dimitri Tarnoff. Terski was the brains back then and Dimitri was the strong arm, a savage killer with no conscience, none at all. He would kill a child in a second if Terski pointed at the kid. This was a ruthless bad man who Terski just found out was recently released from prison in Moscow. All Terski had to do now was pull some strings so he could get him over here and he would have his right hand man and a stranger that the cops weren't looking for. A weapon he could use for revenge.

Tarnoff arrived in Buffalo two weeks later. Got a room at the Hilton and waited for instructions. Terski knew he couldn't be seen with the man or Dimitri would come under scrutiny. Everything was set up on the telephone. Revenge.

Peter called Vito and asked him to meet him at Antonio's for lunch. He wanted to run something by him without any of the men present. Peter got there a few minutes early and sat at the bar waiting for his friend to come in. Vito never showed up.

They found Vito Bansano lying next to his car in the parking lot of the Delaware Grill with two bullets lodged in the back of his head. Terski got his revenge.

Peter looked up at the television from his seat at Antonio's and saw the report:

What the police are calling a war between the crime syndicates hit a new high, minutes ago, when the body of Italian Crime Boss Vito Bansano was found shot to death on his establishment's parking lot. Bansano, known to the police as the Godfather, was seventy-three years old, unmarried with no children. Bansano owned and operated the Delaware Grill located on the twenty-four hundred block of Delaware Ave. On the outside a quaint looking Italian eatery but police have always thought of the restaurant as a front for many criminal activities. The police now feel that a blood bath could erupt from this latest ruthless killing and all officers are on watch. This is a dangerous time to be living in this city. Please stay close to your homes.

Peter sank in his seat for a moment and then simply cried. He had a whole new reason to hate the Russians. He arose from his stool with renewed passion, the scary kind, and the kind that doesn't let anything or anybody stand in its way. Peter Conti didn't exist anymore. The Flower Man replaced him and that persona was back in him with a vengeance. He left that restaurant and headed directly to the scene of the murder.

Cops were milling around like ants. News people filled the street and police were directing crowds away from the area. Tony Sotto saw Peter and yelled to the police, "Officer, let that guy in. He's related to Mister Bansano."

Peter walked into a frenzy of hot-tempered livid Italians ready to load up and finish this war. No one, including the cops, was going to stop them from putting Terski in a grave. No one that is, until Peter walked in. He surveyed the confusion and listened before he said, "Stop God damn it. Think for a God damn minute."

Sotto retorted with, "Your flower man bullshit ain't gonna work this time, Conti."

"This ain't about the fucking flower man, God damn it, Tony. This ain't about killing Terski either. This is about Vito. All about Vito. I understand. You want to go out and kill those fucking Russian pricks right fucking now. I got news for you, running around half cocked and stupidly killing a few of those son of a bitch Russians is exactly what Terski wants. Yeah, he might lose a few men but in the end. The cops take you out and he gets it all. Use your fucking heads."

Frankie Andolino shouted at Peter, "Who the fuck do you think you are Conti telling us what to do?"

"SHUT THE FUCK UP FRANKIE!" screamed Peter at the top of his lungs. He continued, "You want the Russians. I want them too, even more, mark my words. They will die. We're going kill them all. I got a way. I got a fuckin' way of killing every fucking one... all at once! And we won't have to fire a shot."

The room got very quiet very fast.

"I was supposed to meet with Vito a few hours ago. That's where Vito was going. I told him what I was thinking and we were meeting to work out a plan. It will work. I promise you that. I need a few days to work out the details. When it's done so are they. Every one of those sons of bitches will be lying dead at our feet.

"But not right now," Peter said fiercely. "First we avenge Vito. Whoever did this dies. And gentleman I'm not asking you. I'm telling you. I'm the one; I kill the man that took Vito's life. Period. I know you all respected him but I loved the man. The minute we find out who fired those shots is the day that mother fucker dies. One more white rose, he dies and we live to tell about it," Peter said, slamming his fist on the table.

He continued with, "This hit wasn't done by any of Terski's flunkies. They're being watched as much as we are. Terski brought in an outside hitter. I'll bet my life he speaks Russian or if he does speak any English it's with a bad accent. You guys got snitches, friends, even family that work in hotels, motels, cabs, restaurants, shit like that, find out if a stranger recently showed up in town, a stranger with a real bad Russian accent. When we find someone like than we find Vito's killer."

Peter looked every man straight in the eye and snarled, "I promise you this. When he dies I'll watch him fight for his last breath, and when he does, I'll spit in his face and laugh. Then we'll kill them all."

Peter finished with, "Find that fuckin' guy. Find him fast. And for Christ sake don't do a fucking thing about it when you do. Call me. The Flower Man will strike again and then, like I said, we kill them all.

"That all sounds good, Conti, but just how you plan on pulling all of this off?" questioned Sotto.

"A meeting, a truce, that's when they die."

"How? You think they'll just walk into a room and let us shoot them? How?"

"I'm working on it, Tony. I have to locate some shit we need first. And that's where you come in. Vito told me that you have connections in the black market. We're going to need them. Let me tell you what we need. You get your hands on this shit and I'll do the rest. In the meantime we got somebody to find and I got someone to kill."

It didn't take long. Vic Desica's cousin worked at the Hilton and spotted a man that fit the description of the guy they were looking for. He told Vic the guy could barely speak English.

Sotto was on the phone to Peter within minutes. "We got him. His name's Dimitri Tarnoff. Desica's cousin checked him out. He's called the warehouse number several times in the last few days. He's our man."

"Good work, Tony. Tell Vic I owe him. We all do. Let me set something up and then I'll take care of this and get back with you. You able to get your hands on the shit I ask for?"

"I'll have it in two days."

"It's all falling into place my friend, but first things first: Dimitri Tarnoff."

Peter got the room number of his new target from Desica and watched every more Tarnoff made. He didn't make many. He was holed up in his room like a hermit. The only contact he had so far with civilization was getting food from room service. That was it, Peter's way of getting in. He needed to talk to Vic Desica.

Peter was at the Grill the next morning. "Vic, your cousin, how much do you trust him?"

"With my life, Conti."

"How about my life?"

"He's one of us."

"Does he work near the restaurant area in the hotel?"

"What do you need?"

"I need to know when Tarnoff orders room service, and a cart, and a uniform. Possible?"

"Anything is possible. Let me run over there. I'll check it out. Grab something to eat. I'll be back."

"Vic, I don't want your cousin to know me. It's better that way. Understand?"

"I'll handle everything. You just kill that prick."

Desica showed up an hour later pushing a small food cart that had a uniform on top of it.

"When you want to do this, Conti?" he asked.

"Soon as possible. We know where he is for now but no telling for how long."

"Dinner time tonight good for you? My cousin works till eight."

"Perfect. How will I know when Tarnoff orders something?"

"I worked it out. I'll sit in the lobby like I'm waiting for someone. My cousin Gino will get me the info, just be near a house phone. I'll call you and pass on the information. That's the best I can do."

"Perfect Vic. Perfect. I'll take care of the rest. After we talk, get back here quick and get a card game going. I'll sneak back here as soon as I can. We'll all have an alibi then."

"You're a bad mother fucker, Conti."

"Takes one to know one, Desica." They both laughed. Killing was nothing to these men. It was business. But to Peter Conti, it wasn't business, it was personal. Jackie was never out of his mind, not for a minute, and now Vito. The whole ordeal was going to end soon and he was going to end it.

CHAPTER TWENTY-NINE

The plan worked to perfection. Peter got the call, knocked on Tarnoff's door, pushed the cart in, pulled out his silenced .45 and put two slugs in Dimitri's chest. As Tarnoff lay on the floor struggling for life, Peter spit in his face, threw a long stem white rose on him, and said, "This is for Vito."

Then Peter put one between Dimitri's eyes ending the miserable bastard's murderous life. He then slipped out the back of the hotel without seeing another soul and was back at the grill before the smoke cleared.

"He died sniveling like a baby. I put two in him where he wouldn't die right away, I gave him Vito's regards, and then I put one between his eyes. Now we wait. Terski won't know what to do next."

"Nice. You mind telling us now Conti, what the hell this big plan of yours is?" asked Nino Torisi.

"Yeah, you kept us in the dark long enough Conti, and we don't like it. Spit it out," added Vittorio Sordi, basically speaking for the whole group.

"First, I told you, I needed something before I could fill you in. Second, don't ever talk to me like that again, you understand me, Sordi? I hope you do. Here it is in a nutshell, I'm going to set up a meeting, call it a truce, we eat, we drink, and we work a few things out. What they won't know is I'm going to do one more thing at this meeting. I'm going to poison them, I'm going to poison them and watch them all die. All at once."

Gino Paladino laughed out loud, and said, "That's funny. You think you're going to be able to get him to gather his men and come to a meeting with us and you think they're not going to suspect a thing. That is fucking hilarious. This is even funnier; we're going to all be together eating and drinking shit and they're the only ones that are getting poisoned. No fucking way they're falling for that. How you plan on pulling that trick off, Conti?"

"I'm not. We're going to get poisoned too."

"What the fuck, Conti. You losing your fucking marbles?" interjected Frankie Andolino.

"No Frankie. I still got my marbles. I also have a shit load of antidote that we'll all be taking before the meeting. They die. We don't. Done."

"Jesus Christ, where did you get the shit?" asked Frankie.

"Sotto, you can thank your buddy Tony and his black market connections. He's already got the stuff. It's done. All I got to do is set up the meeting. That's the hard part."

"How you plan on getting that done?" asked Tony Sotto.

"Here's what I'm thinking. Terski don't know me from a bag of shit. If any of you tried to meet with the guy he'd off you before you got a word out of your mouth, but me, if I contact him and portray myself as Vito's consigliere, his advisor, he might just listen. I'll give him some song and dance about both sides taking a beating and losing guys left and right. I'll convince him that if this keeps up there won't be anybody left on either side. Everything, all the work, all the scams, all the set ups, and all money, everything we got goes up in smoke. That will get his attention.

"I'll follow that with this idea, we join forces, call it a partnership, let's face it there's plenty for everybody. I'll propose a meeting. I'm going to suggest someplace over the bridge in Canada. No cops there and if we set it up right, no one to bother us. It will be a business meeting out in the country somewhere, no tricks, no guns, no gimmicks, no fucking around, strictly business. I'll tell him we can work out the details together. I'll tell him it only makes sense that everyone from both sides should be there. That way we can make sure we divide up everything fair. We'll eat, we'll drink, and we'll all leave rich men. If he goes for it, they die."

The guys didn't say a word. They all sat there quiet, just nodding their heads until Sotto said,

"Do it, Conti!"

"First we bury Vito. Then we wait. Terski's gotta be going crazy trying to figure out what our next move is going to be. I don't know who this Dimitri Tarnoff was but dollars to donuts Terski knew him and knew him well. We set him back a bit when we eliminated what he thought was going to be his secret weapon. I think we need to give the little man some time. His best move is to let things die down; he knows that, so it just figures he will sit and wait, too. Let's let things simmer down. A deal like this makes sense. I'll strike when the fire is hot. But right now I need to figure out the details in a way that Terski thinks he's making all the decisions. Timing is everything."

A month passed by like it was minutes. Both sides were quiet, too much heat to try anything without bringing the law down on them. Peter felt he waited long enough. He contacted Terski.

"Ivan Terski?" asked Peter.

"Who's asking?"

"My name doesn't matter. Are you familiar with the term consigliere?"

"Who the fuck, are you?"

"I'm the advisor to your competition. I'm the guy who might just be able to make this terrible situation go away."

"Let me ask you one more time before I hang up. Who the fuck, are you?"

"Name's Conti. Peter Conti, and I represent the late Vito Bansano."

"So what. What are you calling me for? I don't even know any Vito Bansano."

"Listen Ivan, do you want to end this fucking war and walk away rich or just keep killing each other until we're all dead. Is that a hard question?"

"What's on your mind, Conti? I'm a busy man."

"What do you say to a truce?"

"I say, go fuck yourself!"

"OK, nice, if that's your answer, remember this, we tried. Thank you for your time."

"Wait, What do you mean by a truce?"

Peter laid out what he discussed with the guys and did it well.

Terski answered with, "I don't trust you and I don't like it."

"If you think this is a trick, you come up with a better idea. One that doesn't end up with all of us dead."

"Let me think about it. I'll let you know."

"Look Ivan, this could be good for everybody. There's plenty to go around here. A meeting, a totally secret meeting, no one knows, I mean no one, just between our two organizations, everybody, all our men, all your men, we talk, we talk about splitting up shit, territories, maybe even profits, it's all negotiable, no guns, no tricks, just business. Call me if you're interested. It's Conti, Peter Conti. You can reach me at the Grill."

"We'll see, Conti," said Terski. "We'll see."

Nothing happened. Two weeks went by. Still no contact from Terski until the phone rang at the Delaware Grill. Peter wasn't there to get the call but Nino took the call and set up a time for Conti and Terski to talk. Terski would call back at four o'clock.

Terski called right on time.

"This Conti?"

"What can I do for you, Terski?"

"Let's talk, here, at my place, tonight."

"Sorry, I gotta say, no!"

"What the fuck, Conti? You said you wanted to talk."

"I do, but not at your place, and not at mine. Let's have dinner. I don't care where, just you and me. You want to be armed; I don't give a shit, carry if you want. You kill me, or I kill you, that just ends a deal that could be sweet for both sides before it even starts. Let's start this off on the right foot."

"That sounds OK by me."

"Look Ivan, I have a private room at Antonio's any time I want it, if you don't mind if I'm the one that pick the place. It's a nice joint, good food, and we won't be disturbed. Is that good by you? If not, you name a place."

"That's OK by me. Tonight seven o'clock, Antonio's. If this is a trick I promise you you'll never see how it ends."

"No tricks. Just business. See you at seven. Alone. Just me and you."

The two men entered Antonio's within a few minutes of each other. Both were cautious and both were suspicious but the end justified the risk, so there they were. They shook hands but neither one was smiling. Peter started the conversation.

"Look, we're not friends. That's not gonna happen. This is a business conversation. Period. But there is no reason to start what could be a lucrative partnership off with a bunch of animosity. Let's eat some food. Have a drink or two. I'm not here to negotiate a deal. Just to negotiate a meeting. I'm just the consigliere for the Italians, not the decision maker. I know who you are. I know I'm talking to the headman. I respect that. I'm not in any way theirs. Let's eat something. Then we'll talk. I'm hungry, you hungry, Ivan?"

"You're a smart man, Conti. I like that. Yes, I am hungry."

They had a drink and then ordered.

"Just so you're comfortable," said Peter as he reached over and took a sip from Ivan's vodka tonic.

"Like I said Peter, you're smart."

After they had a nice meal consisting of an antipasto salad and a nice dish of tut mare (linguine and sea food in a garlic white sauce), Terski started the important conversation with, "I decided that what you proposed at my place a few weeks back is worth discussion. But if we're going to meet, I lay out all the rules and conditions."

"Nope. Wrong start. We negotiate everything, even the meeting."

"How do you negotiate a fucking meeting?"

"Here's how, I pick something that you don't like. We change it until we both agree. And that goes both ways. Everything and I mean everything from where we meet, to what we talk about, who does what talking and when, what we eat, what we drink, and everything in-between. There is no boss. Everything is a negotiation."

"Sounds to me that you're the boss here."

"Nope, just the negotiator."

"Ok, what you're saying sounds fair."

"Ivan, fair is the best word used when negotiating anything. If it's fair to one side and not to the other, there's no deal. But if it's fair to both sides, that's when a good deal is struck."

Peter continued with, "Let's start out with where. We have cops crawling all over us; they're so close we can't even breathe. That's why I suggested Canada. It's a quick ride over the Peace Bridge and the cops are gone. What do you think about Canada?"

"Sounds smart. But I pick where."

"Fine. As long as it's somewhere that we're alone so no one could possible know what we're up to. We all wear gloves, no prints, no one knows we were ever there."

"We have a storehouse on the outskirts of Fort Erie, five miles from the bridge and eight miles from Niagara Falls. Suit you?"

"I hope it's secluded enough so that no one could see us or get wind that we're there? We don't need our current customers knowing what we're up to yet," said Peter.

"We do business there so of course it's isolated and private."

"Great. You getting the picture on how this negotiating thing works?"

Terski adds, "I get it but negotiate this, I decide when."

"OK, again, no argument from me, when?"

"One week from today. Saturday the twentieth at let's say noon. If we're going to do something, let's do it."

"OK. So far so good."

Ivan adds, "Alright then I want one more thing. Just me and one of my guys meet with you and one of theirs."

"Nope, no way, it has to be all the men, yours and ours. Every guy has to have a say. If one guy decides to get greedy the whole fucking thing turns into another war. All guys discuss but only you and I make decisions. Vito gave me that power, the power to negotiate for the crew on all levels and the organization has decided to keep me in that position."

Peter added, "Noon time is good. We pound out a deal and then we can eat lunch together and maybe defuse any hard feelings between the men. That will take time but it would be a start. What do you think?"

"Sure, good idea. I'll take care of the food and drink."

"Good. I have a bottle of Magnum Grey Goose Vodka. It's one of the most expensive vodkas in the world. It's made from French wheat and distilled in a five-step process that involves artesian spring water that is filtered through Champagne limestone located in the Gensac Springs. The water is untouched by human hands. Five hundred dollars a bottle. I've been saving it for a special occasion. We'll toast with it when we strike a fair deal. And, I'm sure we are going to find a fair deal that both sides like. We all get rich and we all live."

"Sounds like you know your vodka. I have some Russian vodka that I'm quite sure you'll enjoy. Let's see if you have wasted your money."

"Looking forward to that. But there are a few conditions we haven't discussed and we need to. None of our men will feel safe. Let's face it. They don't trust each other. So, no one carries a gun except you and me. We stand at the door and everyone gets frisked.

Two of my men are allowed in first to search the place for hidden weapons. After we both are sure everyone is unarmed we both unload our guns and toss them. Remember if something starts we both lose. This is an opportunity for both of our organizations to prosper and grow. It's good business and it's smart. You agree?"

"I'm still leery, but I agree, as long as I have a gun in my hand."

"Done. Saturday at noon. I can feel the money flowing as we speak, partner."

CHAPTER THIRTY

Saturday morning, all the men met at the Grill early. Peter was laying out everything and was nearly scripting what he wanted each of them to say. It was important to win over the Russians but not make them think this is something phony and get suspicious of the whole meeting. It had to sound like a business partnership that everyone would benefit from.

"First things first," said Peter before they even got started.

He pulled out the syringes of antidote and every guy got his injection.

"We'll all take an oral dose before we leave for Canada to be extra safe. The antidote is good for forty-eight hours so we will have no problems. Do not worry. I've checked this out completely."

"Jesus Christ, Conti, this ain't comfortable," said a worried Gino Paladino.

"You end up a rich man, Gino. You risk your life every day, man. This is nothing new."

"Lay this whole deal out again, Peter," asked Tony Sotto.

"Ok, when we cross over the border at the bridge we'll get questioned at customs as usual. They'll ask where we're going and how long we're staying. If you weren't born in the USA make sure you have your passport. You guys have done this a million times every time you go to the racetrack. It's nothing new. We tell them we are going to Niagara Falls. See the falls and a couple of museums, eat lunch and come back. So we tell them we'll be there most of the afternoon. We drive to the meeting. No weapons. Even if you know how to smuggle a gun over we don't need them. I'll have one that I have stashed in the trunk. It's inside my spare tire. If there's any trouble when we get there, stay low and get the hell out of there. If it's some kind of trap, I'll take care of it. But, there won't be."

"How can you be so sure, Peter?" asked Vic Desica.

"Vic, believe me. They had some bad losses, not just casualties, cash. They want this. They need this. They will at least listen. Terski won't let them fuck it up before it even starts.

"Let me continue. Tony and Nino, you guys go in first. Check the place out. Look for anywhere they might be able to hide guns that they could get to in a hurry. You're going to be frisked at the door, we all will. Don't worry about that shit. This ain't a gun fight. Once we're all in there, I'll start the conversation with the same cock and bull story I fed Terski. The share and share alike kind of description that goes along with the splitting up of the territories. Once I have their attention we'll all speak. We will alternate first one of us, then one of them. We describe everything we're doing in every location and how much we're making. List our contacts and tell a little spiel about how to do business with them. Every facet, drugs, extortion, women, guns, gambling, blackmail, everything whatever you got going and they will do the same. That way when it's over we'll have all their contacts and info. It's beautiful.

"Terski and I will work out the splits. It won't matter but I'll argue quite a bit about certain areas. If I don't they won't go for it. If it seems fair when we're finished negotiating, we'll party with the cocksuckers. We'll eat, drink, bullshit, and kind of mingle with the bastards. At the end, to consummate the deal, I'll bring out the Grey Goose Vodka. We all drink a shot. They die. We win.

"Sounds too simple," said a skeptical Al Nazzi.

"That's the beauty of it Al. It is simple. That's why it will work."

Peter continued, "After they drop over dead, we clean up everything like there was nothing going on except these guys having a meeting. We grab the shot glasses and the poisoned vodka, and check everything else to make sure we leave no tell-tale sign that we were there. I'll throw a white rose on the fuckers' dead bodies so the Flower man gets the blame and we'll drive to the Falls to complete our alibi. Fuck those fucking Russians. Good riddance to bad rubbish."

The men all nodded their heads in agreement, drank a little more antidote, and headed to the cars. The plan was in motion.

They had no problem at the border. It went as smooth as silk. The storehouse was just how Terski described it. A small warehouse tucked away nicely in the woods on the east end of the city of Fort Erie, and miles from the nearest civilization. It was perfect.

The Russians were waiting in their cars and Terski was standing in front of one of them, gun in hand. Terski kept his word; he had his entire crew there.

Peter got out of one of their cars first. Gun in hand of course. Tony Sotto got out right after Peter with his hands held high in the air along with Nino Torrisi, his hands up as well. Three of Terski's men exited their cars in the same way, arms up. The rest of the Italians then came out, all with their hands high in the air.

When Tony and Nino came out of the building claiming a clean bill of health, Peter and Ivan had each man frisked and all entered. There wasn't a non-skeptic in the bunch as they sat down across from one another at a large set of connected tables. No one spoke. Peter broke the silence.

"We came here for one reason and one reason only. To end this fucking war and figure a way to do it and make a whole lot more money while we do. Ivan and I have figured a way."

Peter explained the share and share-a-like plan. He included some innovative scams that the Italians had been working on and shared how they all could profit in the scheme. He went over the division of territories and how that would work. He described how it would come about and when. He said that each earner from both sides would have to lay out their agenda and their contacts in order to split up everything fairly. All the things that he and Terski discussed, and finished his spiel with, "One guy, just one, on either side gets greedy and this don't work. We start killing each other again and no one wins. It only takes one.

"Tony, you start. List off how you earn and from who. Tell it all. When you're done, Ivan pick one of your guys to do the same and at the end we'll split the whole fucking thing up and we'll all be rich. No competition."

The meeting went perfect. There was some hesitation but each Russian realized fair was fair and no more competition meant more money for everybody. The Italians played their parts to the fullest. Terski and Peter argued a bit. One gave in a little than the other until both sides felt like this was going to work out great.

When the negotiating was over, they partied. Drank and ate like kings. All provided by the Russians. When the meeting was coming to a close Peter brought out the vodka. He rolled it out on a table full of shot glasses and poured each glass full.

"This is the one of the finest vodkas in the world and a fitting end to a perfect meeting. To our new partners and to a shit load of money for all," toasted Peter as he drank a shot full first.

Then each man grabbed a shot and raised his glass. All but one, Victor Benko.

Peter said, "Victor?"

"I don't drink."

Peter said, "I'll drink one for you my new friend," and drank another.

Terski toasted, "To the end and the beginning."

They all drank. After a minute or two the first guy Mikal Stavro stumbled and as he fell, Peter picked up a fork from the table and stuck it into Victor's throat. Killed him on the spot. The Russians starting falling like bowling pins.

As Terski went to his knees Peter walked over to him, pushed him down to his back and said, "All of this was for my wife," he said as he showed him a long stem white rose.

Terski's last words were, "Fuck you!"

Peter answered with, "Rot in hell you cocksucker!"

As Peter threw a long stem white rose on each body the Italians wiped the place clean, grabbed the booze and the glasses, and headed to the door. Just before they walked out Tony Sotto stopped them all. They all looked at Peter when Tony asked, "What's next, Boss?"

Peter thought for a second before he spoke but realized there was only one answer. He replied, "We're just getting started!"

That's the story. That's how it happened. That's how Peter Conti, a clean-cut all American boy from the suburbs became the Man, Numero Uno, the Don, the Godfather.

The End

Or is it?

Made in the USA
Monee, IL
26 November 2019